~~

death.by.facebook

~~

death.by.facebook

by

Everett Peacock

ISBN-13: **978-1453861936**

ISBN-10: 1453861939

deathbyfacebook.com

cover inspiration by Tarey Dunn

proofreading by Valentina Cano

v.7

republished January 13, 2012

Other books by Everett Peacock

The Parrot Talks in Chocolate

theParrotTalksInChocolate.com

2009

~~~

In the Middle of the Third Planet's

Most Wonderful of Oceans

2010

~~~

Tiwaka Goes to Waikiki

2011

~~~

~ ~ ~

to those hardy souls

that inhabit the rainforests

of

Volcano, Hawaii

~ ~ ~

PREFACE

Like the other half billion or so people using Facebook to keep in touch with friends, family and business I was reading a stream of posts one afternoon. Nothing unusual, just the steady flow of clever statements, complaints about the weather, about being sick, being in love, being lost.

One such person I had added to my "friends" list was a girl from high school I had known, not very well, but enough to say hi on Facebook. She was an active poster with more "friends" than most and you could tell she lived a great deal of her life online, on Facebook. On this particular afternoon she had posted about being sick with the flu and I scanned her last post with the same disinterest that I did about other such complaints.

However, the next day she was posting again, except this time it wasn't her doing the writing. It was her husband using her log-in to tell her friends that she had died during the night. He expressed how much his wife had enjoyed her social life with her Facebook friends, how she would come to bed at night relating all the wild and crazy stories she'd heard there. He signed that last post with his name and I naturally never saw another from her.

Facebook, of course, is just a another tool humans use to communicate. It was this lady's death though, announced online that cemented it in my mind as a tool that had grown up, one that was perfectly suited to announce such a finality. And, it became clear to me that with such maturity it was also a tool that could be expressed with a darker purpose.

Everett Peacock
February 27, 2011
Kula, Maui, Hawaii

1

At this point the only thing in life I truly regret was having my poor Mom read about my death on Facebook. I had finally managed to convince her just a few weeks ago that it was the best way to follow my adventures. Janet was posting pictures of our *sweetmoon* (our vacation *before* we got married) at the volcano in Hawaii and I was posting clever comments, which I had to usually steal from others. Mom loved all of it. Well, she "liked" all of it.

In fact, I had just posted a new profile picture, me up close and Janet with her chin on my right shoulder. Both of us were smiling, but, now I guess, for different reasons.

Being dead is nothing like I thought it would be. Two tours in Afghanistan made me think death was a horrible experience. I know now that it is only horrible for those that see it happen to others. For me, it was pretty quick, a bit of a surprise no doubt, but otherwise a smooth transition.

I suppose I was always a simple man, never bothering to think things through much, and ignoring those things I didn't want to deal with. But, that gave me a lot more time to love the important things: fishing, hiking, the great outdoors and Janet. Too many tours in the Army had let me hit 35 without having had a serious relationship. That and having been adopted by parents who couldn't sit still more than six months or so had kept me from having many friends.

Janet then was my first love, not counting my two flings in Germany. I loved them too, probably still could, but Janet was so much like me it hurt. Hurt real good. She could feel my emotions in her soul she said, and then laughed before I got too confused trying to figure out how she did that. We almost could read each other's minds too. I could almost always tell when she was sad and she could always tell when I was trying to figure something out.

Trouble was Janet had been sad a lot lately, even as we were due to get married in just a few days. And, her headaches were sometimes so severe she got sick, or got the shakes real bad. She told me it was left over from the drugs they had given her in the asylum. It was worrisome to me, and true to my nature, I did my best to ignore it. Bad things, I knew, had a way of disappearing eventually.

Janet suggested we take my signing bonus (yes, another three years of Army life for me, for us) and go to see the lava, the beaches, and the wild papayas you could just pick right off a tree. Hawaii, she said, was good for the soul.

I sure liked the idea of being out in the jungle wilderness. What I didn't realize was that when I died I would be hanging out there as well, waiting for my turn in Heaven. They said it was temporary and that was cool by me.

I guess it was what you might call an angel that told me it would be just a little while. She looked a lot like my kindergarten teacher, Ms. Debbie. That same big smile and soft pat on top of my head when I got lost in thought.

"Jimmy, you got some things left here to take care of, OK?" she said softly, the bright light moving around her like some kind of water.

"Sure," I said. I had the taste of cookies and milk on my tongue just by looking at her. "When is nap time?" I'd asked, probably more from habit than from actually being tired.

Her face lit up just like a Christmas tree when you first plug it in. "Anytime you like Jimmy." She had put her arm around me real tight, just like I remembered and squeezed a little too hard. "You're a good boy Jimmy."

I smiled up at her and she simply glowed and slowly, very slowly moved up and away from me. I was soon all alone. Again. In the rainforest, near the volcano. That was yesterday. So, I walked, or I think I walked. Anyhow I moved through the ferns and the mists. I didn't need to push anything out of my way, I just flowed, past the birds and the blooming ginger. In and out of the lava tubes, cold and dark and long forgotten by their creator; something I was beginning to relate to. Lonely was something I could deal with, though, something I had grown up with.

One thing I must admit to: being dead, or at least not being a human anymore has some distinct advantages. As I wander around I can sense things I have never been able to before; I can feel what people are feeling, like I am in their heads, in their emotions even. I can move easily, anywhere I point my mind. Wandering through the rainforest today I stumbled into some hikers. They seemed interesting, so I simply focused on them. Just for a moment. Suddenly, I was there, inside their minds, feeling what they were feeling. It was something I found entertaining and sadly educational. Sad, I say, because I'd never known people could have such rich experiences. Rich beyond anything I can remember having experienced. It was a good thing no one could see me, see my disappointment.

I looked up above me and I saw that bright light far away, where Ms. Debbie had come from. I knew somehow, that it was slowly getting closer and that when it did reach me, I would have to leave this place and go there.

Finally, for the first time ever, I really appreciated time. And people. People were so cool and suddenly so damn interesting, I just wish I hadn't killed so many in the war. I kinda wondered if I would meet any of them, when I went up where Ms. Debbie was.

Meeting guys I'd killed was scary, so I didn't think about it. I was going to make my way back from the volcano's lower crater, the brochure called it Halema'uma'u, to see Janet at Cabin #94. We still had several days booked at the Kilauea Military Recreation Area. I had to figure out what had happened, and if she was OK. Poor Janet, all alone now. Alone with her headaches, her shakes and herself.

It was now almost dawn, the day after I'd died. I felt I was changing already, even in the few hours since I'd been dead. Now, the landscape was talking to me, like a teacher. I was no longer a tourist, or even a dead tourist. I was a welcome guest in this home of creation, where the Earth herself spoke lovingly to those that would listen. I was listening and watching and very, very curious.

I moved through the 4000 foot elevation Ohia forest until I saw a light go on in a house close by. An interesting house.

2

I watched as his new bamboo curtains slid silently aside. He was studying the Mother of Creation still wearing her white mantle for the rising sun. Dawn on 13,679 foot Mauna Loa started at the top and worked its predictable way down to the Ohia forests far below.

Larry Larson knew a good day to fly when he saw one, especially when he saw so many of them. A large cup of Kona's best, a strawberry papaya from the Hilo farmers market and a kiss to dear Shirley got him out the door.

A sparkling chromed engine sat faithfully in the garage ready to propel him and his parachute wing with a sweetly balanced propeller. Just across the driveway, in an open field, he set up to fly, watching the sun fill the great volcano's height.

The high mountain air sat patiently, heavy with promise, greeting him with a brisk embrace of anticipation. An electric click brought his baby to life, humming a familiar song, hugging him with its vibration.

The wing swung up to dance with the engines breath and rose, ready to carry him up into the gentle flow of the trade winds. Larry pushed the throttle a little higher and felt the tug of the earth, for just a moment.

Rising firmly up into the crispness and soft light of morning he surveyed the familiar ground pulling smoothly away. He had flown this route hundreds of times, moved among the clouds and above the jungle, the lava fields, the sea. Yet, it wasn't anything less than fresh, this dance with the sky. Hula Me Opua was painted on his wing: dances with clouds.

He flew over the lava filled craters, vainly attempting to hide their ferocity with fumes and smoke and over further to the great expanses of desolation. As he, and I, rose ever higher toward Mauna Loa her family stood tall to welcome their visitor. Mauna Kea, her own mother stood to the north, silent and proud. The ancient great ones of Maui, Oahu and Kauai hugged the western horizon and beyond them the unnamed ones rested below the ocean now, forever.

As Larry was greeted with the first lifting morning thermal, he smiled, knowing, like I was now learning, Hawaii reserves her true majesty for those who fly.

3

Below Larry, I could see Cabin #94, next to the road and the gym. There I found poor Janet, still sleeping, beer bottles strewn everywhere. It was as if she had opened every last one we had brought with us. I tried to focus on her, her thoughts, but it was just a lot of haze, a lot of static. Moving over to the floor I tried to pick up the cans, as I might have only a day or so ago. It was disarmingly strange. I had no way of picking up anything. No hands, no arms, nothing I could use to help clean the place up. I tried to focus on the cans, thinking I might be able to do something that way. But again, all I got was haze and static.

After some good deal of time waiting on the outside porch watching the clouds move in from the deep forests across the street I sensed her wakening. I hesitated going inside with her at first, content to watch through the cold glass.

She was as beautiful as I had ever seen her, her hair tossed and perfectly red. She wore only a thin t-shirt and her running pants, her bare feet no doubt experimenting with how much cold they could handle. She moved slowly, like she was measuring her paces, simply pushing the empty beer cans aside like reluctant cats. I could now easily see at least twenty cans, on the table, by the TV and even in the sink.

Her yawn caught my attention as well, not so much by itself, but that she stopped and held her head in both hands as she did. It looked a lot like that famous painting by Munch, the one Andy Warhol copied.

Suddenly, just as what must have been the next moment in that painting, she fell to her knees, still holding her head and moaning loudly. She fell to her side, curling up in a ball and crying now, loudly. Screaming and crying.

I looked around, from my outside perch. The place was practically deserted. Most of the military guys were deployed in faraway places, unable to take enough leave to enjoy these distant mountains.

Looking back in, I just caught a glimpse of her moving into the restroom, and before I could move closer I heard her throwing up. For a long time. Horrible sounds, like demons barking from hell itself. I moved through the wall and to the fireplace and waited. Patiently.

After a while, I heard the sink running and then a curse or two mumbled from in front of the mirror. Soon after that, she emerged, rubbing her eyes. Her hands looked injured as well, with scratches, fresh from some kind of fight. What had happened there? I was really starting to worry now. Certainly worried as she stopped and looked right at me. Stared at me! Her stare was blank, though, as if she was looking right through me. I had to laugh a little at that. Of course, she would be looking right through me! My laugh was short lived.

"Jimmy?" she whispered.

I remained where I was even as I looked to see if I had suddenly reappeared, or had suddenly reincarnated. I had not.

"Oh Jimmy," she moaned and looked at her hands. "I'm so sorry Jimmy."

I found myself focusing on her now, trying to read her. The static was gone, but the haze was thick and I could only sense confusion.

She turned away from me now, and sat heavily at the small round table, sweeping three empty beer cans off to the floor. I watched them fall, all of them, bouncing off the floor once and then rolling contently against the wall. I heard more static as I watched them.

Janet was obviously distraught, and injured. I couldn't remember much about what must have happened to me, but it looked like she got hurt as well. She had her head down on the table now, brought her wounded hand up to her mouth and began licking it, like a dog would. I felt like a voyeur suddenly, watching a stranger. A stranger in her own personal, strange land.

Watching her finish licking her wounds I found myself remembering when I would do the same thing, as a kid. I had even licked that bullet wound before the medics got to me in Kandahar. The blood wasn't the main attraction, though. It was the soft torn flesh that felt good against my tongue and between my lips. Janet seemed to have that same fascination.

Suddenly, she stood up and took two quick steps to the small refrigerator, flung it open and grabbed two more beer cans. Sitting back down at the table, letting the refrigerator fend for itself, she pulled her laptop over.

Opening its lid she waited to turn it on, watching the blank screen for minutes. She drank the first beer slowly as she continued looking at the darkness. Finally, she crushed the can empty and closed her laptop. Reaching over to the far side of the table, she pulled my laptop over to herself.

Quickly she booted it up, the false light painting her face a ghostly sheen which broadcasted the redness in her eyes obscenely. Why would she use my computer? I checked what memory I could and wondered at what I might have on there that she would be interested in.

I had no old girlfriends, no bones in my closet, no pornography even. No banking records, she did all that anyhow. She managed all the number stuff.

My view from the fireplace was getting stale, so I moved. Moved over to her shoulder, her right shoulder, where I might have smiled once. Here I could see her open the web browser. My homepage tabs all came to life. CNN.com, MTV.com, TheParrotTalksinChocolate.com and, of course, my favorite, Facebook.com.

I did love my news and music videos! The parrot that talked in chocolate was one of those light-hearted tiki culture blogs fashioned after a favorite book. I loved that stuff.

She clicked immediately on Facebook, where I was automatically logged on. Over her shoulder I saw the latest news feed. I read it all immediately, soaking it up.

Jim Cannon *"When the call goes to voicemail and the voice of your friend asks you to leave a message after the beep and you are all prepared to talk THEN the automatic cell phone lady follows this with "if you would like to leave a message, blah blah blah, when you are finished, blah blah blah, to leave a callback number press 5, ..."*

That guy Jim was some kind of master piano tuner in Texas but had found his comedic genius nested somewhere between original posts and clever responses to others. I had stolen many of his posts when I couldn't come up with anything on my own.

My favorite tiki parrot had a recent post as well.

Tiwaka.Tiki *"the Tiki bar is rocking tonight! People are dancing and drinking and falling all over each other...it looks like a bunch of drunk pigeons!"*

And finally Mom had a post! It must be like her second one only, and I felt a twinge of pride. She could do it, I'd known she could!

Agatha Anne Turner *"off to play a little bingo with Jessie and the girls."*

Most of the rest were old posts, before we had left for Hawaii. Janet scrolled down the page, looking for something. She clicked on my Friends list and spent a long time looking at the few girls there. Most of them were simply Army buddies, the only people I had ever really spent any time with.

She seemed to get bored after a moment and opened her second breakfast beer. Tipping it high it looked like she downed half of it before slamming it into the table and burping, burping loudly like I might have. I was a bit shocked, but what got me was her next move.

Janet clicked in the text entry box near the top of the page, where it said "What's on your mind?" Immediately those words disappeared, awaiting some clever or more likely inane post. I couldn't quite figure it out. Why was she going to post under my profile?

I pulled back a little from her, in fear mostly, but a fascinated fear. Like the fear I had in Afghanistan when our foot patrol moved into a quiet neighborhood. A neighborhood with no kids playing in the streets, no women carrying bags of who knows what on their backs, no old men sitting around doing nothing. The fascination that comes right before danger, right before a bullet.

Even this far behind her I could see her type the words. Words I can't believe anyone would ever believe I would say, certainly nothing I believe I ever could say. She clicked on *Share* and there it was for all the world to see.

Jimmy Turner: *"I just wanted to let you all know that I am dead."*

4

I remember how happy I was to rediscover my older brother Frank. It had been some years of trying but nothing had worked. Until the Army had been looking for bone marrow donors up Pennsylvania way. Some might have called it destiny. Me? I just call it as I see it: pure luck. I had been up at Tobyhanna Depot training on sniper rifles and Frank had come on post to give a blood sample.

Some young dependent kid had the bone cancer, and every military family east of Mississippi had heard the call. Lucky kid too, both Frank and I matched him. The nurse gave us both a funny look when we showed up for a consult on what they intended to do with us, like we should know each other. Of course we didn't. Mom and Dad, our biological ones, were gypsy souls, drinkers and the world's worst parents, except that they did manage to feed us, occasionally. Apparently Frank wasn't the only one the State of Pennsylvania had to raise.

The nurse finally told us, that we were related. The doctor who came in later, a rusty old guy made no bones about telling us we were brothers. It was earthshaking, at least for me. I had no idea there were any siblings in the family. No one had ever mentioned any. Frank, however, knew better. He just didn't know much where to look, or maybe just wasn't that interested. After all, those had not been happy years for him. I guess I got lucky, with my adopted Mom.

Frank had just returned home from the tire shop where he did it all: fix, replace or rotate. The early winter cold was already invading

October in predictable ways. His old F100 had trouble starting in the mornings; the summer's cracked kitchen windows now demanded repair and the light grew shorter on each passing day.

But, that first beer from the twenty year old Maytag tasted as good as it ever had, right there on the round, white Formica kitchen table. The same that held his computer and his bird watching manual and sometimes a newspaper.

Facebook had become a lifeline out of Cold Hollow, PA for him, a link to the rest of the planet outside the narrow slice of humanity he had fallen into. I thanked all kinds of lucky stars when I convinced him to give it a try. "Older folks are signing on faster than the kids now," I had promoted. "But, be careful," I warned. "You might hook up again with an old girlfriend or two."

He looked at me kinda of funny like, a band-aid still on his arm at the donation center. "That might not be too bad," he had mused. Then he had asked the classic question: "No one needs to know what I really do, do they? I can post any profile picture I want, right?"

I laughed out loud, not at his questions but at my first opportunity to tell that joke I had seen so many years earlier.

"Frank," I said, putting my arm around his large hairy shoulders. "On the Internet, no one knows you're a dog."

Now, in a chilly late afternoon light, on an even colder kitchen table he was reading the post that Janet had made under my name. However many thousands of miles away it was, I could still hear him cursing at me. "What the hell kinda comment is that? For God's sake Jimmy."

I knew he would be taking a big swig of his second or third beer by now, scratching his leg and kicking the dog out from under the table.

"Where the hell is that dislike button anyhow?" He swore out loud. Loud enough for anyone out in the world to hear if they cared to. No one did.

5

Janet was still on my laptop and watching the comments come in from my post, well, *her* post. Frank, my brother, was one of the first.

Benjamin Franklin Turner: *"that ain't funny Jimmy. Your gonna hurt someone's feelings if they believe you. Look for that delete button and erase that shit right now."*

Frank was right of course, it wasn't funny, even if it was true.

There were many others, most of them scolding me for doing such a thing. However, some were kind of encouraging, in a weird sort of way.

Joyce Johannson: *"What part did you kill off Jimmy? Red meat, alcohol, drugs? You know life is richer when you kill off your demons. Congrats! Let us know what you're up to when you can."*

Staff Sergeant Joyce Johannson was probably the only reason I would have even considered re-enlisting. She was spot on, as the Aussies say, on any subject you cared to discuss. Tough, fair and when required, wise.

Another comment from a guy I had shared many a scary moment in combat with, Tommy, got me to thinking about the fear again. Poor bastard, he was still over there.

Thomas J. Jacoba: *"Damn! You beat me to it buddy. I got that same post scheduled every day at 10pm. If I don't get back from patrol it goes live, but so far, God willing, I cancel it every night. Now quit screwing around and post some lava pictures already!"*

Janet read all of these several times, all while drinking a fresh twelve pack of PX beer. The cleaning lady had come in and made a small fortune on the nickel returns for each can and had left a flower on the table.

It was getting late in the afternoon, as the light began fading even quicker beneath another dense cloud settling in all around. Janet finally closed the laptop without any more posts. No explanations, no hints, just her telling the world I'm a goner and using my account to do it. What the hell was that about?

She was in the bathroom now, whistling. Some kind of silly happy song. It sounded like the kind of song you might hum right before an execution. Distracting, optimistic and completely inadequate. Brushing her teeth and forgetting to floss, she then hopped in the shower until the steam challenged the clouds from just inside the window.

Walking out, dripping wet and naked she went into our room and threw open my suitcase. Pulling out a pair of my new underwear, my camo pants and a recently purchased Volcano National Park shirt, she got dressed. Everything fit her perfectly, something we had joked about so many times. Of course, I never tried on her underwear, but we always swapped out jackets at ballgames.

In front of the bathroom mirror, inside the small circle she had to clear with the towel, she pulled her hair back tight, tied it and put it up inside my ball cap. Satisfied with whatever look she was trying to accomplish she clapped her hands for a moment and then made for the door.

I followed her across the parking lot and in between a couple of buildings and right up the steps to the warm glow from the Lava

Lounge. I couldn't quite believe it. I had been dead all of about 24 hours and my baby was already out in a bar.

It wasn't much of a bar, but it met the requirements necessary to drink. A karaoke machine was pumping out all the popular songs to the dozen or so people already in there. No one was smoking, which seemed strange, but it might have been a law here. However, the lights were low enough to do the job smoke used to, keeping the corners dark and those lurking there anonymous. Janet found one of those corners.

I followed her into the darkness. Watching her closely, I could almost feel excitement in her heart. She was quiet, deathly quiet, but deep inside there was happiness. I couldn't sense any static now and the haze was thinner; her mind was opening up a little. She waited for someone to take her drink order.

Most movies I had ever watched where someone dies somehow prompted everyone else to have a drink. As I looked around, at the young people at the bar, the old cowboys opposite them, and five crazy guys with headlamps on, I wondered if they all had seen those movies. Most likely not, most likely they were just there to party, to sing and probably not wear their dead husband's underwear.

After several minutes, Janet got up and went to the bar to order. Despite her best attempts to hide it, her beauty was spilling out everywhere, even if her long red hair remained hidden in my ball cap.

"Two drafts please," she asked the bartender. Amazingly the bartender poured while holding the mike and belting out Prince with plenty of finesse to impress. It only took a minute or so to get the drinks, but that was apparently enough time to get the attention of one of the headlamp crew.

She saw him coming and stoically stood her ground, one of the Lava Lagers moving down her throat already.

"Honey girl, what's the difference between a French Canadian and you?" His bravado was unable to resist that mixture of alcohol and feminine mystique.

"OK, big boy, I'll bite. What?" Janet asked, turning to face her tormenter.

"About six inches, on a good night!" He laughed out loud. Loud and proud, and despite the obvious come on, seemed friendly enough.

Janet set her beer down and looked him over real good. I didn't like that much. I focused on this guy and immediately saw trouble. Trouble for him.

"Dave Lesperance honey," he said sticking out his hand. "I'm a geologist, here to see some lava." Shaking her hand, he noted the deep scratches on her palms. "Whoa girl, what happened here?"

Janet smiled, withdrew her hand, picked up her second beer and turning said, "Why don't you join me in the corner and help me lick my wounds?"

"Did I tell you I was a doctor too?" Dave added, turning to give the other headlamp guys a thumbs up as he followed her to the corner. Just before he disappeared into the shadows he signaled the bartender for two more.

I remained across the bar, unwilling to follow them to the corner. But I did focus on Janet for just a moment. Was she really that callous?

Could she really be out picking up strange men, French Canadians no less, with me less than a day dead? What I saw there reassured me, though. There was no lust in her mind, just more static now, actually a lot of static. A confused sound to me, something I was only hearing from her, no one else I'd run across.

The bartender walked two Lava Lagers over to their corner and returned quickly, a frown on her face. Back behind the bar she briefly looked back and then shook her head and went over to the cowboys. I watched her closely, focused on her for a second. She was upset, really upset, she had....

"What the hell?" Dave yelled from the darkness. I heard a chair fall over and then another. He practically ran into the light and back over to the table of headlampers.

I listened as Dave told his buddies, "Crazy bitch! She had these deep wounds on her hands and she was opening them so they would bleed and then she was licking up the blood!"

They weren't believing him. I looked over at the bartender, still visibly shaken; it must have been true.

"Geez, she wanted me to lick the blood too! What the hell?"

They all looked over to the corner, still dark and unrevealing.

"Maybe that's something they do up here in the jungle?" one of his friends suggested, half seriously.

Dave shook his head and looked back as well, making sure she wasn't sneaking up behind him. "For some strange reason," he announced with his characteristic French Canadian optimism, "it did make me thirsty. Who's ready for another Lava?"

They signaled for more and in record time, the bartender was there with five more.

"I see you got up and left. Smart move." The bartender told Dave.

"Did you see that too?" Dave asked excitedly. "See guys, no shit, that was the most insane thing I have ever seen."

The bartender, all caught up with her dozen or so customers pulled up a chair and sat in between the headlampers. "I won't ask about the lights on your heads guys...but, where are you all from?"

"Well, I'm from the San Diego area," Dave volunteered. Pointing to his friends he introduced them all around. "Pat Kemp there, have you heard his ukulele playing?"

The bartender shook her head no. "No, but lets hear it soon!"

"He's from Texas, you'll most likely hear it no matter what you say. And, then there's John Steinmiller. Honolulu. Realtor to the stars or something like that."

"Nice to meet you," John said. "You pour the coolest Lava I've ever had."

"Mahalo there John, our house specialty. We're lucky it's a good beer." The bartender looked slightly proud saying that.

"That blond guy is Tim Wheeler, an airline captain. He's our designated driver tonight."

"Good thing we're not driving!" Tim said. "We're walking distance to our cabin."

"And last, and some say least is..." Dave looked around. "Hey, where's Everett?"

"I think I saw him head off to the bathroom," Pat said.

Dave turned back toward the dark corner, pointing. "You mean the bathrooms...over there?" He stood up. "That crazy whatever she is might try and chew on his neck." Dave started to walk over there, then stopped. "Pat you better come with me, she can't reach your neck."

The bartender stood as well and went back to her regulars, having said hi to the five strangers in her bar tonight. She looked back to where Janet was sitting and I followed her gaze. She was gone.

6

They found old Everett. Still in the restroom. His neck was intact, but he never could handle his Lava.

I found Janet, back in front of my laptop, two more open beer cans next to the open screen, reflecting the blues of Facebook. More comments to Janet's post about me were coming in.

David Hazlett: *"If you're that tired catch a few winks. I'm sure you'll feel better in the MOURNING."*

Larry McKenzie: *"is it hot where you are?"*

Andy Velasco: *"yo Jimmy. What the heck? How can you post "you're dead" if you're dead? Stick your head in the lava or what? Hey, I just remembered, you owe me money!*

Janet laughed a little at that post. Laughed a little like she was worried, like she was going to have to answer that somehow, and had no idea how. Abruptly, she closed my laptop and found hers. Opening it, she opened Gmail after a moment and began composing an email.

To: Amy Gingerhouse
From: Janet Ashbury
Subject: My Hawaiian Vacation

Amy, I don't know how to tell this to anyone at all, but I will try with you. After all, I owe you after you told me about your uncle and that sleepover. Things are really weird here now, remember what I told you I had found out?

Immediately, she put aside her laptop and reached for mine again. It took a few minutes to reboot it, but another beer occupied that time. She opened up my Facebook again, and began searching. Looking for "Older Posts" she fished for several minutes until she found a Wall post between my brother and I. He had said something there, thinking the Wall was private, when of course, it is not at all.

Benjamin Franklin Turner: *"Good to hear you got yourself a wife-to-be Her picture looks strangely familiar to me though. You know I gotta tell you something. I don't know how to do it, so I'm just gonna say it. We had a sister, Janet, and your fiancé looks a lot like I remember her, before we all got taken away. Both Janet and you were really young at the time, but I was 10. Maybe you should talk to her about it. You know, before...before you have your wedding night and all. Sorry, but I felt like I should tell you. You would want me to right?"*

I had forgotten that, probably like I forget those things I don't want to deal with. I was in love with Janet. Frank must be wrong. Hell, I hardly knew Frank anyhow, he might be looney tunes himself. I took a few days to answer him, but I finally did, and this is what Janet was reading now.

Jimmy Turner: *"Look Frank, I love this girl! She is the best thing that has ever happened to me. No way she can be my sister! But, you know...if she was...well, I wouldn't care! Not too much. Cause I love her man! I love her and that can't be wrong, can it? I know it sounds weird, but if I love her, it doesn't matter right? Besides, we've already slept together and it was frickin awesome! I ain't giving that up for some rumor."*

Janet seemed to take a long time reading that post. In fact, I think she might have just dozed off. It was late, she had been drinking all day, literally, and maybe she was just too stressed out to stay awake.

But, after a few minutes, she rallied and went back to her laptop and her unfinished email.

"Amy, you are my best friend! We have both been through a lot. And, now, I need your words, your friendship. I have done something I cannot undo, even if I wanted to, which I don't. Swear to me you will forever, upon ever, keep what I am going to tell you a secret. OK? I'm waiting for your reply. I'll be up all night...Janet"

Janet hit the Send button, finished off another can of beer and stood up to make her way to the bathroom. Before she could get the door closed, Amy wrote back.

To: Janet Ashbury
From: Amy Gingerhouse
Subject: RE: My Hawaiian Vacation

Girlfriend! I got you covered to the grave! Your secret is my secret! So, what? Did you do it? Really? Was he unreal? Come on, I need all the juicy, nasty details! It's cold here in New Hampshire girl! I need a hot story!

~Amy

Janet came back to the table looking a little pale. Quickly turning and making it into the bathroom I heard her throw up again. I wanted to tell her to lay off the beers if that got to be an inconvenience for her, but apparently it wasn't going to be. She opened a fresh one and washed away the taste.

Stumbling a bit over to the rattan couch and stretching out there I watched her closely. Maybe it was me, being all dead and such, but she looked different. Different like something had changed, deep inside her, something permanent. Her face looked more determined than I had ever seen it. She put her booted feet up on the armrest and closed her eyes to think.

So, I joined her. I focused on my love, my bride to be, my best friend. She was thinking about the night before, when she had talked me into hiking to the crater. It was playing in her mind like a late night TV show, slow but interesting enough to keep your eyes open. I could hear it like it was happening all over again...

"Come on Jimmy, I swear it'll be fun." She said it with a twinkle in her eye that told me she was serious about that promise.

"Janet," I was protesting. "It's pitch black out there, cold and you want to go hiking across a restricted area to the edge of a *boiling lake of lava*?"

She looked at me with a blank gaze for just a second before pouting her lips and swinging her hips. "I want to do it, there, by the lava."

I didn't quite pick up on that for a moment. "Do what baby? It's gonna be a long..." Looking at her while I said that I finally figured it out. "Do it? You mean like get it on?"

She walked up to me with a saunter that answered my silly question with a thousand yeses. Her hands found my neck and brought my face close to hers for a kiss. I closed my eyes, then felt her move away.

"Come on baby, get your jacket. We can share my flashlight."

I opened my eyes, a little hungry for that kiss. Like a puppy dog chasing a bone I did as she told me, following her out the door.

We were both dressed for hiking, having just finished a short one over to the closed for renovation Volcano House. She looked up at the stars once clear of the street lights. There were rivers of stars sparkling brightly. The Milky Way looked to be a cloud stuck in the darkness, the only one anywhere close. Our breaths were foggy reminders of how cold it could get in the tropics with a little altitude.

"Slow down Janet, how far is this crater?" She was almost jogging ahead in the dark, flashlight scanning for the trailhead sign.

"Two miles. We can be there in forty-five minutes to an hour. I checked it out earlier." She stopped to wait for me to catch up to where she was leaning against the sign: Hale'ma'uma'u Crater Trail. "The restricted area sign is just a precaution. We can walk right up to the edge. They even have a viewing area there, with railings."

I remember those railings for some reason, but followed along in Janet's memory as she continued her daydream. We practically jogged along the trail.

That's where I must have met those guys with the headlamps on their heads the first time. They were all hiking out as Janet and I were going in. It must have been almost midnight by then. I thought it funny that their headlamps were turned to red, but one of them, I think it was Pat, said it was because the Park Rangers would spot normal flashlights. The comedian, Dave, said it was a $1000 fine to be caught where we were all standing there, talking. They had pointed up to the crater ridge, some 1500 feet higher and a mile away.

"They sit up there with infrared scanners, looking for people trying to sneak up to the lava pit." Pat said with a bit of adventure in his voice. If not for that I guessed, they wouldn't be having as much fun.

"I doubt there's any overtime in their budget for that," the guy Everett had said.

"I don't know about that," John said. "Rescues can be expensive." He had looked at both Janet and I real hard. "You guys be careful out there. Keep an eye on the wind. If it looks to be shifting, the plume can get you in a moment."

"The plume?" I asked.

"Yeah," John continued. "The smoke, the steam coming up off the lava. It's caustic. It'll burn your skin and your lungs in seconds. Not to mention it's hot as hell too."

The airline guy, Tim, was watching us closely I remember. First Janet, then me, then back to Janet. He seemed to be sizing us up. "Go. Have fun kids!" he said. "I would if I were you," he smiled.

I watched them march off, telling jokes too loudly and laughing like people do when they've had a few too many beers. Or maybe laughing like people who have just cheated death. I thought about that for a moment and how similar those two sounds had always seemed to be.

Janet pulled my arm and got me back on the trail. "Come on!"

The trail was well worn from many years of tourist boots before the big AREA CLOSED signs had gone up. We practically ran the last half mile, Janet throwing off layers of clothing as we got closer. By the time I got to the concrete viewing pad she was naked and standing right up against the railing, facing me.

"Right here baby! Come get me!" Janet's beauty was a bit eclipsed by the insanely radical movement of the plume behind her. It was a dancing mix of orange and gray, twisting and falling, then plunging upward with a ferocity that made me shudder.

Despite my best misgivings I started to strip as well, thinking about the stories I would tell about sex and the volcano.

At this point my own memory was matching up with Janet's daydream pretty well. But, after shedding the last of my clothes, I seemed to forget how I got from being horny to being dead.

I do remember walking over to Janet. She had now turned her back to me, holding on to the railing and shaking her booty like some of those dancers I had seen in Germany. The roar of the volcano was the only thing that could keep me from hearing my own lust boil inside.

"Come on Jimmy," she called out loudly, above the din. "Take me like an animal, by a volcano, in the *restricted area*!"

It was coming back to me now. I do remember coming up close to her. The plume was only yards away, a vertical waterfall of poison rushing up to the sky in some perverse denial of gravity.

She was wiggling her butt left and right and I was trying to grab her hips. Just as I caught her firmly in both hands and thrust my hips forward to meet her, she surprised me, that much I remembered.

Janet was remembering as well. She was still on the couch of Cabin #94, and she was crying now, her hands up to her face. I stayed focused, though, focused on her thoughts and it soon became clear.

As I had grabbed her hips, she had turned quickly and grabbed my arm. I looked up at her, wondering why she was pulling me so hard to her side? Then I got worried, that I remember. Worried that she was playing too roughly near the edge, that we might both stumble in a place you don't really want to stumble. Her other arm had me now and she was pushing, pushing hard with all her strength, pushing me against the railing.

I was totally shocked - at the fact that the railing she had been so seductively posed on had given way so easily, like it was rusted away. In a second, even less, I was moving too fast to stop myself going over. I felt myself falling and I looked up at her, afraid we had both been foolish and gone through the railing, but she wasn't looking at me. She was clawing at the edge, holding on against the momentum she had used to push me...

Push me? I spun once and then I could see her again, this time up on her elbows watching me. Her eyes were big and orange. I was surprised, but more confused. Why would she push me, why would she...

There wasn't much more I thought about that. Suddenly, I was enveloped in the plume and a moment after that I fell into the hot pudding like surface of the lava and for just a microsecond thought one last thing...this was going to hurt.

But, it didn't.

7

The Jagger Museum, perched perfectly above the immense Kilauea caldera and the Hale'ma'uma'u pit, protected Ranger Jack Clovis and Larry Larson from the rain squall moving in from the east. It was late, well past midnight. The museum was closed.

"How many did you count coming out, Larry?"

"Looked like five to me, how many did you see going in?" Larry put down the Class 3 Infrared binoculars.

"Five, but that was the first group. The second group I think I saw just two." Ranger Clovis took the binoculars back and looked to the pit again.

The rain was pelting the steel roof of the museum. It was difficult to talk with the racket.

"Damn rain is hiding my view now, even with your fancy Class 3, Larry."

"Yeah, well, it's not made to see through tons of water, Jack."

The rain was just reaching the edge of the pit as Jack pushed the button again, sending out a laser signal to bounce off anything that might reflect back a heat signature. Of course, close to the plume everything was ghostly white.

"I see someone, I think. Near the edge." He peered carefully, holding the binoculars steady on his arms, themselves resting on the wooden counter. "Yep, one. Leaving the edge and heading..." He put the binoculars down. "Into the rain."

"Yeah, we'll never see the second guy now." Larry groaned. "That doesn't mean he's not there, right?" No one wanted to wake up a bunch of people to do a late night wild goose chase. Both of them knew that the crazy fools that might march up to the mouth of hell itself must assume the risks.

"Not unless we get a call." Jack looked over at his long time friend Larry, and winked. "Unofficial policy these days. Unless someone calls in a missing person, we just let it play. Not enough budget these days to go around chasing crazy people." Jack looked back now toward the pit, completely obscured by the driving rain. "Now if it was regular hours, we would have a couple of Rangers meet them at the trail head with ticket books." Jack put his feet up on the counter and leaned back in his ancient office chair. "But, I'm off duty, and you got cold beer, so in my humble opinion..."

"Let sleeping dogs lie," they both said at the same time.

~~~

Janet's heart, she was remembering, was beating so hard in her chest she could see it bouncing raindrops right off of her bare skin. She had retreated a few feet from the edge of the pit, but had to fall back to her hands and knees as she vomited, over and over. Naked, afraid and completely in the dark, she felt her body convulsing and sobbing. Looking down at the black cinder, where her long red hair, matted with vomit and tears was reflecting the glow behind her, she heard something coming. Loud, insistent and pounding the ground with an incredible force. Rain. Torrential tropical raindrops the size of hail. Just as she struggled to her feet, the rush of wind being forced out of the way by the downpour hit her full in the face. She almost fell back, and for a moment, terrified she was so close to the pit, she screamed.

The lava behind her screamed as well with the onslaught of cold water pummeling it. More steam rushed up and out, increasing the roar in her ears. The roar enjoined with her own heart pounding, her horror at having actually thrown me into the lava and her now increasing terror at being alone, naked and cold. Her mind was on edge, flooded with a chemical especially reserved for fear.

Adrenaline. Nature's organic version of amphetamines. The one chemical that is solely responsible for the survival of the human species. Besides its obvious super power properties it has a far more important quality, memory enhancement. When a human brain is flooded with adrenaline it remembers everything, every nuance, every smell, every single detail, visually. No doubt by design or happy coincidence this allowed early humans to avoid that which had almost killed them the previous time. It also produces euphoria in smaller doses, known as the "runner's high" which encourages endurance and motivates excellence. Some people find it in athletics but many find it in the pursuit of power, in the conquest of what they desire. It has propelled us from the trees to the stars.

It also imprints upon our psyches that which can never be forgotten. Janet was discovering this as she began the long march toward justification and Cabin #94. I could sense it deep inside her even as she made excuses for what I now know was murder. Her guilt was eating her alive, much like the lava had done to me, just slower.

She must have been a sight, climbing out of that crater, up through the jungle ferns in a darkness made deeper by torrential rain showers. Perhaps it hid her nakedness well. It no doubt had washed much of the blood from her lacerated hands. Her flashlight, still by the door, was stained with it even now.

The sadness that moved me now was catastrophic. The woman that I loved, the soul mate I thought I had, the future of my dreams had led me like an animal to slaughter. Her entire idea to visit Hawaii and the volcano was calculated to incinerate every trace of both me and her crime. She had talked me into another enlistment, despite my reluctance, just to get the money to pull it all off.

I watched her now with a fascination beyond my capacity to control. How could this creature, this horrible creature have done this to me? Why? I had seen murderous men in Afghanistan, seen our own soldiers take some pleasure in shooting bad guys, but nothing as devious as this appeared to be. She had enticed me to the guillotine with the promise of sex no less. There must be a special place in hell for such creativity.

However much I despised what I now knew, I found empathy toward her, her loneliness and her desperation. It was a flaw of my own soul I suppose, but it was a fact nonetheless. I didn't understand her but I still loved her, some part of her, somewhere.

Janet had finally stopped crying and climbed up out of the embrace of the couch. Immediately she opened the refrigerator and grabbed two cans of beer, opening them both. She opened her laptop and after a moment her email, still on screen. She found the reply from her friend and began to answer her.

To: Amy Gingerhouse

From: Janet Ashbury

Subject: RE: My Hawaiian Vacation

Amy, sorry to hear it's so cold in NH. It's actually chilly here as well, but only because we are at something like 4000 feet. I have my fireplace going, do you?

You are the first one I am telling this to, so please keep it a secret. I haven't told anyone about your Uncle messing with you. That's because you asked me not to, but also because I can understand it now as well.

Jimmy, my fiancé, my lover, my hope for the future turned out to be even more than that. He is my brother as well. And, he knew it all along! What a creep, I just can't believe it.

He was adopted, just like me. We all went to different families. I guess our parents were pretty screwed up. Anyhow, we had a connection to each other that we confused for infatuation when it must have been whatever it is siblings have. My God!

I found out from our other stupid brother on Facebook, Frank. I was reading Jimmy's Wall postings one night. Frank had found Jimmy and posted something on his Wall, instead of a direct message. How many people have made that mistake? Everybody can read Wall posts, duh! Anyhow, Jimmy was telling him about me, posted my picture and such. Frank recognized me and warned Jimmy. Frank was old enough to remember us, Jimmy and I were just little kids.

Typical Jimmy though, he ignored it, just like everything else he doesn't want to deal with. He simply discounts those things he doesn't want to believe. You would think he was grossed out, but no, not Jimmy. He was in love, for God's sake.

Well, anyhow, we are NOT together anymore and once I get over the disgust and stop VOMITTING I will give you a call.

Janet

8

I had been watching her write that email. Something inside of me screamed out for a little compassion. She could have just left me, could have had me arrested. Shit! Why throw me in a boiling lake of lava? That was hateful beyond what I might ever understand.

She had now finished the second beer and was headed back to the refrigerator for more, two more. Pop. Pop. And, she went for my laptop this time, booting it up and opening Facebook.

It took a few minutes on the slow WiFi connection to bring up the newsfeed, but it finally did and I had something like 36 notifications and 16 messages. Whoa! A record. Being dead sure did a lot for one's popularity.

Janet took her time reading every one of the comments and all of the messages. Many of them were worried friends expressing either outrage or compassion at "my post" that Janet had made. They varied from pissed off about me declaring my death to philosophical interpretations of what I might have "killed" off. There were a couple of wise ass comments though, like "Good luck" and another from a friend of a friend I didn't really know but had accepted anyhow. He said "Good riddance". Of course, he was still in the war and probably had no time for false declarations about what he saw multiple times a day.

Despite being upset with Janet for having killed me, I did find it interesting that people were concerned for me, and I kind of liked the fact that "I" had posted my own death notice on Facebook. That was sorta cool actually.

When I had been deep in-country, hiding in small holes or caves from snipers in the dark I had wondered what my obituary would say. I had envisioned a newspaper clipping that Mom, my adopted Mom, would have on her desk. But, actually, Facebook was better. Here people were saying good things about me. And, you didn't have to travel to some remote military cemetery to read about it.

Three days after Janet had pushed me over the edge, some people were still writing comments below "my" original announcement of:

Jimmy Turner: *"I just wanted to let you all know that I am dead."*

Comment number 18 or so started a trend away from the anger and surprise. Dozens were following that as well.

Alice of Atlanta: *"Well, if no one else has the courage to say it, I will. Jimmy was a great guy! I will miss him forever. Especially the way he used to look at me when I told stupid jokes, like I was completely out of my mind. I'll miss that the most."*

Taylor Secontat: *"Yo Jimmy. I still don't believe you. How can anyone that had as much fun as you call it quits so soon? I mean, don't you remember the time we almost got arrested in Chicago at the Sears Tower, running sprints up the stairwells for $20?"*

Other comments were pouring in, all telling tales of how much fun they had had with me over the years. I had actually not quite forgotten, but had not thought of many of those adventures in years. Hunting Grizzlies in Alaska, white water rafting the Colorado and camping in tents across the southwestern deserts with that old VW bus. Even taking a stab at rodeo in New Mexico for beer money and having to spend more than we had won on a broken arm.

I watched Janet read these over and over, sometimes stopping to cry a bit, or grab two more beers. Always two. Pop. Pop. Always planning ahead, that girl.

After a little while she fell asleep on the table, her red hair flowing over her arms, her face and my laptop.

A chat window opened, the little beep unable to rouse Janet. It was my Sergeant.

9

Funny how being dead has so many advantages. I didn't get tired, or cold, or hungry. I didn't feel a need to drink beers or boast or make rude comments about bad drivers. I think I was actually a nicer person, except that I wasn't really a person anymore.

Moving outside while Janet slept I looked up at the enticing river of stars in the black sky. I could see, but I wasn't doing it with eyes, I guess. I could hear, but not with any ears I might have. I could sense things in people that could tell me stories about them, their dreams and fears and hopes. It was all pretty cool.

I could also sense something completely new as well. For want of a better word I had to call it "nature". I felt like I was actually a piece of it now. In school, science class I believe it was, the teacher told us that people were animals as well, a part of nature, etc. etc. No one ever bought that, though. We were Humans. And Nature was a place we lived in, or exploited, or avoided. Two different worlds.

But now, I felt like I was actually integrated right into the fabric of this thing. It was very much alive. As I quit moving, several hundred feet from the cabin, I listened, like a hunter might in the woods. Something was going on, everywhere. It was not just a silent stand of trees, or a few moss covered rocks some poet might write about. It wasn't just a volcano, a tourist attraction, or a place Rangers and scientists make a living trying to monitor.

It was something like I was standing outside of a window of the Lava Lounge on free beer night. Lots of activity going on, like people talking excitedly, singing karaoke. You might not understand any of the many conversations going on inside, but you could tell they were all having a big time.

The river of stars above was humming, billions of Lava Lounges, all full of voices and songs and storytelling. It was almost too much to focus on, so I followed the trees to the overlook of Halema'uma'u crater and it's steaming lava pools. The glow was immense, lighting the plume from below like a Hollywood spotlight turned red.

Deep inside the canopy of Ohia trees and impossibly prehistoric ferns towering everywhere I stopped. Just beyond, a few feet actually, were the cliffs and the march of devastation leading to the pit. Here the jungle was teaming with sounds, the sounds of souls. Sounds from things that were never human though, things that were quiet different from me. Sounds from the sort of things you would expect from a world without people. It reminded me of a time I was alone in the forests of Montana, hunting deer. I must have been the only person for a hundred miles. I was young then, and a bit afraid, and as I clutched my rifle I felt vastly outnumbered. It was then that I first experienced what I know knew to be true: the world, the universe, is not human centric.

As I listened to the cacophony of sounds flowing around me, through me, rising and falling with some sort of pulse I heard something above the din. A voice. It was clear and distinct, easily rising slowly above the chatter all around. It was getting louder, and, I assumed, closer.

"Jimmy! Jimmy Turner!"

I turned all around, trying to find the source, but it seemed embedded in the flow, like a flower floating in a mountain stream.

"Yo Jimmy, it's Tommy! You must be close by dude!"

He sounded very close now and he sounded familiar.

"Tommy?" I mumbled. I tried to look around, but I didn't see anything but the jungle and the glow of the lava some distance away.

Suddenly, I felt him next to me. But I saw no one there.

"Hey Jimmy, good to catch up with you again," Tommy said, his voice gentle and confident.

I couldn't figure out why I couldn't see him. I knew I could see Janet and the tourists, and the wild bunch at the Lava Lounge. Why couldn't I see him?

"Tommy, help me out here," I said to him, wherever he was. "Why can't I see you?"

He laughed a little at that, making me feel a little foolish.

"Well, Jimmy, I can't see you either dude, but there you are, yes?"

I gave up for an instant on that mystery and moved on to trying to figure out which Tommy this was that apparently knew me, and I him.

"Tommy, I'm sorry. But, Tommy who?"

"No problem. I get that a lot. Tommy after all is a popular name. Private First Class Thomas J. Jacoba ring any bells?"

It did indeed. Tommy, my high school buddy. A friend on Facebook as well.

"Hey," I said excitedly. "Why aren't you in Afghan anymore?"

Just asking the question answered it for me, and before I could apologize or explain myself, he started talking.

"It seems like only a moment ago, Jimmy. You know about that, I think. I was on patrol, like every day, on patrol. The guys were all moving along this wall, trying to reach a building where we heard bad guys were stashing weapons.

"I was just turning to ask the guy behind me for some gum when it happened. Real fast. Real fast, buddy."

I listened to him, fascinated to have someone else talk about it with as well.

"One moment," he continued. "I'm thinking about you over here checking out the lava, and it made me thirsty you know? I turn to ask Horas for gum and boom!"

I felt that hit me hard. "Damn Tommy, I'm sorry."

We were both silent for several moments. The flow wasn't, though, and it pulsed around both of us, like rocks in a stream.

"Yeah, sucks right? Soldiers getting blown up with dynamite. I mean, we have nukes, right, and we are getting blown up with frickin' dynamite?"

I had wondered that too, a long time ago.

"But, I'm real sorry," he continued. "Sorry that I had that post timed for 10 P.M."

"Post? What are you talking about?" I asked, still a bit amazed that I was talking to someone at all.

"I gotta go, Jimmy," Tommy said, sounding a bit distracted. "Take care." He seemed to move away a bit, in the stream of sounds. "I'm real sorry, Jimmy." He seemed to speak louder now as the distance between us increased. "I'm sorry that my Dad is gonna read about me dying on Facebook."

10

I remained where Tommy had left me, in the jungle, near the cliffs, staring at the glow of the lava in the distance. He had long since moved on to wherever it was he was going. Those last words of his were still bouncing around in my mind. Sorry. Sorry that his Dad would read about his death on Facebook. Oh my god, my own Mom must have read that post Janet had made on my behalf by now! It had been almost a week.

The sky seemed to quickly grow lighter, washing away the river of stars and the blackness they bathed in. The sounds I had heard much earlier were quieting and soon I didn't notice them anymore. Perhaps the sun overwhelmed them with its own song.

There were no lights on in Cabin #94 as I approached the front porch and then moved inside. My laptop was still plugged in, and Facebook was still up. Janet, I soon discovered, was asleep still on the bed, fully clothed and on top of the covers, snoring loudly. A dozen beer cans littered the room, one spilling on the floor.

I looked more closely at the laptop, and the chat window was still open. The little box off to the right tried real hard to squeeze as much text as it could into a small space.

Joyce Johannson:

"Jimmy, haven't heard from you.
Hope all is well.
You need to report to Ft. Bragg in 3 days."
Joyce is offline

My Sergeant was looking out for me no doubt. She always found her troops one way or the other *before* we were scheduled to show up after leave. It kept everyone out of trouble. Her especially. Someone didn't show up once, and she cursed the guy for weeks for all the heat she got from the Lieutenant and for all the paperwork.

Well, there wasn't much I could do. So I waited. Waited for Janet, waited for Ms. Debbie and my trip to the light. Tommy sure didn't have to hang around long. I wondered what the deal with me was.

Something was keeping me here, and the more I thought about it, the more it pointed to Janet. Why still mystified me. At this point I could move on easily. Sure I loved her, but the part of her I loved seemed to no longer be there. At least not on the surface.

~~~

Sometime around what must have been high noon, she pulled herself up off the bed to find the cabin all cleaned up. The maid had been a saint, keeping her work silent. Plus she was making a small fortune cashing in all the beer cans.

Janet immediately went to the refrigerator and fished out her last two beers cans. Pop. Pop. No Snap Crackle here, just beer. The first one went down like water and she took the second one into the bathroom setting it down on the counter.

Staring at herself for a few minutes, studying her eyes and running her hands through her long red curls she abruptly started crying. But, she didn't drop her head, or reach up with her hands to cover her eyes.

She just moved in closer to the mirror and watched the tears roll down her cheeks, sobbing.

After a moment, and without wiping her face, she stripped off all of her clothes and stared again at herself, her body. Hands shaking slightly she moved them up and under her small breasts, gently lifting them. She pulled at her nipples for a second and then released them quickly. Reaching to her sides, she moved her hands, gently now, down her ribs and to her hips. She was crying again, but lightly. I could almost hear the tears hitting the counter top.

She felt around her belly for a long time, then moved back around to her butt. She always had a fantastic butt, spectacular, actually, not that I cared much anymore, but I did remember caring at one time.

It was strange watching her. I got the distinct impression she was sad about herself, although I can't imagine why. She had an athletic, muscular build that I had to defend on more than one occasion in a bar. When she was happy and smiling and friendly, she was a knockout.

Finally, she reached up to wipe away her tears. Her hands found her long red curls this time and both of them lifted the mass up and over her head. She turned her left hip inward, posing like a model and trying to smile. It looked forced.

She turned the other hip in toward the mirror, preening for the mirror, for herself. Then she laughed a little and let her hair fall. Lifting one leg up onto the counter she leaned in close to the mirror. I watched her expression change as she moved one hand down low. Her eyes closed gently as she took a deep breath. For a few minutes she tried and tried, but her concentration, her mechanics were off, and she quit.

That's when I saw the anger in her eyes. She stood there, hands on her hips, frustrated and angry about it. Furious. She slapped herself, right across the face, twice. Then she slapped her breasts, hard enough to leave a mark. She was crying again now. Angry tears, pissed off tears.

She picked up the last beer and chugged it, smashed the can with her hands, and tried to throw it out the bathroom window. It missed the small opening and bounced right back into the toilet.

Cursing, she turned back to herself, in the mirror and began punching her stomach, like a samurai might sink his sword. Of course, she couldn't get enough leverage to hurt herself much, but she was going to try.

I was afraid she might actually hurt herself in a minute, if the thought of a weapon crossed her mind. Immediately upon thinking that she stormed out of the bathroom and into the bedroom. She was throwing things around, bouncing shoes off the walls and knocking over a lamp with her jacket.

Still cursing loudly, like I might, but certainly not like any woman I had ever met she apparently found what it was she needed. Slamming the bedroom door open so hard it bounced closed again behind her she held long fabric sheers in her hand as she marched back into the bathroom.

This I couldn't watch, wouldn't watch.

11

The cold gray sand was locked in an immortal battle against the green terrorists. Her bare feet ran quickly over the firmness, just above where the last wave had receded. She saw it easily, knowing the heart of war personally, and recognizing one you could never really win. A battle yes, as the gray sand battled the sea and its jade green pebbles, but never the war.

38 years old, tough, single, and moving powerfully along that indefinite line between the Pacific and Oceanside, California, she never paused. Never slowed down for a breather, lest she drop her pulse too low. Never skip a run, even in the obnoxious winter dampness and cold. Sergeant Joyce Johannson liked it that way. No time to dwell on the impossibility of it all.

Impossibility seemed to permeate everything, at least this morning. All this running wouldn't prevent anything in the long run. Her skin would slacken, her hair would gray and her muscles weaken. She stopped at the pier and counted to 60 before turning to head back the direction she had already come. And, she felt, nothing would ever stop the war. The war in mankind's soul. They could win every battle, every skirmish, every challenge, and still, there would be more. Just from some other direction over some other reason, imagined or real.

It didn't matter at this point anyhow. She was going to continue to run in 40 degree fog and she was going back to Afghanistan. And she was going to gather her soldiers like a mother hen and get them all together at Ft. Bragg in two more days.

There was only one man left to confirm and he had just posted on Facebook that he was dead. She had heard of excuses before, but this one got the award for originality, if not for stupidity as well.

How can you post something when you're dead? That hit her first, but then immediately after she thought it was something people don't normally joke about. So, if it was legit how would you do it? Set a timer or something and then go jump off a bridge?

Regardless, she needed Private First Class James Madison Turner on a plane pronto if he was still in Hawaii. It would take him nearly 20 hours to get from airport to airport. She would try and call the front desk at Kilauea Recreational Area to get a message to him directly.

Up ahead a larger wave was moving in, threatening to swamp her straight line back across the beach. She sprinted as fast as she could to beat the enemy. Her heart, her legs and her lungs all stepped up to make it happen. Only a small splash hit on her back as she won, then slowing down to a simple run, she lost her frown.

~~~

My fascination, well, my fear, actually could finally hold me back not a moment longer. I had been outside Cabin #94 for an hour. Nothing had changed. No lights, on or off. No loud noises, no screams. I sensed the static, the white static of Janet's mind begin to soften and fade. Was she slowly bleeding to death on the bathroom floor?

Instantly I moved inside to the fireplace mantel again, and looked around. Nothing. Nothing indicating trouble. I gazed down the hall and then I saw it, on the floor, spread across the entrance to the bathroom. Red, lots of red.

Hair was spread out across the white tile floor, almost flowing on its own. I moved closer and into the doorway.

She was leaning up against the bathroom counter, still naked. Her lower belly was pressed against the edge and her toes were stretched up. Strong legs held her as she moved the scissors for a last snip or two of what was now a military style haircut. A military man's haircut. Half an inch at best and brighter red than I could have ever imagined. Carrot top, blue ribbon at the fair, kind of red.

Reaching down for a beer, she realized the can was empty. Crushing it swiftly she dropped it to the floor, let the scissors fall to the counter and smiled at herself.

I had never imagined how much her long hair had added to her femininity. Her thin hips and small chest accentuated her now boyish good looks. No makeup parked on her skin or lips.

She turned and marched right toward me, running right through me. That was a strange feeling, being that there was no feeling whatsoever. She moved toward the bedroom and threw my suitcase up on the tousled bed.

Soon she had one of my white t-shirts, a pair of khaki trousers, and finally a pair of my briefs. These she put on experimentally, pulling them up like a pair of training panties. They fit her exceptionally well. Next came the white shirt and then she found my 189th Infantry Brigade cap, which she pulled down low over her brow.

Finally the pants and my Wal-Mart special running shoes completed her. Walking over to the bedside stand she found my wallet, opened it and no doubt found the two hundred dollars I had stashed for a special dinner in Kona.

I wasn't sure, but I think I heard her mutter beer money as she stashed the wallet in her back pocket, *my* back pants pocket.

She practically ran back into the bathroom and checked herself again in the mirror. Damn, she looked a lot like me! Her cheekbones were a little softer and her lips a little fuller, but not by very much. With my jacket on, my wallet in her pocket and a big smile on her face she marched over to the Lava Lounge.

~ ~ ~

Larry Larson had parked just outside the closed gate to the back entrance to KMC. It was only a short walk to the Lava Lounge from there and two miles less driving. Being almost 5pm he figured some of the guys over at the front desk might be game for some karaoke.

As he passed the Lava Lounge, he noticed that it was far too quiet. He needed a couple of good voices, or at least some brave voices, to liven things up. The front desk was only a few yards further through the mist. Larry could see the bright lights on inside.

"I'll make sure we get him the note, ma'am." Alex was looking like it was quitting time, but was tortured with the fact that he couldn't quite quit. "Yes, ma'am, I understand it's very important. No. No, I'm not enlisted, no, ma'am. I just work here." He was nodding yes and gesturing with his free hand.

Larry walked up to the counter and leaned in. Alex looked up and pointed at his watch, frowning.

"Of course, right away. Yes. I understand." He looked at Larry and rolled his eyes. "I'll do it myself Sergeant." Alex hung up, disgusted.

"Can you believe that?" Alex complained.

"What?" Larry followed.

"This Sergeant Janice or something like that," he looked down at his notes. " Sergeant Joyce Johannson wants me to track down some lost solider and give him a note. This guy's about to miss his deployment." He waved his hands in mock desperation. "Like I got nothing better to do at quitting time."

"Let me see that, buddy," Larry said, reaching out for the notes. Reading it quickly, he put the note down and reached over for Alex's paper and pen. "Here, you want me to do it? Cabin #94 is half way between here and karaoke. You're going right?"

Alex shook his head no. "Don't know how, Larry. I got this delivery," pointing toward his notes. "And some boxes to open."

Larry looked over at his drinking buddy with a bit of amazement. "Boxes to open? Are you kidding?"

Alex shrugged his shoulders.

"Look Alex," Larry explained. "I'll take this Sergeant's note over to Cabin #94 and you get yourself over to the Lava Lounge where I'll have two Lava Lagers," showing two fingers, "parked in front of two stools."

Alex shrugged again, and this time smiled. "I'll make it fast, but I need to get this stuff done."

"Great!" Larry said, taking the notes and transposing them onto a clean piece of paper, making a respectable telegram. He folded it and stood up to go as Alex was heading for the storeroom.

The clouds had settled in thick, blocking out the late afternoon sun for the rest of the day, and possibly the stars later. Larry took the steps two at a time and rounded the corner of the old stone building just in time to see someone exiting Cabin #94.

Through the thick mists all he could tell was that it seemed to be a guy, possibly the elusive Private Turner. His cap was on tight and low. Boots and khaki pants topped with a black jacket painted the rest of the picture for Larry. It had to be Private Turner.

He ran a few steps to catch up with the rapidly disappearing figure, headed in the direction of the Lava Lounge.

"Hey," Larry yelled out, trying to temper his voice from sounding overbearing. "Hey Private Turner?" He jogged a few more steps until he managed to catch up. "Yo, Turner?"

Finally the figure stopped and turned. Larry stopped abruptly as well. If this was Private James Turner he sure looked young.

"I have a telegram for Private Turner," Larry said. "Is that you?"

Janet had hoped she could get more than a few steps out the door in Jimmy's clothes before having to actually act like she was him. She was afraid her voice would give her away, either through sounding too feminine or just shaking with nervousness.

"Sure," Janet mumbled. "Yes." She reached out for the telegram, before it was even offered.

Larry noticed her voice and immediately figured this was one of those "Don't Ask, Don't Tell" situations. He reached out to give the telegram to whomever this was. "Please read it. Your Sergeant is in a bit of a panic."

Janet took the telegram and quickly stashed it inside her jacket pocket without reading it. She looked up at Larry and tried real hard not to smile like a girl. She remembered a Tony Curtis movie where the young actor simply raised one corner of his mouth in a partial smile and how macho that looked. Trying that she felt ridiculous and turned away quickly.

"Thanks," she said and began her march to the bar again.

Larry stood there a moment as the soldier walked away, then quickly followed. "I'm headed to the Lava Lounge, you too?"

Janet tried to ignore him but Larry came up beside her again, and managed to open the door just as they both arrived. She tried her best to be polite, but firmly announced to him, "I drink alone."

Larry smiled and let her move off toward the bar. "I know that song dude." He paused a minute as he looked around for his friends. "I never do," he added.

12

Her day had started out just fine. In fact, more than just fine, more like perfect. Sacramento was having an unusually late fall, accented nicely by today's highs in the mid 70s. Walking to her bridge game, four blocks from her tree shaded street, along the cafes and coffee shops and throngs of young people she almost skipped a little. The sky was blue-bird blue, her summer dress, cut a little long, was teasing her imagination back some thirty years or so.

It had been at least that long since she had felt that twinge of excitement in her chest. That tingle of adventure. A little promise of romance colored her disposition better than FTD, chocolate or a few sips of white wine.

Agatha Turner had rediscovered love. She laughed out loud at the thought, catching the momentary attention of two other love birds sharing a cappuccino. Amazing, she thought, she was having almost as much fun on Facebook as she'd had so long ago at the soda fountains not far from here.

It had popped up unannounced a few days ago. A message in her inbox from that tall, dark and handsome rogue from high school. He was headed for Sacramento on some kind of contractor convention junket and said he would love to take her to Burr's Fountain.

She had never told him but that had been her very first kiss, there in the corner booth. Opening the door to Sylvia's little dance supply store where they would soon gossip and brag and laugh, Agatha felt a surge of pride. Her son, Jimmy, had been right. Facebook *was* going to be the best thing that had happened to her in a long time.

~~~

I followed Janet at a distance, hovering beside the quiet trees and inside the unnoticed corners of the recreation area. Janet managed to make it to her favorite booth in the back, on the way to the restrooms, without anyone else accosting her. The Lava Lounge was far below seating capacity tonight, being a Wednesday and the day before Karaoke night.

She turned to look for the helpful messenger guy and saw him at the bar talking with a dark haired guy with a long ponytail. They seemed to be old friends. Good. No trouble from him.

Pulling out the telegram, she immediately noticed it to be simply a hand written note. It was short and direct.

Call your Sergeant about your return to duty date
December 15th, 0600H, Ft. Bragg NC
788-555-4343

She had to check her watch to make sure. December 15th was just two days away. No impossible task was ever accomplished without beer, so she drank. Two at a time, until she had finished twelve Lava Lagers, and the bartender began taking longer to bring new ones over.

I was there, watching her. Listening to her thoughts as best I could between the bursts of static and confusion. How was she going to convince Sergeant JJ not to send the military police when I didn't show up? By my calculations, it had been almost a week since Janet had murdered me, and our reservation for the cabin was just for a week. Soon she would have to leave.

The wild ones were back, with the miners headlamps on. They were drinking and talking and doing both loudly. Tourists seem to have the most fun, wherever they went. The locals always maintained a balance. All these guys filed back and forth past Janet, on their way to the bathrooms.

As I watched her she simply stared out at the tables and the TV, always holding onto her drink. Sometimes I thought I could see her eyes close and that was right when the static got loudest, when she did that. When she tried to hide.

Eventually, someone noticed her. It was the tall guy with the wild ones, Pat. He glanced over at Janet on his return from the bathrooms, did a double take and walked briskly back to their table.

"Hey Dave," Pat leaned over speaking in a loud whisper.

Dave put his headlamp back on but changed the light to red. "Yes, Sir Pat, what?"

Pat shook his head like you might shake off a joke you didn't understand. "Your girlfriend, the bloodsucker? She looks to have gotten herself a haircut."

Dave had a momentary look of terror in his face which drew out some drunken laughs from his crew. "No way!" he proclaimed and then leaned over toward Pat, "Where?"

Pat gestured over to the bathrooms. "Your favorite booth."

Dave peeked around his friends to look. "That's not her, that's a guy," he whispered.

"Why don't you buy her another drink Dave?" Tim asked. "See if her hands have healed yet."

"Here," John offered reaching into his jacket to hand Dave something. "I've got a leftover band-aid."

Dave ignored his friends with a smile and kept trying to get a good look at the person in the corner booth. He pushed back his chair slowly, drawing some hoots from the guys. "I'm going to the little boys room."

"Watch out for your neck!" Pat advised.

Dave nonchalantly went up to the bar, ordered a drink to go to Janet's table and then walked toward the bathroom hallway. Glancing over in his best *'I'm not really looking at you, but I am'* gaze he tried to recognize the girl who only a day ago had shocked him with her crazy behavior. She looked quite different, if it was her. No doubt the long red hair was gone, replaced with what looked like a military cut. The ball cap was low over her forehead, and with long pants and a black jacket on it was hard to tell.

But, as he moved into the hallway, his innate photographic memory, used only when girls were involved, kept playing back the images he had just seen. Just as he pushed the door marked *Kane* open, it popped into his mind.

"Shit," he mumbled. "Her hands…"

~ ~ ~

Agatha Turner stood outside the bookstore, just down from Burr's Fountain, looking at her hands. They still had that delicate beauty she had always prided herself on, but now the age spots and wrinkles had claimed much of the surface. Her left hand looked a bit naked, without the wedding ring she had worn for … forever.

Watching as stealthily as she could for any tall handsome man that might enter Burr's, she sighed a little. It had been decades since she had let such emotions drive her behavior, such as shyness at being alone in a booth. Waiting for someone to show up sucked, especially when your confidence was down. She really missed her husband right now, and the comfort she had had in such a long, stable relationship.

"Those days are gone girl," she whispered out loud to herself.

Every Taxi that stopped and cast out its fare was studied closely. First, a young couple, obviously too young to drive but with enough money for a ride, jumped out. Another taxi showed up with four adults, all dressed in some kind of black and red matching outfits.

Her watch confirmed what her heart was screaming. He was late, unfashionably late at this point. She thanked her self esteem for coming up with the idea of standing in front of the bookstore instead of sitting alone at a booth in front of all the happy couples enjoying their time, and their ice cream.

Finally, afraid she would wilt from the stress, she promised herself she would leave at the next taxi that produced disappointment. From a distance she saw another approaching, and after a moment, saw two more right behind it. All three pulled up in front of Burr's.

Four people piled out of the first one, then five from the next and amazingly six from the last, all laughing uproariously and talking loud. She tried to scan all the faces quickly before they disappeared inside. Several were women, mostly beautiful and a bit younger than her, but not by much. Everyone was piling inside Burr's quickly and she missed a few of the men's faces.

As the last of them went inside, one man stopped and before going in turned to look down the sidewalk in the other direction from her. Turning he glanced across the street, and then as if in slow motion gazed toward her for several moments.

It was him! He didn't seem to recognize her. Probably, she chided herself, because she appeared to be an old homeless woman hanging out in front of the bookstore. Turning back to the door he went in last and the sidewalk was bare. Bare and cold.

Agatha's heart was racing with all the emotions and fears of any seventeen year old girl on a first date, a first date some thirty five years later. Her nervousness was overwhelming but her loneliness had driven her to go out, and now to go in the front door of Burr's.

Standing there for just a moment, she recognized the feeling again, just as she had when first diving in online at Facebook. The entire world was there, watching. Watching and waiting for her to say something clever or funny or stupid.

She scanned the crowd and found the large group that had just come in and suddenly there he was, standing up and waving at her, a big grin on that handsome face she had kissed so very, very long ago.

Forcing her hands apart, she took one last good luck spin of her wedding ring, now decorating her right hand, reminding her there was always hope for another grand adventure as great as the first.

~~~

Janet couldn't finish her beer fast enough. This had been a bad idea, coming out in public, albeit a public of a dozen or so hermits in a rainforest. That good looking French Canadian was lurking around again and must have been the one who had sent over a free beer.

"Thanks, of course, but I have to go," she murmured to herself as she stood to go. This was no time to explain her change to anyone.

A $20 bill stuck nicely to the table with all the beer condensation and she made her way for the rear door. She glanced over at the table where they wore head lamps. "What the hell is that all about?" she wondered. Too much time in the woods no doubt. And that meant too much stored up ... well too much of that attention hormone.

Dave almost ran into her exiting the hallway, but stopped short. He watched Janet closely, and tried to look at her hands, but they were tucked deeply into her black jacket pockets. As she passed he caught the eyes of his buddies, waving madly at him and pointing to her. He practically ran back to the table, but remembered it foolish to run with scissors or in bars.

"That was her!" he said in a loud whisper sitting back down.

"No way dude, that was a dude," Everett said, between sips of his fourth Lava Lager.

Pat reached over and grabbed Dave's neck. "Looks OK I guess," laughing he added. "Any other injuries we are not interested in seeing."

"Guys, that was her. I don't know what the deal is with her hair and clothes," Dave excitedly reported. "But her hands, they were cut up just like last time."

"No shit, were they bleeding still?" Tim didn't quite believe Dave, especially having watched him keep up with Everett on the Lava Lagers.

Dave sat back, folded his arms and waited for the friendly insults to stop. "No, they were scarred." He leaned forward, looked over to the door to make sure she was gone now and added, "I gotta tell you guys, if we don't get outta here soon," he looked over at the bar stools. "We just might get a little bit crazy too."

Pat stood up to begin the march to the bathrooms himself, but stopped behind Everett. "Dave, in case you didn't notice..." he touched the head lamp on Everett's head. "We're already there, buddy."

~~~

Cabin #94 was cold inside. For some reason the maid always turned down the heat on her way out the door. But, she never failed to pick up the beer cans. God bless her.

Janet was shaking so much she could barely get her key in the door lock, as the cold mist of the cloud insisted on finding each and every vulnerability in her clothing. Her head was freezing! It had never been so exposed, it was like her neck had ice cubes parked all over her skin.

Finally the door relented and let her in. She flipped on as many lights as she could, thinking it might warm the place up, if only with some reassurance. It wasn't immediately working. She moved to find the heaters, and after some time located them along the base boards.

Bending down to turn them on finally brought on the sickness she had been fighting now for weeks.

Rushing to the bathroom she barely made it before vomiting yet again. She thought she had not done this so much since she had that bout with bulimia back in high school. Perversely enough, as she continued throwing up she remembered what an old girlfriend had told her. Get rid of that much beer and you are ready for some more.

Two minutes later she had two beers and two laptops open. Then my cell phone rang.

~~~

Sergeant Joyce Johannson listened to the ring of Private First Class James Madison Turner's cell phone even as sweat still streaked down the side of her face and onto her phone. Grabbing her towel, she wiped her face and the phone and then listened as it went to voice mail.

"Jimmy here, and you're not. Leave a message."

She was in no mood for jokes, even as she noted his clever outgoing message. "Private First Class Turner. This is Sergeant Johannson. You got less than 48 hours to report to Ft. Bragg. You missed your call in last week and again this morning. Don't make me come out there and drag your ass to Leavenworth." She paused a moment and changed her voice from hard-ass to a bit more friendly. "Hope you had a good time in Hawaii. By the way, what's up with that Facebook post about being dead?" She paused again, and then went back to hard-ass, "You're a good soldier. Be there!"

~~~

Janet was full of confusion. Watching my phone ring then go to voice mail had made her cringe even further. It had to be related to the telegram she still had in her jacket pocket. She, for the first time in weeks, was too nervous to drink.

The cabin phone rang this time, nearly giving her the heart attack she was already working up to. Immediately she picked it up. The ring itself was worse than whatever conversation might occur.

"Hell...hello?"

"Hi, this is Amy at the Front Desk. Can I speak with Private Turner please?"

Janet paused a moment, then consciously tried to deepen her voice a little. "This is Turner."

"Great, we see you're due to check out in the morning. I wanted to let you know you can extend if you like." The Front Desk clerk sounded friendly despite such a mandatory call.

Janet thought about that. She really had no other plans, and honestly had not even considered her next move beyond Volcano.

74

"Sure," she almost let her voice rise back up an octave. "What do you need?

The Front Desk clerk was easy. "Just come by and sign the credit card slip. How many days would you like to add?"

"Lets make it a week," Janet said. That should give her time to figure out a better plan than the non-existent one she had now.

"Great, sir. Come over now if you would, I'll have the paperwork waiting for you."

Janet hung up without any further formalities. She walked back into the bedroom, rummaged around for my wallet, checked for the credit card and then ducked quickly into the bathroom.

I followed her closely now. The static in her mind was suddenly clear and that caught my attention. What could have swept the noise away?

Looking closely in the mirror, she adjusted her jacket and her hat. With sunglasses she could easily pull it off, but it was still a cloud forest outside. Fishing around my shaving kit she found my glasses with their tiny correction for far-sightedness. Putting those on seemed to complete the look she wanted.

Spinning around quickly she marched out the door to the Front Desk. Moments later she had signed my name on the credit card slip and the reservation for Cabin #94.

"OK, that's got you extended until December 20th," the teenage Front Desk clerk said. She looked up at Janet and smiled. "So, whatya doing for Christmas?"

Janet, afraid to look anyone in the eye dropped her head a bit. "I believe I have a lovely tent awaiting me in Afghanistan."

The Front Desk clerk's face faded. "Oh, sorry about that, sir. Good luck, sir."

Janet turned to leave, walked several steps toward the large double doors and then turned back to the clerk. "What are you doing?"

The clerk stared a moment.

"For Christmas," Janet said. "What are you doing?"

"Oh! Thanks." The clerk was beaming now. "I'm going to Maui, gonna hit those beaches."

Janet nodded and turned back to the door. She went down the steps and back into the gloom of the cloud, still thick and drizzling.

By the time Janet got to Cabin #94 she was freezing. Her hands were shaking a little as she pushed the reluctant door open. The heat was still on as she stripped off her jacket and sat back down to her laptop.

Opening a web browser she found Google and typed in *Maui beach condos.* Several results came back up, mostly in someplace called Kihei. She clicked on one that looked nice and had an online reservation system. Their first open day was December 18. Two minutes later, Jimmy Turner had a studio rented all the way until January 9th.

Janet sat back in the light of the two open laptops and smiled. Maui sure sounded nice, and warm. Now all she needed was a plane ticket. Hawaiianair.com made it easy. They had a direct flight between

Hilo and Kahului, which she learned was on Maui, that left pretty early in the morning of the 18th. Jimmy Turner had a seat by the window.

She pulled out my military ID and looked at it closely, then walked into the bathroom to look into the mirror. She grinned and said out loud, "I guess I do look a lot like my brother."

Heading back over to the small refrigerator she pulled out two beers. Pop. Pop. As she quickly drained the first one, she smiled at her new plan.

Sitting back down at the table, she pulled my laptop over to her and opened Facebook.

My profile had several more comments, mostly about my post of two weeks ago about being dead and all, but also about my not saying anything after that.

Larry McKenzie: *"So, if you're really dead, show me a sign."*

David Hazlett : *"Come on Jimmy. I can see right through you!"*

Larry McKenzie: *"are you still dead?"*

Janet clicked in the box that asked 'What's on your mind?' and typed a brief sentence. Having waited this long to say anything would be dramatic no matter what she said, but she found an elegance in simplicity that was uncharacteristic to anyone that knew me.

Jimmy Turner: *"Sorry. Only part of me died. The rotten part."*

13

Larry Larson loved a mystery, if for no other reason than he was good at solving puzzles. Mysteries, though, unlike their odd shaped cardboard cousins had a distinct thrill. Mysteries never let you see all the pieces at once, they seemed to trickle in one or two or a few at a time. That lack of information only made the game more fun, for it was the pursuit of a clue, the chase of a theory that gave it life.

The bartender at the Lava Lounge had seen a lot of strangeness, more than her share for such a small outpost. Her early years in Chicago had shown her all the typical dark sides of humanity, but here, in the high jungle, darkness had a different set of shadows. She attributed it mostly to the remoteness of Volcano town, some to the vog - volcanic smog - and more than she would care to admit to the spirits. No one here called them spirits, they used the term energy, vibes or "the presence", but either way in her mind it was spirits.

She caught Larry's eye and brought over another Lava Lager. "So," nodding over to the headlamp crew, "what do you make of these guys?" She took the bar rag off her shoulder and wiped the koa counter around Larry's coaster.

"Those guys?" Larry glanced over, catching the tall guy playing his ukulele again while the other guys, headlamps blinking red, nodded. "Tourists. Crazy tourists no doubt, but they seem harmless enough."

"Not as crazy as that redhead with the cut up hands." Turning, the bartender looked over at the empty corner booth. "She was in here a moment ago, did you see her?"

"No," Larry nodded. "Cut up hands?"

"Last night, I don't think you were here, but this girl with long red hair was in here, drinking like a fish. Her hands looked to be sliced up pretty bad like she had fallen down on the sharp lava. She was using a lot of napkins as they looked to be bleeding a little. I finally got to cutting her off from any more beers when one of those crazy head lamp guys made a move on her."

"These same guys?" Larry asked.

"Oh yeah, same group. One of them went over to her booth and before I knew it he was yelling and falling over chairs to get away from her.

"She left right away, but I could hear him telling everyone she wanted him to lick the blood off her hands. Crazy shit like that."

"Whoa," Larry mumbled, pushing his empty mug right past the incoming full one. "Thanks."

"She just left a minute ago. You didn't see her, in that corner booth?"

Larry looked around the bartender toward the empty dark corner booth where Private James Turner had sat immediately after coming into the bar ahead of him. He knew his bartender friend occupied the sober side of the bar, but for a moment he thought she had her story mixed up.

"You just said this crazy red head girl had long hair. The guy I walked in with sat in that booth and had a crew cut."

The bartender had both her elbows on the bar now and was listening intently. "You gave the telegram to the redhead that sat in that corner booth?"

"Yeah, that's right." Larry said, suspecting a problem in the tone of the bartender's question.

The bartender straightened up, put her hands on her hips and sighed. Shaking her head a bit, as seasoned bartenders do when they occasionally see something they haven't seen a million times before, she looked back at Larry. This, she kept to herself, was another example of bad spirits, bad energy amongst the jungle dwellers.

"That there redhead, in that booth over there tonight, crew cut or not, is no James Turner."

Larry leaned back on his stool and laughed. "Ah come on!" He looked over at the empty booth again. "Then who was it?"

The bartender looked over at the headlampers and pointed to Dave. "Why don't you ask him? He'll tell you a story."

She walked over a round of mugs to that table and pointed out Larry at the bar. Dave got up and came over.

"How you doing there?" Dave asked, extending his hand to Larry.

Larry turned a bit in his chair, took his hand and asked "Great, how about yourself?"

"Not bad, but I wanted to ask you, being a local here in this bar and all, do people usually come out of the jungle a bit," Dave paused and looked around, then added "crazy?"

Larry tried not to take insult, being a jungle dweller himself. "Well, Dave, define crazy." He was staring up at the blinking headlamp on Dave's head.

Dave got the hint and quickly pulled off the head lamp. "Well, not *this* kind of crazy. The oozing open wounds bleeding in a bar asking me to lick up the blood kind of crazy. You know, *real* crazy."

Larry looked back to his beer for just a moment and laughed. "Yeah, well, that *is* pretty crazy. I don't know. I didn't see that."

Dave tilted his head a bit in confusion. "Well, you walked in with her tonight. She sat in that booth over in the corner."

Larry turned in his chair to face Dave now, frowning a bit. "That guy with the short military haircut?"

Dave nodded. "Yeah, that was her. She cut all of her hair off, who knows why? Maybe got tired of cutting her hands. But that was her alright."

The bartender was back and leaned up to the bar as Dave continued.

"I saw her hands tonight. Same *crazy* chick," Dave put some more emphasis on crazy.

"See Larry, I told ya. Dave here had a close up," the bartender laughed. "Too close maybe?"

"I'll say!" Dave said a bit too loud. "Hey, good meeting you, I'm going to go back and finish my hot wings."

The bartender watched Dave put his head lamp back on and make his way back to his table. Turning she leaned in toward Larry. "So, that redhead actually said she was Private James Turner?"

Larry nodded.

"And, she took the telegram from you?"

"Yep."

Both of them stirred the silence with their own private thoughts for several moments. There had to be some kind of explanation, but neither of them could fashion one.

"You know," Larry began. "I just thought it was one of those Don't Ask, Don't Tell cases. He did look a bit effeminate, or she did, of course. I mean, if you're gonna put your ass on the line who cares which way you swing, right?"

The bartender glanced quickly around her tables and caught an eye of the headlamp crew waving wildly for more beers. "Look Larry," she said as she was forced to go back to work. "I agree. People do a lot of strange things that I don't understand. But, I do know this: Private James Turner has not been in my bar yet." She turned, poured six Lavas and carrying them like they were popcorn headed for the flashing red lights.

Larry couldn't get an angle on this mystery so he waited, waited for the next puzzle piece to appear. In his experience another one always did.

The macadamia nuts on the bar were almost gone and as he picked up the last one he saw his friend Alex, from the front desk, walk in.

~ ~ ~

Agatha found herself getting antsy in the soda shop. Burr's was obviously the place to be if the center of the social universe was your goal. Every happy person in Sacramento must be in here, she thought, laughing, talking and enjoying all the commotion.

On any other occasion this would have been fun, she had to admit. Just not now. She had spent practically every ounce of her will power to propel her soul into this adventure, and she was aching. Any further delay in talking to him would torture her further.

Obscenely big ice cream floats were being placed on the table. Apparently, they all had one, some kind of signature thing he had ordered for everyone.

She was watching him. It was all she could do if conversation was impossible. Watching him closely, and replaying every word of their Facebook chats, messages and emails, she reviewed what he must now know of her. She was a widower, still lived in the same neighborhood, had adopted a boy who was now in the Army, drove an early Prius and had three lovely cats: Tahoe, Reno and Truckee. He was divorced, some ten years now, had no kids, worked for a defense contractor at McClellan Air Force Base and had just bought a fully restored 1972 Camaro convertible.

For just an instant, and really not a moment longer, she felt the same manic anticipation, the full force of teenage angst she remembered having the first time he picked her up on a date, in an old beat up 1972 Camaro convertible.

He was still a handsome man. Time had done him the same favors it seemed to reserve for every other middle aged man: the touches of gray in his hair, the fine lines in a slightly tanned face and the sparkling eyes that still hinted of promise.

Stopping her thoughts before they took her any further beyond reality, she finally tasted what made Burr's so famous. The ice cream, with fountain soda fizzing around every sweet molecule was surprisingly good.

The large diameter straw was perfect and she glanced over at him again, feeling giddy now, the ice cream moving her to grin. Just then, he stood up, waved his hands a bit and smiled over at her.

"Everyone, everyone, please," he was saying, trying to get the table's attention. "I have an announcement."

Agatha became one with the ice cream, and froze.

~~~

Alex took the stool next to Larry. The Lava Lounge was unusually noisy. As he looked around he saw all the regulars, then he saw the headlamps.

"Who are those guys?"

Larry leaned back a bit to check them out again. "Tourists. Or escapees, not quite sure."

"Thanks, honey," Alex said as the bartender slid a perfectly frosted Lava Lager in front of him. "Been waiting on this all day." He took a full minute to slowly down the entire contents. "Another, por favor!"

"So, did you get those boxes sorted out?" Larry asked.

Alex's eyebrows rolled a little. "Yeah, it looks like we have files from twenty years ago in that storeroom. Amy came in a bit early so I was able to finish up quickly.

"Hey, did you get that telegram to Private Turner?"

Larry looked over at the bartender and nodded. "I gave it to a guy who said he was Private Turner, but we were just talking about that."

Alex frowned in confusion and took a short swig of his second beer. "Funny thing that guy. His Sergeant was telling him to get his ass back to Ft. Bragg and Amy just told me he extended here for another week."

Larry stared at Alex for a moment and then over to the bartender.

"No way!" Larry and the bartender both exclaimed in perfect unison.

"What's this about not being so sure it was Turner?" Alex asked with just the slightest hint of trouble in his voice. He could hear the Sergeant yelling at him from some far off place.

The bartender turned to get the ten gallon bag of roasted macadamia nuts and proceeded to refill all the bowls at the bar, while keeping her ear finely tuned to Alex and Larry.

"Look," Larry recited. "I left your office after talking to you, walked out and around the corner and saw what I thought was Private Turner come out of Cabin #94. Dressed in khakis, boots, Army issue jacket and an Army ball cap. I ran up to him, saw the short hair, asked if he was Turner and he said yes." Larry took another long drink of his rapidly disappearing beer. "So, I told him it was important and put the telegram right into his hands."

Alex grabbed enough of a handful of macadamia nuts that the bartender came back around and refilled the bowl a second time. "So, what's the problem? Sounds like you did it to me."

"Yeah, well, everyone in this bar is telling me that guy is no guy. Our illustrious bartender says so. One of the headlamp guys over there tried to pick her up."

Alex cringed a bit at that.

"Well, in his defense, it was before she cut all of her hair off. Apparently last night she was quite the looker. But, tonight she looked like any other farm boy recruit ready to ship out." Larry shook his head a bit.

Alex studied his beer a few moments, captivated by the impossibly infinite supply of bubbles rising to the top. "Strange. But hey," he raised his mug toward Larry in toast. "Another Lava Lounge mystery eh?"

Larry smiled, raised his mug and tapped Alex's mug so hard it made the bartender look around. "To Private James Turner, wherever he may be."

~ ~ ~

The table of middle aged revelers at Burr's soda fountain finally calmed down a bit as he stood there waving his hands lightly.

"What is it Adam? Do I need another drink first?" One of the guys was asking above the din of the place.

"No, no more drinks quite yet," Adam said.

Agatha finally moved her head enough for the ice cream filled straw to fall back into the tall elegantly carved glass. "My God," she thought. "Is he going to embarrass me with some kind of reminisce?"

"Look," Adam said, beaming toward Agatha. "We all came back to Burr's tonight for a special occasion. Yes, the ice cream is worthy of a road trip, but tonight I want to introduce an old, but apparently not so old, friend of mine."

He held out his hand toward Agatha.

She stood up to take it, wishing with all her might that he would keep this short. Public displays of anything, even friendship were quite beyond her pain threshold at the moment.

"Back when I was younger and my friend Agatha was still as beautiful I drove an old '72 Camaro to the high school dance one starry, starry Friday night."

Adam raised Agatha's hand a bit and then gently let it go, allowing her to sit back down, a few shades redder.

"It was by far the best night of my life!" Adam remained up but reached down for his half full glass of ice cream soda. "A toast if you will..." He paused for everyone to raise their glasses. Agatha smiled as she did.

"To the graceful nature of time that lets us occasionally enjoy again the highlights of our youth."

A rousing clinking of glasses followed with several cheers from the other men.

"Now, someone move over so I can sit next to Agatha," Adam demanded in a friendly tone. "We have some catching up to do."

Agatha watched him move in next to her, almost as if they were both sitting in the back seat of that Camaro again. Close and comfy.

"I thought you were going to just kill me standing up and introducing me, Adam."

"Oh that? Sorry, but if I didn't say something all those other guys were going to ask you out."

She laughed lightly at the compliment, something deep inside her heart exploding clear and bright with happiness. Remembering their favorite dish she asked "Shall we order the apple pie?"

Adam reached under the table and gently took her hand. "Of course, my dear. Let's save the best for last."

14

North Carolina was not known for its balmy winters, especially this particularly frigid December 15th. The twenty five men and women lined up in the cold 0600 morning air appeared to Sergeant Johannson like so many steam vents. Their breaths floated above them in an ever increasing fog.

She walked up the line, two deep, barking out the last names in roll call.

"Beninate?"

"Aye" was the answer, forceful and strong.

"McHenry?"

"Here!"

"Samson?"

"Aye"

"Turner?"

Silence followed, then the soft ruffle of necks turning inside of tight collars against the cold. The rumor was out that Turner was still in Hawaii, and despite the attraction of that thought at this moment, everyone knew it to be big trouble for the Private.

"Turner?" Sergeant Johannson yelled more forcefully.

No answer.

"God dammit Turner!" Johannson swore, then continued down her list.

"Yamaguchi?"

"Here!"

~~~

I hovered, as best I could make out, above Janet's fitfully sleeping form all night. Try as I might I couldn't read through the rapid bursts of static and noise coming from her dreams. She had risen twice during the darkness to throw up. Shivering each time, she crawled back under her covers into a fetal position, snoring with exhaustion.

At daybreak she roused herself, dressed in my clothes again, pulled on my Army cap and made her way to the cafeteria. She had to, there wasn't anything but beer cans in the refrigerator.

Showing my military ID card to the cashier, she loaded up on scrambled eggs, toast and steak. A large ice tea and ten packets of sugar, a fork and knife and two napkins filled the rest of the space on her tray.

I wasn't sure why I was so interested in her every movement, but I was. For some reason I couldn't quite fathom there was an intense need for me to keep an eye on her.

About the time she was finished with her breakfast she stumbled and fell twice on her way to the bathroom. I was curious which one she would have gone into but she didn't make it halfway. She was throwing up blood right before she passed out.

Five minutes later she was in the KMC infirmary getting her temperature taken and about to get her shirt removed. The nurse there had read my dog tags around her neck, made note of them and turned back to find her sitting up, staring with eyes redder than my friend the lava.

"Hey there soldier. You had a bit of a spill. Are you feeling any better?" The nurse, a big football player type, asked the question in a relatively demanding tone. He was a civilian volunteer.

Janet shook her head a little, not so much as a no, but to clear the confusion out of her mind. "I'm good. No worries."

"Really? You were barfing blood in the cafeteria. Not a good thing." The nurse wanted to place a call to the base commander, but knew he was in Kona on a shopping trip. There were no other commanding officers available until tomorrow at the earliest.

"Yes, yes. Just drank too much this vacation." Janet looked up at the nurse, an alcohol induced sadness in pitiful eyes working to her advantage. "I'm shipping back to Afghan tomorrow morning. Just celebrated too much." She looked down at her hands, still scarred but healing up. "You know what I mean?"

"Poor bastard," thought the nurse. In his opinion Private Turner could do damn well whatever he pleased by his measure. "No problem. Look, if you like I can check you out now. Real quick physical. See if you're up for duty, if you know what I mean?"

Janet knew very well what that meant. He was going to give James Turner an excuse to avoid deployment, but of course would discover that a naked James was really a naked Janet. That wouldn't work.

"No thanks, but thanks!" She looked up at him and went to shake his hand, anxious to get this over with.

The nurse shook her hand, amazed at how non-masculine it felt, but disregarded that thought. Most hands he shook were smaller than his anyhow.

"Good luck then Private Turner."

"Jimmy, you can call me Jimmy for the next 24 hours," Janet joked.

"Right on Jimmy!" The nurse laughed. "Give 'em hell!"

"I will," she said.

"I did," I heard her say to herself, thinking about pushing me over the side, killing me a little more.

~~~

"Hey Larry, are you up yet?" Alex asked over the phone about an hour earlier than would have elicited a positive answer.

"Well, I guess I am," Larry answered. "Why? Why are you calling me so damn early Alex?"

"Sorry Larry. But, it is 10:30."

Larry sat up quickly, looked around his room to find Shirley and the dog both gone. The drapes over the massive picture window view of Mauna Loa had been drawn shut. "Geez. OK, that's cool. I should be up already." Larry ran his hands through his hair. "I guess it's too late to go paragliding now."

Alex listened to his friend wake up with half his brain while the other half was reviewing the reservations list. After a moment or two of silence, he asked again. "Are you up now?"

"Yeah, yeah. I'm up." Larry coughed once. "What's up?"

"Good, hey look. That Sergeant Johannson called me about two minutes ago, all pissed off about this Private Turner deal."

"Yeah, so?" Larry tried to find more importance in Alex's statement, at least enough to have woken him up.

"Well, she's about to call the police to come pick Turner's ass up, but God love her, she is going to give him one more chance. If we can get the guy on the phone she said she would hold off one more day."

Larry sat there for another long moment trying to figure out his part in all this drama. He couldn't. "Okay, so...?"

"So," Alex made his request. "You can come with me to Cabin #94 and tell me just who you gave the telegram to. This whole cross-dressing thing has me confused."

Larry had gotten out of bed and walked out onto his west facing deck with the cordless phone. The wind was looking too squirrely to fly anyhow. "You want me to drive all the way over there, Alex?"

Alex laughed. "Yeah, the whole three minute drive will earn you a free buffalo steak lunch, on me."

"Well then, since you put it that way. See you in ten."

~~~

Sergeant Johannson knew her troops had returned from leave from all over the U.S. Some from Florida, some from California, and many from the Midwest. Despite whatever weather they had enjoyed, or not, they all knew that Afghanistan was brutally cold in the winter. The 15 or so degrees they had enjoyed at roll call would have been a welcome respite if they'd been already in Kunduz or even Kabul. This was a good run up to one of the shocks they would experience back in-country.

As she dismissed them for breakfast and ran back to her temporary office she hoped frigid weather would be their only shock. She didn't let her mind debate such frivolous thinking. Right now she was pissed off at Turner. Not only was his ass in trouble, but hers would be as well. This would be her third AWOL, deserter or whatever they wanted to call it, in three years. Promotion was slipping farther and farther away.

She was so mad at him she had an overwhelming desire to fly to Hawaii and ring his redheaded neck. She should have done that last week when he posted that inane Facebook post about being dead. Her only good last chance was for some guy named Alex to pull off a miracle and get Turner on the phone.

~~~

The weather around the volcano, specifically Halema'uma'u was getting wet. trade winds, normally steered north by the "long mountain" Mauna Loa were coming in more from the east today. Their moisture laden blessings were easily appreciated by the hundreds of families depending on rain catchment for their water. The jungle seemed to like it as well, and the lava pits grumbled with increased hissing and crackling.

Larry loved the rain as much as the usually perfect weather. It gave him a chance to feel a part of the tropics again. One could soon believe this was all a high desert what with the barren lava plains, clear and dry weather and of course the cold nights. The jungles were tucked into fortunate valleys and ridgelines that had both avoided the lava flows and could catch the little rain that regularly visited. Besides, his papaya trees doubled their production after a couple of days of good drenching liquid sunshine.

The drive to the National Park gate was literally four minutes and it was another four to Alex's office in the military recreation area. Larry pulled his F-250 into the spot next to the flagpole, grabbed his jacket and hat and walked briskly up the ancient steps and into the brightly lit lobby.

"Thanks, Larry," Alex greeted him, already with his coat on. "I appreciate this."

"Lunch?" Larry confirmed.

"Steak!" Alex beamed. "It's my favorite dish up here."

"OK then, let's go."

Alex and Larry marched down the steps and into the light rain, rounded the corner toward the small stone and wood structures. Cabin #94 was already in view.

"So, follow my lead on this Larry. I'm going to knock on the door and ask for Private James Turner. Regardless of who answers the door,

I want you to tap me on the back if you see the same person you gave the earlier telegram to."

"Got it," Larry confirmed.

"Turner rented this cabin for two people. Himself and a Janet Turner, presumably his wife."

"Cool," Larry said. "Looks like the lights are on."

Alex took a deep breath and quickly climbed the three steps up to the small covered porch with a much too large chair on the deck crowding a garbage can.

"Game faces," Alex whispered and knocked three times on the door.

~~~

Janet seemed to be dreaming hard when the two guys came knocking on the door. I was still on my self-imposed duty of keeping a watch over her, not that I could do much.

She was sprawled on the floor having rolled off the couch during the night having never made it back to bed and having thrown up three times. Poor thing.

Beer cans littered the place, some twenty plus, and both laptops competed with the overhead lights to see which could outlast the other. I would imagine that the place reeked by this point too.

The knocking continued, growing louder and more persistent as well. Suddenly my phone began to ring and that frequency seem to rouse her from her comatose slumber. About the third ring she opened her eyes, and then she heard the pounding on the door.

"Hold on! Jeezus." She mumbled it as loud as she could, picking herself up off the floor. A couple of beer cans got mixed up under her feet and she fell back to the floor with a thump.

"Are you OK in there?"

"Yeah, sure. What the hell do you want?" Janet still had a good touch of belligerence in her, no doubt from the alcohol. She finally managed to get to her feet, wipe her mouth with her sleeve and pull a sweater over her stained t-shirt. At least the alcohol had deepened her voice with its toxic effects on her esophagus.

"Private James Turner. It is very important I talk to you immediately!" The voice from outside the door sounded serious.

"Yeah, yeah. Hold on a minute will ya?"

At least the knocking had stopped. Janet looked at the phone and saw the Ft. Bragg area code, again. "Shit!"

"Turner! Are you OK in there? Please open the door!"

Janet frantically looked for my Army cap, found it under the couch, put it on and took a quick look in the mirror. That must have been a bad idea, since she almost started to cry. She splashed some water on her eyes, toweled off as much hideousness as possible and went to the door.

"Game face," she whispered to herself.

~ ~ ~

Alex gasped when the door flew open. Larry squinted to make sure he was seeing what he thought he was really seeing.

"What the hell do you guys want kicking on my door like that?" Janet demanded.

"Sorry to bother you, of course. Private James Turner?"

Larry was already tapping Alex on the back. They both noticed Janet hesitate.

"What is it?" she demanded again, not directly acknowledging the question.

"Look, I'm not here to judge or make trouble. But, I have a message for Private James Turner from Sergeant Johannson."

Janet just stared at both of them.

"It's pretty god-damned important!" Alex yelled now, somewhat out of frustration and somewhat, he would reveal later, out of fear.

That got her attention.

"OK, what is it?" Janet said softly. "I'm Private James Turner."

Alex could smell the reek of stale alcohol, dirty hair and some other whiffs he was trying hard not to identify. Larry was still tapping him on the back until he shrugged his shoulder to tell him enough.

"Sergeant Johannson says you missed roll call this morning in Ft. Bragg. She says if you get on the phone with her right now she will hold off calling the MPs. That's the military po..."

"I know who the hell the MPs are!" Janet barked. Her eyes slowly drifted, as in the pull of gravity itself, down to look at her feet.

No one spoke for at least a full minute, but Larry thought it was ten. Alex was shaking. He had never seen a human being in such bad shape and still breathing. This guy, or whoever it was, looked like death warmed over but left to cool a bit again. Dark purple circles were under the eyes. The hair, short cropped as it was, still looked dirty and there were various scabs on the arms and neck.

Finally Janet looked back up from her feet to guys, snarled and slammed the door hard in their faces.

"I'll be there in ten minutes to use your phone!" she yelled from behind the door.

Alex and Larry looked at each other and turned around. They stepped down onto the sidewalk and both let out audible sighs.

"That went well I think," Larry said.

"OMFG!" Alex pronounced.

Larry took a moment to spell that out. "Oh-My-Frickin'-God?"

"Something like that," Alex acknowledged. "That was the biggest freak show I have *ever* seen."

Larry nodded. "Yep, and they say crack heads are spooky. I'd say alcohol is probably worse, just slower."

As they entered Alex's office he turned to ask, "So that was the same person you gave the telegram to?"

"Sure was, a bit worse for the wear." Larry noted.

"And, our friendly bartender confirms then that this same person was a long haired female red head only a couple of days ago?" Alex continued.

"Sure enough."

"And you heard her just say she was indeed Private James Turner, didn't you?" Alex asked.

"Yes I did indeed."

Alex pondered that for a moment. Larry turned to look out the large office window at the gathering cloud moving into the jungle across the one lane road.

"Well, I'll be interested to see how she explains all this to the Sergeant," Alex mused.

Larry was quiet for a long time, lost in thought. His hands were tracing little circles on the cold window, condensing the moisture into little sad faces.

"Larry?" Alex interjected. He watched his friend take his time to answer.

"So," Larry whispered, then spoke a bit louder. "I guess we can presume Private James Turner is dead."

~~~

Agatha and Adam were in love again. Thirty some odd years of separation in the middle had done little to quell the flame, or so it felt, anyhow.

After apple pie they had taken a ride in Adam's remodeled '72 Camaro convertible, when he finally admitted it was *the* '72 Camaro convertible they had actually dated in.

"I know, I couldn't believe it either. I had heard a couple of years after I had to sell it, that it had been in a crash at Burning Man. But, when I looked at the VIN number, which I had actually memorized, it was the same...I almost cried with happiness."

Agatha looked at him a long moment.

"OK, I did cry a little," he admitted looking away from her a moment. "It was absolutely amazing."

Agatha looked around at the details of this classic ride. It was all so familiar, so historical, but it was her history and that kept it from being dated and old.

After a long night of talking and even singing along with their favorite songs, now on the Oldies Channel, they found themselves awkwardly at Agatha's front porch.

Adam had his arm around Agatha on the porch swing, her head comfortably resting on his shoulder.

"You know, I would. I want to of course. But, we shouldn't. Not tonight."

Agatha lifted her head a little and looked at him quizzically. "What are you talking about Adam?"

"Oh, nothing, just rambling on about nothing."

Agatha secretly smiled to herself. It was as perfect as if it'd been written. "Why don't you sleep on the fold out couch, and," she sat up excitedly, "in the morning, let's head up to Tahoe!"

Adam grinned and let his head drift back a bit to watch the ceiling move lazily back and forth. He couldn't have asked for a better script himself.

~~~

Janet was in a full on panic. I could feel it in the static she was broadcasting, in the noise from her soul.

She shooed the maid away when she showed up, extra cleaning supplies and garbage bags in tow.

"They're on to me, they have to be," she mumbled. "Shit, I gotta get out of here." In five minutes she was packed and in her rented car. Fighting the urge to speed away, she kept pulling her foot off the accelerator after each urge to flee. Staring straight ahead she hoped that if she didn't see anyone then they wouldn't see her either. She did however, feel the sweat moving down her forehead, her neck and back.

Only a mile down the road, feeling no one following her she looked out toward the volcano. There at the scenic outlook overlooking Halema'uma'u crater she stopped a moment, out of some long lost respect. Some kind of perverse curiosity led her out of the car to the short rock wall at the edge of the two hundred foot cliff. Looking down, she could see the path, still closed, that she had led me down.

I moved in close to her, at her very shoulder as she looked at the very edge of the large lava pit, where she had decided to push me in, to kill me. This close I could feel so much more of her mind, so much more of the energy she had within her.

Her vibe felt different lately, different than the first day I was dead. Something was changing inside of her, some sense of hope twisted deeply with the despair. I still didn't have any idea why I was still lurking here when others like me had moved on in the stream, like Private Thomas Jacoba. I took a moment to look up in to the sky and saw that the light there was a little closer than before. This of course wasn't the sun, it was something entirely different, it was where Ms. Debbie had returned to. I found it more intense than the sun and as different from the sun as I was now different from Jimmy Turner.

Suddenly Janet started to sob. Heavily. Heaving her shoulders. She had to lean on the railing for support as grief washed over her.

An elderly lady close by moved in to comfort her out of some immeasurable amount of kindness. I feared Janet would rebuff her, but I was wrong. I think she probably didn't even notice.

Several minutes later, when the rain moved in again, and the kind lady's husband pulled her away, Janet stood tall for a moment and walked back to her car.

Minutes later she was turning left on the Belt Highway and making her way to the Hilo airport.

~~~

Alex's phone rang a full three times before he or Larry noticed it. The shock of meeting Janet and the inevitable demise of Private James Turner were weighing heavy on them.

Finally Alex snapped out of it and picked up in the middle of the fourth.

"Kilauea Military Recreation Area, Alex."

"Alex, this is Sergeant Johannson. Is Private Turner standing next to your phone by some miracle?"

Alex paused as Larry turned around and gave Alex a salute with the question on his face of 'Is that the Sergeant?'

"No he is not, I'm afraid to say."

"Damn it! Why not?" she demanded.

"I..."

Johannson interrupted his excuse, "Save it! I didn't really think he would."

"Look, Sergeant," Alex wanted to explain. "We never saw James Turner. In fact, we haven't ever seen him. We thought we were dealing with him but it turns out to have been a woman masquerading as him, perhaps his wife."

"What the hell?" Johannson yelled. "Where's my soldier, then?"

Larry motioned that he was going to Cabin #94 to get the red headed girl to hurry on up to the phone.

"Larry, the guy who first delivered your telegram, and I have a bad feeling about the Private. This girl who says she is the Private is in bad shape. Drunk, sick, looks like a walking corpse."

Alex waited for a response but only heard silence. He continued.

"She's supposed to be here any minute to talk with you."

"Oh, really? This masquerading wife of his is going to do what? Pretend she is him, to his own Sergeant?"

Just then Larry ran back into the office.

"She split! Took off, car is gone and her bags too!"

Alex stared at Larry for a moment, feeling like an idiot for thinking she would show up. Reluctantly he told the increasingly angry Sergeant on the other end of the phone.

"Yeah, no shit! No matter, I have military police on their way already as well as what armed Rangers I could find. They should be there, in your office, any moment. Please do show them around. The airports are already looking for anyone using Private Turner's ID." Sergeant Johannson continued, "And Alex..."

Alex stood up now, three burly Rangers already entering his office. "Yes..."

Sergeant Johannson was furious but had planned ahead anyhow. She knew she couldn't rely on a civilian to carry out orders in any predictable manner. Two days had been wasted waiting on this guy to get a simple message to someone who evidently was never there. She took a deep breath and finished her sentence.

"Never mind." The phone went dead.

~~~

Janet was speeding, which she knew wasn't a brilliant idea, but she was scared and couldn't keep her foot under control. The traffic was light, but so was the rain, and the roads were getting a sheen.

Finally, her luck, what little there may have ever been, ran out with the entry onto the road of a school bus. She hit her brakes to keep from running into the big fat diesel exhaust pipe, but wasn't going to make it. She swerved into the oncoming lane to possibly go around, but a tour van was coming up quickly.

There wasn't much to do but to swerve back into her lane, behind the looming butt of the bus, downshift to low and keep on the brakes. She felt the tug of deceleration and soon felt her tires grabbing some pavement but pulling hard to the right. The bus was rapidly accelerating, probably having seen the speeder coming up fast, but it was too late for Janet's rental car, now with the front right tire in the soft jungle mud.

The steering wheel came out of her hands demanding to follow the front tire into the shallow ditch between her and the Ohia forest a few meters to the side. In a matter of some small slices of one second, Janet pushed the air bag remnants out of her face and watched in some fascination as the big yellow school bus continued down the road. The tour van passed her going the other way and never stopped. It was like she didn't exist. No one else's little bubble of reality had been sufficiently disturbed to stop and help.

Janet could see a whole lot of mud and ferns up on her windshield, but when she tried to open her door, the mud and ferns there prevented it. Rolling down the window she looked out and saw she was nicely plowed into a ditch that would require a tow truck and more motivation than she might ever be expected to muster.

The rain had at least let up a bit she noticed, so she began climbing out of the window with her one bag. She had to crawl up the steep embankment to the road, her hands, knees and feet now muddied.

Finally on the edge of the pavement she turned to look at her car. The two front tires were flat as well, and the side window on the passenger's side was broken.

"Great, just fucking great!" She looked in both directions. The stretch of road ahead of her was empty and the hill behind her hid whatever might not be there. Nothing and no one. Pulling the Army cap down low on her head, she continued walking in the direction she had been going.

Her shoes were shedding the mud slowly. With little traffic she felt safe walking on the edge of the pavement. Breathing a little more normally now, she could hear the Coqui frogs chanting in the deep cover. Large ferns lined the edge of the jungle protecting the darkness behind them from the casual view of anyone cruising down the road.

Something made her focus on the sounds. It sounded strong and it sounded, she thought, as if it were running straight for her. Coming quickly through the woods was a mass of heavy rain, pounding the Ohia and Koa trees. The curtain of dense rain crossed over onto the road, making it sing. Instantly she was soaked. Her Army cap held the deluge away from her face, similar to how a snorkeling mask did underwater. In true tropical fashion it actually got a little warmer with the rain.

"Perfect! Just perfect!" Janet was yelling holding both arms high up in the air, daring the gods to strike her down.

A car she never heard passed her from behind and hit the brakes, stopped and backed up to her, window slightly down.

"Hop in, I'm going to Kapoho."

Janet stared at the older woman inside of an old Toyota Tercel. She had beads in her hair and was wearing some kind of hippie print dress

"I wasn't hitchhiking," Janet deadpanned.

"Well, you should be! Hop in before you get run over."

Janet stood and stared another long moment, almost in a daze. However, when the lady put the car back into first gear, she rallied and reached down for the door handle.

"Honey, you're soaking wet," the lady exclaimed, seemingly surprised. "Reach into the back there and get my beach towel. I won't need it now anyhow."

Janet couldn't quite read this lady. Did these rural people really pick up strangers in the rain? "Thank ... thank you."

The Toyota struggled through the first few gears getting back up to speed, before the lady let it coast a bit in the heavy rain

She looked at Janet for a long moment before watching the road again. "Who you running from honey? Not that it's any of my business. I just want to know who might be coming up fast in my rear view mirror."

Janet immediately turned around to look behind them, but saw nothing, but heavy gray rain.

"Seriously, is someone looking for you, now?" The lady looked in the mirror herself and sped up a bit.

Janet looked over at her again and saw something friendly, something that moved her to the first bit of honesty in months. "The military, I guess."

The lady looked up at her haircut again and then back to the road.

"OK," she said, pausing just a moment. "So where are you going then?"

Janet fidgeted a bit with her bag. These were sure a lot of questions. The rain was still coming down hard and she would rather ride than walk, even if the questions were coming fast.

"The airport. Hilo I think is what they call this one up ahead?"

The lady looked at her again with a bit of a confused expression. "The airport honey? Are you kidding? The military will certainly have that covered don't you think?"

Janet had not considered that in her haste to leave Cabin #94. No doubt they would have police looking for her soon. They would find her abandoned car and soon figure she had caught a ride to Hilo.

"So where are you going, again?" Janet asked, trying hard to smile just a little.

"I'm going home, to the Kapoho area." She looked at Janet one more time before putting on her right blinker for the turn into Pahoa town. "You're welcome to come with me. I live with several old hippies you might find interesting. Some of them are *still* on the run, some forty years later." She laughed out loud.

Janet felt ten thousand weights lift off her chest. What she needed right then was a good idea, and here was an excellent one. "OK, that sounds good." She looked at the beads in the lady's hair again, they gave her hair a rainbow of colors. "I'm James..." she coughed a little. "I mean Jimmy."

The lady looked over at her again. "Jimmie with an ie on the end?"

Janet nodded.

"Cool, I'm Starshine Aloha." In another moment she turned the old Tercel sharply to the right and punched the reluctant accelerator as they found a good long stretch of downhill road ahead of them. "Nice to meet you Jimmie," she said fidgeting with the windshield wipers. "You can just call me Star." She looked down at her car and punched the dashboard slightly, "I think I've got at least one headlight working." She was right.

Janet saw the dark blue of the ocean ahead at the bottom of the long road they were on. Star glanced over and caught her looking.

"We live at the end of the road. I'm going swimming at Champagne pond before dark. You want to come along?" Star asked.

The clouds seemed to be lifting as they descended from the higher altitude Belt Highway, the rain suddenly disappearing. Janet could feel the air warming up as well. The road was increasingly lined with pregnant coconut palms, guiding them toward the sea.

"Do you live near the ocean?" Janet whispered, incredulous.

Star smiled. She flipped off the windshield wipers and rolled down her window, letting her hand surf the airstream like a kid. "Yes. Yes we do Jimmie." Star took a long deep breath of the fragrant air, something Janet was doing as well, having rolled her window down as well. Star always loved going home and probably loved it more when she could share it. Proudly, she announced to her new friend their destination.

"We're headed for the very edge of paradise."

15

Paperwork would kill her before the Taliban ever did.

Sergeant Johannson hated it as much as any enemy sniper, perhaps more so. At least she could make an enemy sniper go away. AWOL, Absent WithOut Leave, was bad enough, but going AWOL to miss a deployment was far worse. Yet, you could still top that by going AWOL to miss deployment to an active war zone. Old timers called that desertion in the face of the enemy, garnering a death penalty.

Modern America didn't pursue that but the Sergeant could see the point. If one man fled and made it more difficult for the others to survive, an argument could be made for manslaughter. She would be one head short on this deployment because of the absence of Private James Madison Turner. She wrote his name out with disgust and a rapidly fading spark of compassion.

One man short meant everyone had to pull a little extra weight until a replacement could show up, if one even did.

"Turner," she spoke softly to herself. "You better be dead."

~~~

Still I followed Janet.

Still I didn't quite know why. It made me think for a moment whether I had become what we had always called ghosts. Maybe.

Maybe I was in that Catholic thing called purgatory, but not having ever set foot inside a Catholic church, I wasn't sure. My Catholic friends had talked about it once or twice, just enough for me to understand it meant something like being stuck.

The light above me had moved a bit closer, so I had that feeling that whatever it was I was in, it wasn't going to last that much longer. Funny though, I didn't care a bit about the delay, nor did I dread the inevitable whatever it was coming my way. I simply went with the flow of things, and honestly I wished I had enjoyed that freedom when I had been alive.

Janet and her new friend Starshine Aloha had made it to the small grouping of very modest dwellings she called home. They were haphazardly placed between towering coconut palms and rested on a thin layer of sand just above the hard lava. Papaya trees decorated the space beneath the canopy with brightly colored fruit.

"Look Jimmie," Star said pointing them out. "Breakfast in the morning." Janet, I could tell, was in better shape now. The static from her mind was missing now, her muscles seemed less taunt.

"Everyone must already be at the tidal pools. We're going to a heated one just off the Champagne pools."

Janet tried to figure out how a tidal pool could be heated, but finally gave up and asked, "Heated?"

"Oh yeah. We're pretty close to the volcano, as you know. And, all that mountain rain has to go somewhere, much of it underground into lava tubes, where the rock is perpetually molten or almost so. Eventually, it exits to the sea still hot. This little place we're going has a perfect mix of cool seawater and heated rainwater."

Janet was quiet for a few minutes, standing there in a strange, but wonderful place, unsure of her luck. She clutched Star's beach towel tightly to her chest.

"What's wrong, honey?" Star whispered. "Here, take this new towel. Do you need a swimsuit?"

That question broke the spell but released a fair amount of embarrassment. She took the fresh towel and admitted something she had never thought she would ever be ashamed of. Star had to get her to repeat it, and she did, this time slightly higher than a whisper.

"I've never been in the ocean."

Star looked at her for a long time, amazed to have met someone who had never been to that part of heaven. She felt an upwelling of compassion for this messed up young person.

"Ah, then this will be very special." She turned to hang her car keys on a hook and grab a towel herself. "Full moon tonight too, how fortunate you are indeed."

Star reached into a trunk just inside the porch of her place and pulled out a long oversized t-shirt. "You might not have a swimsuit, or you might not need one. Either way, here you go."

Some moment or two later she and Star were walking toward the sea, just before dark and I found myself moving above the trees.

To the east the horizon shimmered under the weight of the approaching moon, ready to burst forth any instant.

Suddenly, in the dark air ahead of me came a shock, a rush of blackness.

Seemingly just ahead of the moon's light, racing ahead, was something from the mainland, to the northeast. Something I could feel as much now as I might have when I was alive - a warm wind. A sudden burst of grief from across the sea just before the moon crested the horizon.

Instantly I was there. Trying to comfort her, impossible as that was. I had to close my eyes, as it were, when I saw that it was my Mom reading my Facebook posts.

~~~

Agatha thought that she might never breathe another breath. She had gone onto Facebook to pull up some pictures of Janet and I, to show Adam.

The little bar on Lake Tahoe Boulevard had two computers with Internet access for the price of two Coors Lights. Adam liked that. He could use two cold brewskis while Agatha went hunting around for pictures.

As the second beer washed away the day's dust he noticed Agatha crying at the computer. Walking up behind her he saw Facebook was open.

"Honey, what's wrong?"

Agatha couldn't talk, having just now only caught her breath. She dragged her finger across the screen to point out something. Finally, Adam saw it.

Jimmy Turner: *"I just wanted to let you all know that I am dead."*

~~~

Alex had spent the better part of his day telling various law enforcement types the same story. He wondered if it would have been easier to Xerox something and hand it out. Park Rangers, County Police and finally four Military Policemen had driven down from the Pohakuloa Training grounds near Mauna Kea.

Everyone wanted to see Cabin #94. Everyone wanted to interview the nurse. And finally they had all visited the Lava Lounge and the booth in the corner.

Alex remained at the Lava Lounge as the last MPs left and his presence was required no other place. Larry soon showed up with plate lunches from the Lava Rock Cafe, having missed the free lunch he had been promised.

"Did you have enough money?" Alex asked.

"Yeah, but I gave the change to the Salvation Army guy outside." He sat the boxes down, pulled up his stool to the bar and nodded to the bartender as she slid a cold frosty one his way. "Besides, Alex, I figured it would do us both good to balance our karma a bit."

Alex shook his head. "I guess so. But, we didn't do anything wrong ourselves."

"True, true," Larry conceded. "But, we were in the presence of evil or lunacy or some other bad mojo." He put a good dent in his fresh drink. "Besides it was only a dollar fifty."

Alex laughed out loud. "Good, as long as we were only near a dollar fifty worth of evil, we're cool!"

Nodding, Larry laughed lightly. "No worries. I've got an emergency twenty in my pocket if we need it."

~~~

Adam was horrified. What kind of thing was this Facebook? He had heard of it, never gave it a second thought and now was seriously doubting it could possibly be a good idea. What would people now consider proper etiquette? Announcing suicides? What else could it be? He had heard of kids getting in trouble with nude pictures or bullying or proving their indiscretion any number of ways. But this! This was a measure of poor taste unlike anything he had ever seen.

Agatha was simply sobbing quietly to herself. Adam didn't quite know what to do, mostly because there wasn't much he could do. He delicately leaned over her shoulder and looked at the Facebook post again. No clues, except it was posted over a week ago. Agatha had mentioned that Jimmy had been calling almost every day while on leave between Afghan tours, but hadn't called in a while.

"Look Agatha, let me get you in the car and we'll go back to the lodge."

Agatha nodded, trying to keep her sniffles from attracting more attention than they already had. Once to the car, Adam helped her in and returned to the bar to pick up their food. The computer was still displaying Agatha's Facebook page, so he quickly sat down to read the post again.

Scrolling down a bit he saw another post by Jimmy.

Jimmy Turner: *"Sorry. Only part of me died. The rotten part."*

Adam stared at that for a moment. He noted the time stamp was a few days after the first one. From what he had heard of Jimmy he would never invite his Mom to Facebook and then pull a stunt like this.

Something was fishy. Adam felt he was on to an explanation that might comfort Agatha. Obviously Jimmy's Facebook account had been hacked. Some bozo, an evil bozo, no less, was posting hurtful things.

He would call Jimmy first thing in the morning and have him change his password.

Walking back to the car he found Agatha sobbing again.

"His phone...his phone is not answering," she finally managed to say.

Adam shook his head at that, privately. "Well, they do have poor cellular coverage out in the boonies there. Maybe?"

Agatha was not comforted.

"I'll try and track him down in the morning. It's must be midnight there now. He might even have his phone turned off."

That did seem to help.

An hour later they pulled into the lodge parking lot. The old pines beams and thick oak doors offered Agatha the privacy and quiet she needed now, and the majestic view of the lake that might absorb all the pain. Adam settled her in and watched her gently drift off to the protection of sleep.

As she slept in the bed next to his, he could almost hear the nightmares chasing her, chasing a mother and her son.

~~~

Lately, things were changing again for me. I wasn't just in Volcano anymore, but rather at my Mom's side in California as well. Wherever my interest was, then so was I, even if we were separated by a great ocean. Distance between places was no longer a problem of separation. It was as if being dead was really being alive in just a different way.

This James Turner that I had been when alive seemed very distant now. It was something I had done long ago, rapidly fading from my detailed memory. 'Been there, done that' kind of thing. Gave the t-shirt away.

At some moment, I wasn't exactly sure when, but I felt that I wasn't especially different from everything around me, only that I was just woven into the fabric a little deeper. It seemed so natural, as if I wasn't so stuck anymore between what I had been and where I was to eventually find myself.

Mom's sadness somehow created a great empathy within me, but one I felt had a smile. She must have loved me. Her sadness is that of a mother for her son, and as such was a great and wonderful thing, even if it had to manifest in grief.

Janet's fear and confusion drew me as well into that space I might call compassion. Now, here she was experiencing great relief and a bit of joy in the discovery of the magical sea.

The static in her mind was still absent; she even seemed a bit serene luxuriating in the warm pools of Kapoho. The full moon moving higher through the palms cast kind fingers of light and shadow across the clearness, reaching even down into the water to touch her naked skin.

I felt that calmness move from the jungle up and into me. The frantic worry and confusion was fading away. Looking around, all around me, I could now see a bigger place. The vastness of beauty was beckoning, the approaching light above me was shimmering with promise. It would take me to amazing places, but I still had to wait. For Janet, somehow.

Ms. Debbie came to me again, again in her cocoon of light. She looked so proud and came up to me, never saying Jimmy, or James. She spoke to me, but never called me a name. We both felt exactly who she was speaking to. Me.

"It is beginning to look so absolutely beautiful for you, isn't it?"

I watched her closely, moving lightly in my vision. "Just now, actually. It is."

"That is perfectly wonderful my dear," Ms. Debbie announced. "Welcome to the universe." She moved away and up again, toward the light that I immediately noticed was quite a bit closer. Turning a bit she grinned and said "See you soon."

~~~

Star and Janet sat quietly in the moonlit pool, listening to the distant roars of both the outer reefs and the Coqui frog invaders deep in the nearby jungles. Behind Star, in the direction Janet was looking a great glow lit the sky. Greater almost than the moon itself.

"Star, what is that, over there?" She pointed into the dense jungle behind them and up into the sky.

"Ah, Jimmie, that would be the great Mother. She who must destroy in order to create. Nature at its most enduring. Our volcano."

Distant ultra low vibration booms could be heard filtering in through the dense darkness around them.

"Ah, Jimmie, do you hear that? She calls you." Star was smiling broadly, apparently convinced of the lack of coincidence.

"Who?" Janet asked, slightly put off with a tinge of fear. "Who calls me?"

Star let herself slip under the warm waters and after a moment resurfaced with her hands already on her face, moving the water away from her eyes. "Mother calls you Jimmie, she welcomes you to her bosom."

Janet didn't know what to make of that. Hippie-talk she figured. "You mean the volcano?" She slipped under the water for a moment as well, then after lingering a full minute surfaced and asked "Is Mother the same as the volcano?"

Star nodded silently. "They are indeed."

Both of them sat quietly for several more minutes before Star started a story.

"None of this amazing..." she spread her arms wide up and out of the water, unashamed of her nudity. "...absolutely amazing paradise around us would be here without the great Mother. If she had not destroyed what was here prior, then this beauty would not be possible."

Janet looked around, trying to imagine how this place could have ever been anything but awesome.

Star continued, intent on sharing the reasons for her and the others devotion to this area. "Our Mother is a kind soul. For when she does destroy, she only takes a little at a time. When I was just a young girl, she took a section of Kapoho, swimming ponds and coastline." Star ducked under the water again and lingered long enough to make Janet begin to wonder if she was OK. Eventually, she surfaced and exhaled loudly like a whale might have or a porpoise. Wiping the water from her face again, it seemed she had to recall what she had been saying, but the sudden smile on her face showed she remembered.

"When Mother took part of Kapoho, she left this section, where we are now, making it even more special because of it."

Janet listened intently. She had never imagined nature could be so powerful in one stroke or as gracious in another. The glow of the volcano in the distance seemed to flicker like a candle might, followed by low growls, or maybe, Janet thought more accurately, low moans.

Star watched her new friend closely to see if she was listening with her heart or just with her ears, or listening at all. It was hard to tell, but she was sure of one thing. She had determined that the obvious must be true. Jimmie was a woman, despite some awkward attempts to mask it. They both sat across from each other in the warm pool, nude.

"So Star," Janet asked. "How do you know when Mother is ready to destroy again?"

"Ah, Jimmie, she doesn't quite work that way. The question should be when is Mother ready to create again?"

Star let that settle into Janet's mind for a moment. "We have small earthquakes..." The volcano let a few loud booms loose just as she was speaking. "...she moans loudly, like that. It's almost like childbirth. The placenta is destroyed but the baby is born."

Star watched Janet even closer now. She had lived communally with young women since she had been one herself, and had seen many a case where some didn't understand their bodies. Perhaps few ever did realize the Goddess in themselves, the power of creation and the magic of nurture. This young woman, she mused, had never had the opportunity to explore herself, had probably been lost and confused her entire life, short as that had been so far.

Janet was enjoying the solitude and safety of her and Star's remoteness, but she was getting queasy again. "Star," she warned. "I must get up, I think I'm going to be..." Janet stood quickly and turned back to the worn lava behind her at the edge of the pond, and vomited.

I felt sorry for Janet then, and moved a little closer to them both there at the warm pools. Star was certainly a loving creature herself and it was good for Janet to be away from the alcohol and near some kindness. I focused a moment on Star with that. She was looking at Janet as she moved across the pool to help her.

"Here here, Jimmie," she was soothing as Janet vomited again. Star moved in to pat her gently on her still dripping back. "You'll be fine, dear."

I could feel Star's thoughts as she looked at Janet's small but full breasts and her poochy stomach. Janet did not have an ounce of fat on her otherwise and so Star determined, again, that the obvious must be true. Janet was pregnant.

~~~

Immediately, I moved in very close to Janet, still leaning over from the pool, waiting for her next upheaval. Closer still I went, ignoring Star who was hovering over her, words of comfort moving like poetry. The sounds of the pool, the jungle, the frogs and even the wind in the high trees above all became silent, as I listened.

There was Janet's heart beating, loudly thumping, racing. Moving closer still so that I might tune that out as well, I became very still, very attentive.

Nothing. I moved into a trance, completely ignoring every possible thing except that I was listening for. What that was I didn't know, but I did know I would recognize it if it was there.

Star was overwhelming my sense, though, with her kindness to Janet. Her love for this strange human soul she had only just met was pouring and pooling and cascading everywhere. That was something I found impossible to tune out.

Maybe Star was wrong. I don't know. I followed them both back to the small cabins a short distance away, where Star gave her the one bed she had.

"I have a date tonight anyhow and won't be home til dawn. You rest here, darling," Star advised.

Janet looked a bit worried and asked, "Where are you going?"

"Only next door Jimmie, to my friend Wally's bed. We share as much time as we can when he isn't fishing." She smiled broadly, like a teenage girl might describing her older boyfriend. "If you need anything, just call my name outside, I will hear you."

Later, when Star had left and Janet had fallen into a deep sleep I moved in close again. Again, I moved the sounds of the jungle, the sea, and Janet's breathing away. Star was still detectable at a distance, laughing and cooing, but quite easier to silence.

I listened intently and waited. Waited. A coconut fell from a nearby tree outside and thumped the ground deeply, a small bird squawked immediately and then it was quiet again. I focused deeply inside of her, beyond even the physical confines of her body and deep into her essence.

That is when I heard it, beginning softly and tentatively. A young voice was singing. Singing in the dark.

~~~

Moving back, and out to the steps of the cabin I saw the early indications of sunrise to the east, over the sea. Janet was sleeping soundly behind me, her breathing strong and steady.

Star was up already and had come to check on Janet. Moments later she and her friend Wally were off to the beach, coffees in hand. I watched them holding hands as they picked their way through the coconuts, overripe papayas and shadows.

The trade winds were light but strong enough to bring in the little puffies already lit with the sun's rays from below the horizon. The sky looked a bowl of deep blue rapidly draining its color into the approaching light.

I looked above me and there was my own light, now so very, very close. Perhaps this was why I had not already gone into it, I was here to see my child get its start. Instantly I tuned everything out again, all the sounds around me and focused inside of Janet.

I only had to wait a moment before I heard the faintest bit of laughter. Playfulness and maybe, I wasn't sure about this part, a listening ear. Perhaps it could sense me as well.

I turned back to the sea and saw Star and her friend kissing there on the small beach, just as the sun leaped above the waters. Whales were splashing gently just beyond the reef and small seabirds began darting back and forth.

As a very light wind stirred the palms into song I felt as if the entire universe was full of love, something I never would have thought of when I was still James Madison Turner. I laughed a little at that. I had grown up now, spiritually. Turning toward Janet again, and the baby, my heart grew bigger. Bigger than any man's heart could ever be. I felt as if I was the entire world all at once, part of that infinite love that seemed to now be everywhere. And I forgave her.

16

Shirley gently roused her sleeping husband from the couch, where she had found him before dawn. She was up early, as always, to read and enjoy the peace of their mountain-view home. Fresh coffee was steaming in her other hand.

"Honey. Larry," she lightly pushed his shoulder. "Wake up." Nothing was working, so she pulled the cover off of him and put it on the chair next to his couch. Walking back over to the kitchen counter for another dollop of cream she said softly, knowing he would hear it, "You said you were going to go *flying* this morning…"

"Huh? What…what time is it?" Larry groggily asked.

Shirley smiled to herself. The magic word in this house had always been "flying". She could say it from across the large custom built home and Larry would hear it across the yard and down inside his old lava tube wine cellar.

"It's about twenty minutes before dawn," Shirley said. "Did you stay out late?"

Larry was sitting up now and running his hand through his hair, waking up. "Not too bad. Alex and I had quite a day." Standing up and making toward the coffee he picked up a sweater hanging over a chair and put it on. "It took a bit of debriefing at the Lava Lounge."

Shirley had a fresh cut strawberry papaya and a steaming cup of wake-up waiting for him. "Did you drink a lot, debriefing?"

Larry laughed a little. "No, honey. But we did stay there past closing, trying to solve this wild mystery."

Shirley picked up her other half of the papaya and her coffee and moved to the outside deck. "Coming?"

"Sure, let me find my slippers."

Moments later they were both in their oversized chairs, watching the first rays of the sun reflect off Mauna Loa, still holding onto her winter snows. They took the luxury of time, only couples with history can, to enjoy their coffee moment before talking.

"So, what's all this talk about mystery? Is this something going on at the Lava Lounge?"

Larry finished his long sip of the exquisite Kona bean before answering. "No. Actually it's something Alex was dealing with, with guests at one of the cabins."

He took another long sip. "It's almost too crazy to believe."

"What could possibly be happening in Volcano that would be crazy?" Shirley asked with a raised eyebrow. "Is it vog related?"

"No," Larry shook his head. "This is way beyond vog."

~~~

Hilo airport was normally a very quiet place. You could park your rental car, drop the keys, get your boarding pass and be at the gate in under 12 minutes. No tourists expected this and so everyone was always far too early. Waiting on a plane after that was a lot like waiting on a car ferry, there was a lot of time to waste, with few stores to explore.

"Well guys, this year's adventure was outstanding!" Pat said. "And, thanks, Everett, for the blinking head lamps. I think we made quite an impression on the locals."

Everyone laughed at that, subconsciously reaching into their packs to make sure they still had their head lamps.

"I know Dave sure made an impression on the locals," John laughed. "They want to initiate him into their bloodsucker club!"

Dave demurred to his friends humor, expecting a razzing all the way back to San Diego. "You know," he added. "Another couple of beers and I could have overlooked the bleeding hands."

Tim shook his head and added "Now Dave, you know you've always said you would never go out with a girl that could out drink you - in case she decided to paint your toenails. Again."

"Hey!" Dave exclaimed. "That only happened once!"

The airport bar was closed for some reason no one seemed to know. The lone security guard said it might be because it was Sunday. The five guys, friends since high school in Honolulu, watched their interisland plane land on a nearby runway and roll out of sight.

"You think that guy Larry will ever figure out what that crazy Private Turner mess is all about?" Everett asked no one in particular.

Pat shook his head no. "I doubt it. But, he did seem to light up a bit when we told them we first met her hiking out to Halema'uma'u that night."

"Oh, yeah," Tim said. "That was definitely the same good looking redhead from the bar."

"I wonder what ever happened to that guy she was with that night?" John pondered. "We never did see him at the bar, did we?"

Dave looked down at his shoes a moment and shook his head no. "That poor bastard must be the guy they're all looking for. Private Turner."

Their Hawaiian Airlines Boeing 717 finally taxied up to their gate and the rapid activity on the ramp began. The picture windows had a great view of Mauna Kea and her observatories, all topped with brilliant white snow.

"Well Dave," Tim said. "I think your record of never hitting on a married woman is still safe."

Dave looked at Tim with a confused look, begging explanation.

"How's that Tim?" Pat asked.

"She was already a widow when she showed up at the bar," Tim said.

"What?" Dave asked. "How do you know that?" John, Pat and Everett all listened in.

"Easy guys," Tim laughed. He sat down in a chair facing the far off snow. "This guy was last seen by who? Us. Where? Hiking out to the lava pit, at night, with no one else around. She had probably never planned on seeing even us, but fortunately for her we were just leaving."

"No way..." Everett murmured, thinking ahead.

"Yep, she took him out to the lava, to Halema'uma'u and pushed him in somehow."

The Hawaiian Air gate agent called the flight for boarding of small children, their parents and any military members.

"She must have fallen, or the guy fought her," Tim continued. "That's how she got those hands that Dave was so attracted to."

"What a bitch!" Pat said. "Wait here, I'm going to go buy my wife a gift real quick."

"Yeah, but why try and pretend she was her husband?" John asked. "I mean cutting her hair like that and telling people she was him."

Tim shook his head. "I can't figure that out."

"Maybe," Everett offered. "It was to buy some time, or to steal his money. The ultimate identity theft."

"More like just plain crazy," Dave offered. "If she were calculating enough to do an identity theft thing, she would have left Volcano right away. The fact that she was a drunk monkey wanting me to lick up bloody wounds was nothing short of..."

"Boarding all rows now!" The gate speakers bellowed.

"Crazy!" Dave repeated. "Nothing else can explain it."

They boarded last, getting a few looks from some military police types but garnering none of the admiring female glances they used to a decade ago.

Fifteen minutes later, their friend Captain Reid Emminger was taking them through fifteen thousand feet, carving a slow circle around the majestic peaks of the Big Island.

Tim watched the spectacle through his window, the peaks of Mauna Kea and Mauna Loa appeared to be islands themselves, surrounded by their own ocean of clouds.

These two magnificent volcanic peaks appeared different depending on how you looked at them. If from the ocean bottom where they really began, they were the tallest mountains on the planet. If from the coastline they were the familiar wonders everyone had grown up with. And, now, as Everett leaned over to look as well, peeking out from a mass of clouds the tops appeared as two small lost islands in a sea of gray and white.

"There's another side to that crazy Private Turner story Everett. We're just not looking at it from the right angle," Tim mused, still watching the mountains as they fell farther and farther away.

"I hear that buddy," Everett said, his head back in the seat, eyes closed. "I hear that."

~~~

Several outstanding mornings had drifted down upon Janet and her host Starshine Aloha. The weather had, naturally, been absolutely perfect. Warm days, but not hot. Cool nights, but never cold. The stars had been putting on a show and the moon slept in a hour later every evening, eventually so late that it graced the mid-morning skies.

Janet had discovered a ravenous appetite for papaya and coconut, and the occasional sashimi treats the guys brought back from spear fishing. She swam in Champagne pools every day and in the open ocean at night.

Star worried about her a little. Whoever she was and whatever her story was it was clear to Star that the young woman needed this place.

Idyllic tropical splendor - well everyone needed some of that, or so went the theory. Star had seen many a visitor come, snorkel, throw a BBQ in a vacation rental and leave. Sunburned. Yet, there were always the few that might under different circumstances move here, and fit in just fine. They could be seen stopping to pick up a plumeria blossom from the path through the old lava, or leaving the salt water on their skin as long as possible before showering. Star had seen them sitting alone, sharing a papaya with the mynah birds, or shifting through the beach sand with their fingers, not really looking for a shell, but enjoying the textures.

Those visitors, she could sense, almost felt that they must have been here before. How else could it seem so comfortable and so familiar? Familiar in a fashion that their hearts told them this was how they were meant to live, by the sea, under the moon, awash in wonder.

Janet was one of those, Star thought. One of those most fortunate lost souls that had stumbled upon this place before it was too late.

Too late came in at least two different flavors here. The first kind of too late was where a visitor or a tourist had become so jaded by the harshness of the outside world that they couldn't appreciate what Kapoho had to show them.

The other kind of too late could be observed by simply looking across the small bay to the thirty foot tall lava flow that had covered one half of this pristine paradise back in 1960. Star's parent's house was under there somewhere, what hadn't been burned. They had lived right on a beautiful sandy beach, with a peaceful little stream flowing from a large pond to the ocean. Star used to catch little fish there as a child and release them up stream again.

Her parents had never really recovered, emotionally or financially. They moved to Honolulu, soon divorced and eventually both fled to the mainland. Her younger brother had ended up in Flagstaff.

Star found herself thinking about that too much for her liking and tried to redirect her thoughts. It was what it was, she figured. Mother had to destroy in order to create. As noble as that might sound, she thought as she chased a yellow striped butterfly fish, it was still painful.

Star continued to watch Janet swim in the pools long after having climbed out to sun herself in the late morning warmth. No one else was around. No one else on the entire planet but Star, Janet, the baby and of course, me.

~~~

I had been sensing the baby every moment I could. Janet was still clueless, but Star sure seemed to be paying a lot of attention to Janet and her situation.

It was an enchanting situation for me. The baby could now tell when I was focused on it, well I mean him. I now knew a little bit more about him. He would always laugh when he felt me there, then would start his singing again. Of course he wasn't singing any words, so humming was probably a better analogy.

The light above me, the one I figured I would eventually have to go to, was getting a bit closer. Now, with my discovery of the baby, I wasn't so keen on making my way there. I figured I could just hang out, maybe be one of those helpful souls that whispers into the ears of the living.

Janet sure seemed happy; at least the static had been gone for many days now. Perhaps it was some of the baby's energy leaking into her emptiness that helped. As I moved slowly through the papaya trees following her, and the baby, I could feel them both changing. Janet was becoming calmer and the baby was now looking for me, seeking me out before I would come in close to focus. We were having a big time, and I was as happy as I could ever remember being.

~~~

Star noticed Janet suddenly get out of the water, take a few steps forward, stumble and fall into the ferns. Immediately she jumped up and ran as best she could over the boulders lining the pools to where Janet was now vomiting.

"Jimmie! What's going... Are you OK?"

Janet looked up briefly, some fear in her eyes, before pointing her face back down to the moist jungle soil and heaving again. "I don't understand," she managed to say.

"What Jimmie?" Star asked, stroking her back until the convulsions stopped.

"I quit drinking over a week ago...why am I still..." The spasms rocked her again, and then right before Star, she collapsed, unconscious.

"Jimmie!" Star yelled, the nervousness in her voice quickly moving to fear. "Jimmie!"

Two of Star's fishermen friends heard her and rushed over to help.

Moments later Star and Janet were in the car, headed up to Pahoa town, fifteen minutes away. There Star had a doctor friend with a small lab. He was known to all who cared to ask, as a doctor who gave the uninsured a break. Cash and often barter of some kind could secure enough expert advice to keep everyone's low-rent lifestyle going.

An hour later, with Janet comfortable and awake on a couch Star was called into his office.

"Starshine," he said in his booming voice. "This was no false alarm, you did the right thing getting her in here when you did."

"Really? I just met her a week or so ago, walking in the rain, on the run from some heavies. I just guessed she was strung out and detoxing a bit."

The good doctor looked up at Starshine and smiled. She would have made a great social worker, or a nurse. "Well, there is some confidential information I can only release to a relative." He walked around his desk and sat on the outer edge. "Are you her mother?" he suggested.

"Perhaps I am," Star smiled. "I sure feel like it, anyhow."

"Good," the doctor laughed. "Well, you're about to be a grandmother."

"I knew it!" Star exclaimed. "I knew it. How far along is she?"

"Well, I must say her prenatal healthcare seems to have been not only non-existent but almost abusive. She is probably twenty pounds shy of where she should be at five months." He went back to his desk and sat heavily into his chair. "Her blood work says she is nutritionally deficient on just about every point we measure.

And, I would guess she has been doing some kind of drugs. Most likely alcohol."

Star shook her head. "You know doc, I don't even think she realizes she is pregnant." She looked up at him to see just how crazy that sounded to him.

"Yeah, well I wouldn't be surprised. She's not showing much, she was probably drinking like a fish I would guess, and she seems a bit disconnected. I asked her several questions, you know, about who is the President, what month it is. That kind of thing.

In my opinion she is probably not competent to take care of herself, much less a baby."

The doctor leaned back in his chair, put his feet up on his weathered desk and asked "So, Star. Whatya doing for the next eighteen years?"

Star laughed out loud, perhaps a little too loud. "I probably don't even have eighteen more years in me, Doc!" She looked toward the closed door separating them from Janet. "Why don't you give her the good news?"

He looked down at his desk for a brief moment, not wanting to, but knew it was part of the job. "How do you think she's gonna take it, Star?"

Star reached up to scratch her head and hunched her shoulders. Walking over to the door to open it, she mumbled. "Let's go find out."

~~~

Larry had his feet up on the small handmade bench he had crafted for just such a purpose. As such it was perfectly comfortable.

"Shirley, if you wanted to get rid of something, forever, what would you do with it?"

She looked at Larry for a moment longer than he had expected and with a bit of a frown she scolded him for asking such a thing.

"Larry! First of all, I don't have such things that need to be disposed of *forever*. Second, what could you ever be talking about?"

Larry didn't answer. He took a long sip of his coffee, hoping his silence would answer her question.

"You were saying something crazy was going on at the cabins," Shirley reminded him. "Is that what you're talking about?"

Larry took another big scoop out of the pinkish red papaya and slipped it into his mouth as he looked over at his wife with a mischievous grin.

She lowered her eyebrows at him and he raised his at her.

"Well?" she asked, losing just enough patience for her interest in the story to wane.

Sensing his audience about to leave, he decided to step it up a bit. "Look, Alex got a message from some Sergeant at Ft. Bragg. A soldier that was supposed to show up there didn't, because he was still registered at a cabin there at KMC."

Shirley took a sip of her coffee and watched him over the edge of her cup, half expecting him to say they found someone dead inside the cabin.

"Well, this missing soldier, apparently, hasn't been there for a while, and a girl, some crazy redhead that was staying in the same cabin has been masquerading as this same soldier."

Shirley nodded a bit. "OK, this is interesting. What else?" She set her coffee on the table next to her and picked up her papaya and spoon.

"This missing soldier was last seen, supposedly, by some tourists from the Lava Lounge…" Larry paused there, quite possibly for dramatic effect.

"Yes, yes? Last seen…where?" Shirley demanded, now quite interested.

"Last seen hiking into the Halema'uma'u crater restricted area, at night…" Larry continued, pausing yet again.

"OK, what? What?" Shirley was leaning on the arm of her chair now.

"Heading to the lava pit with this same crazy redhead, never apparently, to be seen again."

"No kidding?" Shirley sat back in her chair thinking about that one. "Wait though, I thought the Rangers kept a lookout on that kind of stuff. No one can get to the crater without getting spotted. Right?"

"Yeah, well, it looks like they did. I was up with Jack in the Jagger the night those tourists spotted them. We were counting heads to make sure whatever insane people hiked in would also leave. But, the rain got heavy and we lost count."

Shirley shook her head a little. "Why are some people so intent on tempting the volcano?"

Larry stood up to get more coffee, and Shirley followed him inside to the kitchen.

"I think," Larry answered. "They don't have the same reverence, the same respect you have Shirley." He poured a second full cup of the still steaming Kona magic.

Shirley was putting her papaya shell into the composting bucket seemingly concerned about this story.

"Larry, if this crazy girl did indeed throw this soldier into the lava pit there, at Halema'uma'u..." she paused.

"What honey?" Larry prodded.

She shook her head a bit. "The stories I've heard, from the ancient days anyhow, was that when criminals were punished, thrown into the lava pits in execution, the volcano reacted."

Larry looked at her closely, trying to read her obvious concern. He hadn't expected this story to bother her this much. "Reacted? How do you mean?"

"Well, lets just say they quit punishing criminals that way." Shirley walked back outside with a large glass of orange juice and a bagel.

Larry followed her out with his coffee, anxious to find out more.

"Why? Come on Shirley, tell me. Why did they stop punishing bad guys by pushing them into lava pits?"

Shirley looked up at the magnificent summit of Mauna Loa, the mother of all the lower volcanoes of Kilauea, Halema'uma'u and no doubt dozens of unnamed ones from the distant past. Larry was watching her closely when she turned to catch his eye.

"They got tired of losing their fishing villages to lava flows."

~~~

Ranger Jack Clovis had just received a phone call from the Hawaiian Volcanoes Observatories lead scientist. A rather frantic call as he would later tell his friends.

"Look Jack, we need your friend. Larry is it? To fly his paraglider upslope from the vents and drop some sensors for us. We're kinda in a hurry."

"Sure, no problem Alice, Larry's usually up for that." Jack confirmed. "Anything going on?" He knew something must be but tried to keep his voice slightly uninterested to coax an exasperated answer out.

"You'll get a page as soon as I can finish typing it up here. Look, I need to get Larry airborne within an hour, OK?"

Alice was trying real hard not to shake with excitement, or perhaps it was fear, so she slowed down her typing to one finger at time. The seismograph next to her was wagging its tail excitedly recording dozens of small quakes no one could feel. She went back to her memo, reading it over before sending it.

"At 0420 Hawaiian Standard Time this morning sensors at the summit of Mauna Loa recorded unusual activity centered around significant and rapid re-inflation. A record swarm of 1200 long period earthquakes have been recorded in the past 36 hours. All of these have been measured at 2.5 magnitude or less. Indications are that a large pool of magma is heading upward from the vast magma chambers below the volcano."

Alice was about to send that out when a window shaking 4.8 magnitude rattled her office. She added another paragraph.

"We can expect larger than normal and more frequent earthquakes in the vicinity of Kilauea, Mauna Loa and Halema'uma'u."

17

Janet tried to read the eight month old Time magazine, but decided to just look at the pictures instead. She could feel her stomach churning like something was bumping around down there.

Voices were discussing something on the other side of the door which her friend, her now dear friend Starshine had shut behind her. She figured they were talking about whatever it was the doctor had found out, and that was just fine with her. If someone else could handle the details then she didn't have to.

Still, she was a bit nervous. Standing up finally and going to the large window facing west she looked out over the vast Ohia forests and jungles. The second floor office had a fantastic view toward the rising terrain leading up to Hawaii Volcanoes National Park.

She hadn't noticed before, perhaps because she had never paid any attention to it from down at the ocean pools, but a large plume of steam was rising vertically above the trees. Nothing like what she had seen on the History channel of course, but something more akin to what they showed in Iceland. Something like a healthy column of steam, slowly dissipating into the blue crispness of the calm morning.

Star opened the door and walked out with the doctor, both smiling broadly, their eyes glittering like someone holding on tightly to a secret they were about to let loose.

"Jimmie," the doctor began, sitting on the edge of his desk, giving Star a moment to go to Janet's side. "I've got some exciting news for you..."

The windows just then began a complaining rattle and the wooden structure on which they sat atop swayed just slightly. Several car alarms, rental cars obviously since no locals here would tolerate them, began squawking.

Janet jumped a bit and Star gave her a little hug.

"Ah, I hate it when that happens," the doctor laughed. He looked at Janet's big eyes and added. "Just a little roller, not to worry. We get one a month or so."

"It's OK Jimmie," Star whispered softly. "The doctor has some news for you." Star caught herself repeating the doctor but could put it no other way. She had a touch of dread and didn't want to lose her new friend by being the dark messenger.

I hovered close by, watching Janet, and talking with the baby. Janet seemed a bit nervous, but I was having a great time. The baby was enjoying our little "talks" which I must admit were little more than mental goo-goo eyes. I would find him and smile, he would hear me and laugh. Naturally, it was nonverbal, but it was a flow of love back and forth nonetheless. I kept broadcasting my name to him, as Daddy. Although neither of us really needed a name, since we seemed to be the only ones in the room as it were, it was fun. My mind wandered a bit trying to find him one. I guess since I had met him at Star's cabin I would give him a name that was a variation of the place. Poho. Poho from Kapoho, Hawaii. Very masculine, I figured, and somehow very strong.

As Poho and I were cracking each other up, I was interrupted, well, we both were, by a burst of static. Janet was screaming, loudly. Both the doctor and Star were holding her down, as she was thrashing around and yelling in between her screams. I couldn't make out much but I did hear something that brought me back to a state of fear.

"My brother did this to me! My brother!"

Star was shaking, afraid to see Janet like this. The doctor seemed quite surprised.

"Jimmie, Jimmie!" He said loudly until he got her attention. "I have to ask, but how do you know your brother got you pregnant?"

Star looked at him like he was an idiot, and he had to admit to himself it was an idiotic question. He knew that, but he knew he had to ask anyhow.

"Don't you think I would know who…"

"Wait, just stop!" Star demanded. "Sit down, please."

The doctor moved back to his desk visually shaken as well.

"Now Jimmie, did he rape you? Your brother?" Star spoke softly.

I was already answering "No. NO!"

Janet shook her head no. "No, our family was split up when we were young. I ended up with what I thought was a nice guy, fifteen years later. But, it was him, my brother!" She looked up at both of them and I saw deep pools of tears in her eyes. "He knew too. He was told by our other brother." She burst into tears again.

Star looked over at the doctor and then back to Janet. "He knew and still had sex with you?"

Janet shook her head no. "No, not then. But he knew later and never told me, almost married me. He didn't care. He didn't..." Janet reached over quickly for the small plastic trash can near the doctor's desk and began vomiting.

Star walked over to the doctor's desk and whispered in his ear. "Can't you do a test of some kind? To confirm the baby, you know, is from a brother and sister?"

The doctor didn't like the implication of where such a question was leading. "Look Star, if it's true, there's only a 25% chance of deformity or some other DNA incompatibility."

Star stood up straighter next to him, put her hands on her hips and stared down at the man. "Are you suggesting she keep such a baby?"

The doctor looked quickly over at Janet, who by now was watching him closely even as she wiped her mouth with a large box of tissues. "I suggest nothing. I can initiate a test though, if you think it's a good idea."

Looking to Janet directly he asked, "Jimmie, do you want to keep this baby? I have to tell you the odds are that it would be healthy and viable. However, in the State of Hawaii, in such a circumstance as yours, a termination of the pregnancy could be had."

Star looked at Janet as well, studying her face for a reaction.

The doctor continued. "But, I have to tell you, the baby is twenty two weeks, some five months along. It might be able to survive an early birth now." He was trying to offer as many solutions for life as he could. "But, if you could wait another month or so, or even go to full term, we can arrange an adoption."

I could feel the massive amounts of static ramp up again in Janet, like they had back in Cabin #94. Poho was real quiet.

Janet's eyes got all wild, pools of insanity spilling up through the pale blue of her stare. "Get this..." she hissed loudly, spit flying out of her mouth. "...monster out of me!" She spit obscenely into the waist basket. "Now!" She was breathing heavily and cursing under her breath. Suddenly she stood up and started beating her fist into her stomach. "I'll kill you twice, you bastard!"

Star and the doctor quickly grabbed her arms while some of the office staff and another doctor ran in after hearing the commotion.

"Sedate her," Star cried. "Please," she whispered through her tears. "Please, sedate her."

Star was horrified at Janet's reaction but tried to tell herself she understood. How would she feel in such a situation, she asked herself. The doctor, being a man, had no firm grasp on the emotional turmoil, but had seen enough of it to understand the stress. Still, neither he nor Star could attribute Janet's wild behavior to such news alone.

The doctor followed Janet into the examination room where they strapped her down on one of those paper covered couches. He swabbed a cotton stick inside her mouth, put the stick inside a tube and sealed it.

"Star, we need to do an amniocentesis, to determine the baby's DNA. Do you approve that?"

"I can't say, I just met her a few weeks ago. Can't you call someone?" Star complained. "I don't want to do something wrong here."

"Look, it won't harm Jimmie or this baby. She's going to need one anyhow, to make her case for such a late term abortion."

Star sat down in the chair next to Janet's now sleeping form. She was crying softly. Covering her face with her hands she spoke quietly. "She called it a monster." Star sobbed for a moment and then repeated Janet's words. "She said get this monster out of me." Her tears overwhelmed her.

The doctor went to comfort Star and wondered to himself as I did too. Which monster was she speaking of?

~~~

Larry's phone was ringing before he finished figuring out whether the earthquake was just a coincidence or not. Shirley had immediately looked him the eye and raised her eyebrow high.

"Larry! It's Jack."

"Who? Your connection is bad…" Larry could hear what he thought sounded like a lot of wind. Wind close to a motorcycle.

"Jack, it's Jack! Look I'm on my way up to your place. We need you to drop some sensors for us."

"When? Why are you coming up here right now?" Larry said loudly so Shirley had fair warning.

Shirley watched Larry shake his head a little, lean into the call and smile, then walk up to the large picture windows and look out. "Sure, Jack, I'll meet you outside, across the street."

Larry looked across the room to Shirley after hanging up. "I've been drafted, again. HVO needs some sensors and a transmitter dropped upcountry. Seems urgent."

"What, right now?" She sat her coffee cup down. "I thought ... what's he doing coming up to the house then?"

Larry had already started his subconscious checklist, feeling in his pockets for his spare glasses and sunglasses. "He's bringing the sensors now. They want me over the drop site within the hour." He couldn't find his sunglasses yet.

~~~

Janet's DNA mouth swab had been administered while she was still sedated. Star sat by her side the entire time, crying.

"OK, we've got Jimmie's DNA and we can get the baby's after we get the father's." The doctor had the sample placed carefully in a mailing container. "How are we going to get that?"

Star looked up at him, and shook her head.

"Star, we can't determine if this baby is hers and her brothers without the father's DNA."

"Well," Star said. "Do you have any doubt? After that performance?"

The doctor stood up and walked over to his desk. "No, of course not. I don't." He stopped at his desk, still facing the wall. "Star, I don't perform abortions. Period." Sitting down heavily in his chair he rubbed his forehead and continued, painfully explaining the options.

"I understand when they are necessary. Of course. But, I don't perform them. I can't do it. Personal thing, you must understand.

"Jimmie is really at the limit of any kind of discretionary action at this point. In another couple of weeks, only a threat to the mother's life or a proven debilitating disability would make it happen."

He turned to look out the window, trying to wish this part of the human experience never again crossed his doorstep. "The best I can do without the father's DNA is to recommend a mental health evaluation and possibly an adoption of the baby by the State."

Star was gently stroking Janet's unconscious hand, humming some old tune from her childhood. Something comforting.

"Did you hear her?" Star asked, looking up at him. "What she said?"

The doctor tried to recall but all he got was screaming and wild insane eyes. "No, what?"

"She said," Star spoke precisely, as if daring herself to get it right. " 'I'll kill you twice.' "

The doctor put his head down into his hands and moaned a little. "You think that means…" He looked up at Star, over to the still unconscious Janet and then up to the ceiling, hoping the revolving fan could somehow make it all more palatable. It didn't.

"You think she has already killed the father, then? Her brother, as she claims?"

"Yes," Star confirmed quietly. "And, she will kill this baby as soon as she gets a chance. One way or another. You saw it, in her eyes."

The doctor turned back to his desk, found a pen in his top drawer and on a piece of paper wrote something quickly. Almost frantically handing it to Star, he acted like it might burn his hands, or perhaps it was his soul.

"Take this. It's a clinic in Hilo. They'll do it. Ask for Dr. Zhung."

~~~

Larry heard the motorcycle long before he saw Jack speeding up through the fog. A morning mist was beginning to form, threatening his launch. Worse, though, was the fact that is was threatening his eventual landing back home.

Ranger Jack Clovis felt the backpack contents shift with every turn and lurch with every bump. Normally, he would never drive this fast, but then this was the first time, he thought as leaning into a hard left, that timing had ever been this critical. Alice, the lead HVO scientist was not known for enthusiasm in her voice or ever a hint of hyperbole in anything she might say or predict.

Jack, though, heard the stress in her voice when she'd said "I need to get Larry airborne within an hour". Something big was going on and these sensors, to be dropped from the air over inaccessible terrain upcountry of Halema'uma'u and Kiluaea, would immediately begin reporting acoustic data that related to inflation.

Inflation was one of the last hints you got before stuff started pouring out of the ground, or shooting high up into the air. It was the very ground itself swelling with the introduction of large pools of magma. It was also the signal for down slope evacuations when it reached a certain point. Civil Defense would begin closing the only road going around the island at either side of the predicted flow zone as soon as the HVC gave them the alert. Without these new sensors though it would be a guessing game that almost guaranteed embarrassment.

Larry had his wing deployed on the ground behind him and had done his preflight check, twice. What had him concerned now was coming home. He could take off into a fifty foot high fog in no wind and quickly rise above it. Landing, though, would be impossible. He double checked the hookup to the additional ten gallon fuel bladder he had just strapped on.

Jack roared up, dropped the kickstand on the Harley Davidson Superlow 883, leaving it in the middle of the street. He hopped off while taking his backpack off and opening it.

"Captain Larson!" he teased. "Ready for departure?"

"Yeah, well, departure is cool, but arrival looks a bit messy."

"I see that." Jack looked around at the thickening fog. "We'll send up a spotter plane for you, like we did before. I'll call it in." He handed Larry the backpack. "Just monitor 123.45 and the spot plane will advise you as to landing spots as well as where to drop."

Larry was looking inside the backpack, trying to figure out what all the tennis balls were about. He pulled one out and showed it to Jack, silently asking for an explanation.

"Cool yeah?" Jack laughed. "I invented that myself. You drop those from what...three hundred feet or so? The tennis ball is sliced open, we put in the wireless mote with acoustic and accelerometers built in and sew them back up."

Larry shook one a bit and felt the movement of something small inside. "Florescent yellow? So you can find them later?"

"Yep, plus they were on sale." Jack was beaming.

"OK, where do you want these?" Larry asked, strapping the backpack on backwards, onto his chest.

"Pretty easy, just get on a 360 degree north line just above Halema'uma'u and drop one of these tennis balls every two hundred meters or so. No further than four hundred meters, or they can't find each other. You should run out of tennis balls about three miles up the mountain. Then, drop this soccer ball."

"What's in the soccer ball, Jack?" Larry was already laughing.

"Yeah, that! So cool! It's the mothership. All these wireless motes talk to each other as well as transmit their own info. Only one of them needs to find the mothership. All of the motes can relay for any or all of the others.

"The soccer ball can transmit four to five miles. We already have one deployed about where you will start, so we feel with your drop we will have a good live feed on what this mountain is up to."

Larry nodded, confident he could help the scientists out. "And, so Jack, what is this mountain up to buddy?"

"More than we know, that's for sure. That's why we have you ..."

"I know that Jack, for God's sake. Tell me what the hell is going on!"

Jack put his helmet back on and straddled the Harley. He didn't have a problem telling his friend, but he didn't want him to freak out right before his important mission. Nevertheless he had to say something, and he was sure Larry needed to hear it.

"I'd have Shirley prepare for an evacuation."

~~~

Star was half way to Hilo when Janet finally woke up, groggy and grumpy. I could feel the static roaring through her as I did my best to keep up with the old Tercel hatchback. The Ohia forests were slowly giving way to mango, monkeypod and palms. Orchid farms were interspersed with the small tomato and taro patches of the local farmers.

"What...where...what are we doing?" Janet managed to say through the haze and nervous hangover of anesthesia. "Why does my damn head hurt so much?"

Star quickly glanced over. "We're going to Hilo, to get your abortion." Her fingers tightened on the steering wheel as she said it.

Janet seemed to take a moment to put that into some frame of mind that made sense. Suddenly, she looked down at her belly, put her hands there and began a slow wailing. After a few seconds she began short yelps, almost barking and then just good old screaming.

"Goddammit Jimmie, shut up! I found you on the side of the damn road, and I'll kick your ass out on the damn road again if you don't shut the hell up!" Star had already been at her wits end when she'd convinced herself to drive Janet to Hilo. Add a little crazy from the passenger seat and it became overwhelming.

Janet did shut up, except for the low moaning she continued to make as she now rocked back and forth in the front seat.

Poor Poho was not yet awake, I couldn't roust him yet. The anesthesia must have worked him over good. How could I warn him? How could I do anything about it?

Star passed the airport and turned left toward town, crossed the bridge just beyond tsunami park and turned left up Pauahi Street. Soon she took a right and then another left and pulled up into the parking area of an old two story house, with a view of the harbor and beyond, the ocean.

The sign outside said simply "Dr. Zhung, OB GYN". Star pulled up under the large canopy of an avocado tree that must have been as big as the house all by itself. One other car was just pulling out, leaving them to choose from any of the parking spots.

"Poho! Poho!" I screamed with my voice, silent as it was. This place looked like death, especially with the small metal chimney rising from the back of the building. I watched as Star got out of the car, leaving Janet inside. She walked up to the building, opened the door and disappeared.

Moving closer to Janet now, alone in the car, I could still hear only the static. Her mind was in a turmoil of chaos, hiding any chance I might have of hearing my Poho boy.

Her head was back against the head rest, her eyes closed tightly and she had both hands against her stomach. Breath came to her deeply, her skin taking back a little color as I watched. In a moment her hands relaxed, one of them falling to her side onto the car seat.

It was there, in the shade of the massive avocado tree, brilliant sunshine painting the tropical sky just beyond, that I think I finally got through her static storm. My focus had been improving constantly as time went on, probably with all that practice talking to Poho.

Several mynah birds began squawking in the tree branches just above us. It might have been their racket that brought her up and out of the pit of static. It might have been me, trying to reach her, but in any case I felt her begin to listen, tentatively.

As she opened to me, a flood of fear and sadness poured out of her. It was amazing that so much could fit inside of one soul. Tears filled her eyes from behind her closed lids, pushing their way out at the corners. Her brow furrowed deeply as she squeezed her eyes harder. She was still a young, very young woman, confused by forces outside her control.

Surrounding all of that was a weak request for help, for peace. Her deep subconscious was a well of clear thought now bubbling through the static, pleading with whatever forces, whatever miracles might help her.

It felt to me like she was praying. Each tear finding its way out as another supplication. I listened intently, drawing her out with a compassion and empathy, with a love that came from beyond even me.

The sky around me was filled with light now, the same light I had been watching get closer for some time now. It was so very close. Then, in a moment of intuition it became clear to me that I was certainly not James Madison Turner anymore, but an extension of that light descending ever closer. It reminded me of a lava lamp, where I was a distinct glob separate from the mass but the same stuff, soon to return, and probably soon to move out again.

The lava analogy wasn't lost on me, though, and that brought me back to Janet. Her heart was open, floating on an underlying sea of static that was trying to swallow this rare moment of lucidity.

I found myself expressing to her, to her very soul, that which I had already felt earlier, but which I now seemed to communicate from the larger light moving so close to me. My role felt as that of a messenger, but as one who intimately understood the message, had helped fashion it.

I moved closer even as I could sense the static rising again, threatening to overwhelm her moment of prayer and hope. I spoke to her clearly, feeling her grasp at the words, at the answer, as she began to drown again in the rising static.

I spoke to her from the light itself. Her mind ravenously grasped at the message as it slowly sank back into the depths.

"You, Janet, are loved by it all, and so you are forgiven, in advance."

As she sank away, I heard a new voice.

Poho was awake.

~~~

The electric start fired quickly and only once to get the large fan spinning behind Larry. Immediately, his wing, a skydiver type of parafoil, began filling with the forced air and lifting slightly up off the ground.

Launches are always a critical part of flight, and this was certainly the case with a paraglider, but even more so in an ever thickening cloud fog. Larry could see, faintly, the edge of the Ohia forest marking the boundary of his launch area, toward the Volcano Vineyard. Unless he had a mechanical failure, this would be flight # 3,376.

Quickly but perfectly going over his checklist he double checked his fuel readings, looked behind him to insure the parafoil was off the ground, and slowly pushed the throttle forward one third.

The engine behind him didn't so much roar as hum with a power that indicated flight was inevitable. Larry took a moment to confirm all was well as he moved the throttle to full take off power.

The parafoil wing behind him immediately fully inflated as he began rolling forward quickly. He only need 25 knots of headwind to generate enough lift to get off the ground. That took about two seconds with this engine and off he went, letting that little tug of gravity go silently and without any remorse. It would be waiting for him later.

Still fully engaged in safely getting off the ground, he watched the approaching Ohia trees. If his engine failed he could still land straight ahead without much danger. However, there was a point, very soon in fact, where that opportunity would evolve to one that required an emergency landing spot. Without much altitude he would have to rely on a special combination of skill and luck.

After just one minute of flight he reached that point where it was safer to continue rather than abort. Things looked good. His altimeter and compass had now joined his best friend list, along with the wing and the engine. With this group he continued up through the fog to break through into brilliant sunshine only 150 feet above the ground.

Jack was already calling him. Larry moved his thumb over to the control stick panel to answer the cell phone call inside his integrated helmet. Built in were his Bluetooth paired phone, an iPod that had more music than he had fuel to enjoy, an aviation radio for talking to Hilo tower or Air Traffic Control and a direct walkie talkie link to Jack as well as Shirley at home. Another walkie talkie unit was in their four wheel drive. However, with all that he still hadn't figured out how to install caller ID.

"Hello!"

"How's it look up there?" Jack asked, with an obvious touch of jealousy.

"Clear sailing! I'm well above the layer of cloud now. The entire area is blanketed, but as I turn toward the west southwest I can see a white plume of steam or ash popping through."

It was quiet a moment as Jack considered the weather issues.

"Are you going to be able to find the target area, Larry?"

Larry was still climbing in a slow circling corkscrew. It was getting chilly even as he was only 500 feet above the ground, but 4500 feet above the ocean. Glancing at his gauges quickly he saw 44 degrees outside air temperature, 42 kts forward speed and a climb rate of 150 ft per minute.

"I'm headed up to 6000 feet Jack. I'll call you on the walkie talkie from there."

"Roger that. We just had another little shake come through, about a 4 or so."

Larry looked down at the spectacular vista below him, reached with his thumb to switch to the walkie talkie. Home was somewhere beneath the rolling white textures beneath him.

"E.T. Phoning home!" Larry called.

It took a few seconds for Shirley to answer. She was tending to her award winning Taro and 'Awa and had to clear the mud from her hands before answering. When Larry was airborne she kept the walkie talkie on her waist.

"Are there any more aliens with you, go ahead?" She looked up into the milky gray fog half expecting to at least hear his engine.

"Only me. Hey, Jack says you just had a little shake. Over."

Shirley put down her tools and stood to get her water bottle. "Yes, a small little shiver in the ground. I think it actually helps aerate my garden, over."

Larry was still in his climbing turn, now looking south toward the open ocean. "Listen Shirley, Jack says HVO might recommend an evacuation, over."

Neither of them had ever had to in the twenty-two years they had lived in the village of Volcano. They were perched on a ridge a few hundred feet above Halema'uma'u. A thousand foot deep valley separated them from Mauna Loa, and they were miles from the sea and any tsunami. The only event that could realistically threaten them was a new vent opening up across the street, from a massive earthquake. Anything was possible, but everything was improbable. For now.

"When are they going to do that? Over." Shirley asked. If there was one thing they were good at in Volcano it was avoiding false alarms.

"No idea. But they seem pretty excited over at HVO. I think they suspect some inflation along the ridge above Halema'uma'u, over."

Shirley, Larry and practically every resident on the Big Island of Hawaii knew that "inflation" could only mean one thing. Lava. Magma was upwelling from the hotspot in the Earth's crust many miles below, pushing the landscape up in measurable amounts. Sometimes it deflated later. Sometimes it didn't. The real question, as always, was where it would exit. Currently there were three active areas, Halema'uma'u, Kilauea and a small vent near the sea. With those established pressure releases the odds were that one, or all of them would become more active. But, there was another option for the volcano.

What everyone dreaded was another Kapoho type event. There in 1960, when young Starshine Aloha and her parents were living the idyllic hippie dream of papayas and the beach, the unbelievable happened.

Deep within a five hundred year old jungle, rich in koa trees, native ferns and surrounding banana farms a series of small swarm earthquakes alerted HVO of magma movement. A few days later on January 13th, a crack opened up in the jungle floor. That same evening lava fountaining was reaching above tree height and within a week 900 foot lava geysers built a 160 foot tall cinder cone. All of this was feeding a carpet of devastation that engulfed an entire village, farms and the beaches. Dozens of acres of ocean were claimed by the island, extending the coastline outward.

Shirley was holding the walkie talkie up to her chest now, looking out at her garden, at the beautiful yard they had created out of weeds and non-native bushes. Uncertainty was, she knew, a reality of living next to an active lava pit on the side of the planet's most active volcano. Hawaiian volcanoes, though, were probably the most predictable of the bunch and were benign enough, for the most part, to allow humans to enjoy complimentary space around them. But the privilege came with precautions, and a precautionary evacuation was one she could live with. Lava would probably never overtake their home. Probably.

Larry had almost reached his first altitude step of 6000 feet. From there he could approach the climbing terrain uphill of Halema'uma'u safely. Shirley's silence told him she was upset by the news. No one ever wanted to evacuate their home. The world, Larry knew, was a volatile place. There was always something that could chase people away: tsunami could force beach dwellers to higher ground, as well as flooding rivers. Snow avalanches cleared out valleys, earthquakes knocked over buildings, fires ran Californians out of the hills. At least the sky was smooth and safe where he was.

"Shirley?" Larry whispered as best he could over the noise of his engine.

Shirley broke her focus and walked back inside her kitchen. "I'll put some things in the car, Larry." A few moments of silence followed before she added "Over."

"Great, listen, it's just precautionary. But, would you please put my 1945 Haut Bailly and some of my Bordeaux in the car first? Please? Over."

Shirley rolled her eyes, but agreed. They *would* need wine.

Larry found his mark on the GPS and verified it with the steam plume behind him as he turned his paraglider on a heading of due north. The massive Mauna Loa loomed ahead, her white crown of snow glittering in the clear air.

Descending slightly to just above cloud level he opened the backpack Jack had given him, and set his timer to sync with his speed giving him a ground speed of 200 meters per minute.

He picked out the first sensor, held it over to the side and dropped it. This terrain was remote and extremely difficult to hike into, no one would be below. But, the birds and other creatures that lived there would no doubt find it strange to see florescent yellow balls falling from the sky in the middle of a foggy morning.

~~~

Poho was cooing quietly, waking up I suppose. I could now easily penetrate poor Janet's static field and communicate directly with my little boy. My entire being had that tingle I used to remember getting on my scalp when I felt ecstatic. My boy! Poho!

He laughed a little when he felt me there, then seemed to stretch and take a moment to move himself around. So cute! Could my heart get any bigger for him?

Star's return to the car quickly reminded me, though, that Poho was in mortal danger. Quickly, I tried to find Janet again, her lucid mind that I had touched a moment ago. I dove deeply into the static, leaving Poho behind for just a moment. There was nothing. I followed path after path of her thoughts, her emotions, but all I was finding were nightmares and horror.

"Jimmie," Star was saying softly. Her hands were folded in her lap, her gaze out the window ahead. "I explained everything to them. Everything." She looked over at Janet, still rocking slightly in her chair, eyes shut tight and moaning. "They said they classify this as a late term abortion."

Janet continued rocking back and forth, oblivious by the looks of it to what Star was telling her. I had some hope that maybe she would back out of it, or even better that Dr. Zhung would refuse to do the procedure.

My optimistic nature, as I had always suspected, had very little connection with the darker sides of reality.

"They want $5000 before they'll agree to do it," Star said softly, tears streaming down her cheeks. She watched her own hands shake with nervousness, one borne, no doubt, from the pain and suffering that was occurring. And, I thought, from that which might soon occur.

Janet kept rocking, clutching her stomach now and moaning. Star just watched her, for probably a full minute. Convinced Janet was too out of it to make a decision, she started the Tercel.

That's when Janet reached for and opened her door. I felt a darkness pouring from the car, and her. She stepped out and stood up straight, reached into her back pocket, pulled out a wallet and threw it onto the hood of the car.

Star just stared at it for a moment. Horrified. She wanted nothing to do with this, had hoped for a way out, but saw now that her commitment to another sister was assured.

Janet walked around the front of the car now. Her eyes searching Star's.

Star turned off the engine and reluctantly opened her door. She watched Janet closely as she reached into the wallet.

"Here," Janet said. "This debit card has $20,000 on it." She then turned and began a slow march up the dozen or so concrete steps.

My signing bonus for another enlistment! My money for signing up to send bad guys to the other side, and now it was going to be used to send my son there instead.

Star put the debit card back in the wallet and followed her up, leaving tears on every step behind Janet.

I moved to the top of the stairs and with all my will tried to keep them from going inside. My focus was as strong as I could manage, but there was, of course, nothing I could do physically. Star seemed to hesitate as I begged her to take the wallet and throw it away. She did stop at the top of the stairs and looked at it in her hand.

"Throw it away," I repeated into her mind a million, billion times. I was probably breaking every rule in heaven by doing so, but no one was going to blame me, that I knew.

Her hands seemed to change grip, from one of carry to one of toss.

"Here, give me that!" Janet snatched it out of her hands. "Let's do this." She turned back toward the door and walked right through me.

~ ~ ~

Agatha Turner had never flown on an airplane for this long. Four hours had been a record when she went to Miami once. Now, she was on a six hour marathon to Honolulu, with a plane change and then another hour to Hilo on the Big Island. She was intent on finding her boy James.

In her mind she replayed the good days. When he was just becoming a teenager and all the other kids were getting in some kind of trouble, her boy James was volunteering at the Boys and Girls Club. He kept his room clean and washed the car without being asked. He had never given her any trouble, in fact some of her friends made comments what an angel he was. Of course he was, she murmured to herself, of course, he was her son. James Madison, James Madison, she repeated over and over.

"Agatha dear," Adam whispered. He could hear her repeating something. "What are you saying?"

The first class cabin on Hawaiian Air flight #19 was spacious but it was also quiet. Adam feared that Agatha's murmuring might disturb the other passengers.

Agatha shook her head a little waking up. "Am I snoring again?" she asked, embarrassed a little.

"No," Adam comforted her. "Not anymore."

Agatha sat back in her large leather seat and found her feet up on the seat rest, another new experience as well. Looking out her large window, the ocean had a tropical color to it already, brushed lightly with the white of waves far, far below.

"Thank you so much for coming with me Adam," she leaned over and kissed him on the cheek. "And for these excellent seats!"

Adam had considerable resources at his disposal. He had more money than he could probably spend on himself, plus he had connections throughout the military and defense industry. Finding lost people was a challenge, but one that money and intel could usually solve.

"My pleasure dear," he lifted his guava, papaya smoothie up in toast. "My absolute pleasure."

One thing Adam had forgotten about oceanic crossings – there was no Internet access. He would have to wait until they landed in Honolulu to get the emails he expected would tell him more about one Private James Madison Turner.

~~~

Star refused to fill out the paperwork in Dr. Zhung's office. She insisted Janet do it herself. That gave Janet the opportunity to lie about every single detail it required, except she matched her name with that of our shared debit card. Dr. Zhung was never going to check it anyhow, she could see that. After they had cleared the card charges it was all a done deal.

A nurse came out and took Janet back for a quick physical.

Star sat in her uncomfortable chair and watched the carpet. She felt that it at least would not offer up anything stressful. Her tears had slowed but still marched out, one by one, each carrying another drop of sadness from her soul.

Moving close to her I nudged her mind to open to me. She was one without many walls and soon she was daydreaming. There, in her memories, were the magic days of her youth, playing on the sandy beach by the ancient lava coves. She was smiling up at the birds above and the little fish below. Her mom was next to her, singing some sweet hippie love song, while her father was husking coconuts close by. The air off the ocean was warming her skin with tingles.

"Starshine," I said with a voice she would remember as her mom's. "Did you feed the little fishes yet?"

Fully engrossed in her memory she looked to her feet and found the frozen peas in a plastic bag. The fish loved these, she remembered fondly.

"Go ahead baby, they are hungry," I whispered. "Look how happy they are that you are here."

Star sat quietly in her uncomfortable chair in Dr. Zhung's office lobby, dreaming. She remembered how the little fish darted back and forth in the shallow water snapping up the little peas long before they could ever sink the few inches to the bottom. Sixty years later she could see it in her mind as clearly as I was seeing it. This little moment, this memory was one of the most beautiful things either of us had ever felt.

"Good Star," her mom's voice said to her. "You have shared some love." One thing the hippies got right was love.

"Mom, can I keep some of them? Take care of them in a bowl?" Star asked, as she had no doubt asked so many years ago.

The light I had been watching for so long was now slipping inside the windows of the office, easily penetrating the canopy of the avocado tree. I felt it warming me as well.

"Star," I said one last time in her mom's voice. "You must let them take their own path now," a vision of her mom holding some sand in her hands filled her dream. "Let them swim where they will. It is, you know," reaching over to tickle little Star, "what makes them free."

Star stood up and walked to the door, opening it and moved down the stairs to her car. She suddenly felt good having helped out this lost kid Jimmie, had given her as much love as she could, sharing her Kapoho cabin by the sea. Jimmie was free though, she now felt, and would swim where she might.

I followed Star to the shaded spot in the parking lot where she sat, waiting. Here I would wait too.

I knew the doctor was now talking to Janet, counseling her on the options they both knew she had already rejected. I knew the nurse had entered the room now with a tray of tools and drugs. I knew Poho was awake and looking for me.

"Poho!" I sang to him. "Poho my boy!"

His laughter was infectious, even in this saddest of moments for me. He called out to me, "Let's play!"

I knew they now had Janet lay down on the table, her legs strapped down. I knew a second nurse had come in. I knew the doctor was wearing a mask.

"My Poho," I asked. I needed to distract him somehow. "Have you ever seen a bird?"

He giggled a little at the strange idea I had sent him. When he felt the feathers with his little brand new fingers he laughed out loud again, forcing me to laugh as well.

I knew the doctor was injecting Janet with a drug now. I knew that one of the nurses was holding her shoulders. I knew that Janet was so full of static that the room she was in vibrated with it.

"Poho, my boy! Have you ever seen a fish?" The slippery creature fascinated him, especially when it wiggled right out of his grasp. He squealed with delight.

The light was coming closer to me. I could almost reach up and feel it. It felt so wonderful to have it so near. It felt so wonderful to know I could soon be with it. Yet, I resisted going to it. I needed to help Poho, help him get through.

I felt some confusion in him. His laughter had stopped, and I could sense worry.

"Poho, it's OK, my son," I cried to him, trying to sound brave on his behalf.

I knew the doctor was telling Janet to push. I knew the nurse was pulling the tray of tools closer. I knew his little feet were kicking.

"Poho! Have you ever played in the ocean?" He immediately responded with a small whimper. "Poho, it is so warm, and the sun is bright. You can see the sky full of blue!" He hummed his approval but whimpered again.

I knew the nurse had handed the doctor his tool. I knew Janet was screaming and squirming. I knew the other nurse was holding her shoulders tightly.

The light was now just upon me and I could fight it no longer. I felt myself lifting into it, softly, with welcoming voices. Star seemed to look up a moment and then blinked when the branches let the sun through to her face.

"Poho, my boy!" I said one last time. I couldn't feel his presence there anymore. I searched and searched but I was moving deeper into the light, away from them. "Poho! Poho!"

"Yes, here I am."

There next to me. He came close to me, both of us moving into the light. He was with me, at my side, smiling.

"Thank you for waiting," he said as clearly and lovingly as anything I had ever heard before.

"Ah Poho," I cried with joy. I looked ahead of us to the greatness of the universe, the immeasurable happiness. "Poho, have you ever flown through the sky?"

~~~

Jack was sitting next to Alice, the Lead Scientist at the Hawaii Volcano Observatories. He would have much rather been up in the air with Larry.

"Can you call him again? I need to know if he dropped the mothership yet." She stood up quickly, pushing her chair back so quickly it fell over. "Damn it," reaching down to pick it up, she mumbled loud enough for Jack to understand. "I need that data right now!"

"Roger that, boss," Jack turned to walk outside so he could escape the steel roof of the building and it's perverse habit of destroying radio signals.

"Hey Larry, how much fuel you got left? Over."

He listened for something to come through the static. Looking to his tuner he fidgeted with the frequency. It sounded like he was off frequency, bursts of low frequency hums were coming over his walkie talkie.

Holding it up to his mouth to speak again, he was interrupted.

"Howzit Jack. I've got another hour, easy. Over." Larry's voice sounded hollow in the rising interference.

"Good. Great!" Jack turned back quickly to see Alice pacing back and forth, glancing his way. "Look Larry, I don't mean to hurry you or anything, but Alice is anxious about that data. Over."

A moment of silence followed, another burst of low growls of static, then some high pitched pops.

"Just dropped the soccer ball Jack. Damn Jack, I dropped the ball!"

172

Jack could hear him laughing above the noise of his engine and the static. He would have to tell that one to Alice. Tomorrow perhaps.

"Over." Larry finally added.

"Thanks, Larry, we really appreciate it. All done over here. How's it look for landing? Over."

A long, almost howling, mid tone raced through the static now, drowning out any human communication. Larry must hear it as well Jack figured, as he waited until it was done to attempt answering.

"Lot of weird static yeah Jack? Over."

"Yeah, buddy, got an earful from all angles down here," Jack looked at Alice now running to her workstation as the soccer ball mothership must have begun transmitting. "Over."

"Looks like the cloud is dissipating. I'll just circle around and enjoy the view. Probably land at home in an hour or less. Over."

Jack was only half listening to Larry as he began walking over quickly to Alice's computer screens. She was now standing up again, but this time covering her mouth with her hands.

"What ya seeing Alice?" Jack asked, glancing up to see Alice's eyes wide with fear.

She looked to her seismograph feed on the screen to her right, already bouncing wider and wider.

"I don't think...I never thought I ever would..." Alice stammered.

Jack moved next to her and put his hands on her shoulders to calm her. "What Alice, what is it?"

She stared at him blankly for a moment. Blinking she seemed to gain her composure and answered, "I never thought I could predict a major earthquake. But, I am now." She sat down heavily into her chair, leaning her head against her desk.

"When? Come on Alice, you're freaking me out a little here," Jack demanded. "When?"

Alice was shaking her head back and forth as she reached for her red desk phone. "Any moment."

~ ~ ~

Shirley was back in her garden, taking advantage of the cool fog to get some especially hard work done. Checking her watch she figured Larry would get another check-in ten minutes from now. Her dogs were out in the yard with her, chasing imaginary mice or something similar.

The taro required a lot of hands-in-the-mud time which usually meant arms in the mud. She heard Larry and Jack talking and wanted to join in, but would wait until she was finished with the planting of the new roots.

She was reaching deep into the mud when she finally felt it at her armpits. The dogs were barking and running around in circles, something she had never seen them do.

"What's up, little guys?" Her hair fell from her bun and spilled into the mud. She might have cursed at that, but the dogs were really acting strange now. Frantically trying to dig into the ground, barking into the dirt as they did. It was the strangest...

It was just at that moment that she felt something moving in the mud. A rumbling far away, but strong enough to shake the mud like jello all around her arms. Terrified, she pulled her arms out just as she heard deeper rumbling coming from the slopes of Mauna Loa. She tried to stand up, but for some reason kept falling down, once, twice, until she saw the mud sloshing out of her taro patch and up into the air.

Her thoughts immediately said 'Earthquake!' Stay on the ground. At least she was outside. The dogs had quickly gone quiet and were running toward her. Shirley could have sworn she was hearing the earth growl low and powerfully as large rolling waves moved under her.

Large amounts of glass could be heard shattering, but when she looked back to the house, the windows were still there. They were flexing quite a bit, bending the increasing light from the sky as the clouds were breaking up. More shattering and then she figured out it was Larry's wine cellar built into the lava tube in the yard.

"Thank god I got his Haut Bailly out of there."

~~~

Larry was circling higher and higher just in case he needed to make a run for Hilo, some twenty five miles away. His iPod was his only companion now that the walkie talkie was quiet.

8000 feet was plenty high enough, especially since it was getting downright cold. 41 degrees was beyond his comfort level, even with down flight gear on. He had checked in with Air Traffic Control, just to let them know where he was, in case some VFR student pilot in a rented Cessna decided to come barreling over his way. At least they would tell him, and the intruder, that there was traffic in the area.

The Brad Paisley song playing never seemed to have that much bass in it. Larry reached into his jacket to see if something was wrong with the iPod. He turned it off, back on, and then noticed something very strange. He turned it off again. The low bass rumbling was still there, and getting progressively stronger.

"What the…"

Looking down into the thinning soup of clouds far below he saw the entire layer of moisture vibrate back and forth quickly. Several times. Loud booms were flying up at him. The clouds were vibrating about as fast as an open beer would on his paraglider seat if the engine was running. That had been a mistake during that garage tune up. The beer had spilled.

As his turn took him toward Mauna Loa, he heard loud cracking and watched as a massive slab of snow avalanched down the brown lava slopes. It quickly split into a thousand fingers, spreading out twice as wide as it had been before slowly coming to a stop.

"Holy shit!"

Larry almost fumbled with the walkie talkie to the point of dropping it. His hands were shaking as he pushed the talk button.

"Shirley, Jack, what the hell is going on down there?" He completely forgot "over."

He waited twenty seconds and asked again, this time with quite a bit more worry in his voice.

"Shirley, Shirley, can you hear me?" He looked down at the hand held to make sure it was tuned to the correct frequency and had the power light glowing. It was and did.

"Jack! Come in. Jack! Can you hear me? Over!"

Nothing but static for a full minute, and then as he descended, "Larry, Jack. Over."

Larry wanted nothing more than to get down to a few hundred feet above ground level to see what was happening. He hadn't figured it out until he played it back in his mind. The snow mass shaking loose.

"Earthquake," he said out loud to him and his audience of zero. "Big damn earthquake," he whispered quietly, in awe.

"Jack, was that an earthquake?"

"Oh, yeah. Big. We've got damage here at HVO. Windows out, and it looks like some roof damage as well." Jack was already outside, having fallen right out of the floor to ceiling window next to Alice's desk.

"How big, Jack, how big?" Larry asked, knowing what to expect at certain magnitudes.

As Jack tried to make his way inside the building, through tons of broken glass and shattered dry wall pieces, another big rumbler approached from the south. He could hear it coming about a second and a half before it hit them.

Something was moving inside the earth, something big. Jack held on until it passed and then quickly made his way over to the seismographs. The electricity was out, but the generators had fired up. That had to be some good luck.

The seismographs all sat on relatively earthquake proof independent columns of special material designed to keep them from moving relative to whatever building housed them. Their sensors were not in the column but outside the building. Naturally none of the scientists wanted false readings in what was probably their most effective measuring tool.

"Alice!" Jack yelled as he saw her on the floor next to the seismograph. Her arms were bloodied. "Alice, are you alright?" Obviously not, he thought. He pulled out his cell phone, attempting to dial 911 for the first time ever. As he held it up to his ear, he gently tried to rouse Alice, pushing her a little. He felt her head out of habit, as if she might have a fever.

Nothing was happening on his phone. Looking at it for some clue, he noticed that he had zero bars. "Damn, the towers are down."

Alice was moaning a little, coming out of her stupor. Jack instinctively began to move his mental train elsewhere as he saw that Alice was only lightly scratched. He stood up and went back to the seismographs.

They were still working and still recording hundreds of aftershocks, including the big one just a moment ago.

"Wow, Alice. That aftershock was a 6.1!" Jack was astonished. That was huge by any measure for an aftershock. He looked back at the paper record, to see if he could find the main quake.

Alice was standing next to him now, trying to wipe off the blood on her arms with her sweater. Her cuts were apparently from the same window Jack had fallen through.

"Where is it?" she asked Jack. "Where's the damn main?"

Both of them stopped just as it came off the role. Jack whistled for dramatic effect, even if it wasn't needed. "7.4 Alice. Not a bad prediction at all." Jack patted her lightly on her good shoulder. "Good job."

Another smaller aftershock rolled on underneath them, coming from the north and exiting out to the east.

"Jack," Alice wondered out loud. "Where is all this magma headed?"

As if in answer the large lava pit at Halema'uma'u sounded as if it would do something dramatic any moment. It was rapidly filling with lava, being fed well from the now very active ancient lava tubes. Booms and cracking could be heard from a mile away.

Alice was back at her desk trying to get her computer back online but with little luck.

"I need a picture, I need some observers right now. Halema'uma'u, Kilueaua and the sea entry. All this lava is going to come out somewhere."

"Larry. You still here?" Jack asked, turning back to his walkie talkie. "Over."

"Yes. Look I can't get a hold of Shirley, can you call her on the phone? Over."

"Larry, our lines are down, we're on backup power. Look, how much fuel did you say you had?" Jack turned to Alice and moved his index finger against his thumb in the time honored symbol of "more money". Alice nodded her head yes.

"Got an hour, maybe 1.2. Over."

Jack looked at Alice and smiled. "Great, can you go observe Halema'uma'u and the ocean entry? I don't know if we can launch any helicopters at this point. Got a feeling things are messed up everywhere."

"Love to you all of course, but not until I can find Shirley." Larry had his priorities straight.

"Hold on, cowboy!" It was Shirley.

"Hey honey! Are you OK?" Larry yelled above the noise.

"Good to go, but I've got some bad news and some good news Larry. Over."

Shirley was happy she had her two tiny dogs with her in the car and that it was relatively full of supplies.

"Go ahead, the bad, baby. Over."

"Well, your wine cellar collapsed, all the bottles seem to have shattered.

Jack could be heard whistling a low salute to the now dead darkened bottles he had once hoped to have enjoyed.

"And, the good?" Larry's voice had quite a bit of hope in it. Maybe the lava tube had collapsed and in its place a hole full of gold bars had been discovered.

"I got ten bottles in the car before it happened. Over."

~~~

Adam was on his cell phone while Agatha stood in line at the Honolulu counter for Hawaiian Airlines. All flights to Hilo and Kona were postponing and canceling. The TV monitors in the bars of the gate areas were all talking about the massive earthquake that had just rattled the entire state. The power was out in many places, even on Oahu. The airport emergency power was up, so Starbucks were doing a brisk business.

Finally Agatha walked away shaking her head.

"What are they saying?" Adam asked, putting his cell phone away as another call failed to connect.

"Nothing much," she said, holding back tears. "They don't know much more than us." She looked up at Adam. "The airports there are closed, that much they do know."

"What a mess," Adam swore under his breath. Their luggage was trapped as well, leaving them with their meager carry on supplies.

"I'm going to use a landline, honey," Adam said, putting his worthless cell phone into his pocket and walking over to stand in line at the eight payphones against the wall. "I've got some favors I could call in with some boys at Hickam. Maybe we can weasel a military hop down there."

Agatha smiled weakly, turned and walked over to the huge picture windows facing the ramp area and the distant Waianae mountains. She watched the gentle trade clouds, small and fluffy, move lazily across the deep blue of the tropical sky. Her heart reached out, looking for any sign of her son. Closing her eyes she began to listen as only a mother can do for her own children.

Several little songs she had often sung to him long ago came to her mind. She let them play gently in her mind as she continued her search, looking for any sign, any signal of her boy. She had always touched him this way when he was at war, in Afghanistan.

The gate announcement of another canceled flight interrupted her concentration. Opening her eyes she noticed a lone bird flying by, climbing higher and higher. It seemed to be carrying the same song she had in her heart, carrying it away.

~~~

Several powerful aftershocks were still pouring out of the earth, shaking everything off the walls of Dr. Zhung's office. Star had watched several hundred semi-ripe avocados bomb the parking lot on the first big shake, as she had trouble standing next to her car.

Even the doctor's sign had fallen off its evidently rotten post. The office staff were exiting the old two story wooden structure with their belongings.

From around the corner, where the parking lot disappeared into a well kept lawn, came Janet in a wheelchair, pushed by the doctor himself. A nurse followed them both with a small shopping bag full of something she couldn't make out.

Star rushed over to them even as a smaller trembler rolled a few of the avocados around the pavement. "Is she OK?"

"Yes, yes, she will be fine," the doctor said, happy to be getting rid of her, so he could flee as well. "Here, you can have the wheelchair.

We are leaving." He turned and marched off to his Mercedes parked in front of the building.

Star was disgusted to the point of spitting at him as he left, but as she watched him climb into his car she was pleased to see several large dents in the roof of his car, no doubt from the avocado rain.

The nurse with the bag walked up and touched Star on the shoulder gently. "Look, she will be fine, but she did just give birth. She is sore, tired and should be watched closely for any excessive bleeding."

Star stared at her with a confused look on her brow.

Handing her the plastic shopping bag, she added, "These supplies will keep her for a week. There are pain meds as well."

The nurse looked deeply into Star's eyes until she saw a glimmer of comprehension, then stood back.

"Good luck." She turned and left as well, walking down the long sidewalks toward the harbor.

Star turned to Janet and saw her slumped over in the wheelchair, breathing steadily, but heavily. Grasping the chair she wheeled it over to the passenger side of her Tercel. She reached over to open the door and pushed the wheels up against the car, set the chair brake and walked around to her side.

There she reached through and tried to get Janet into the passenger seat.

"Jimmie! Jimmie, come on and wake up a bit. We have to get going."

Janet didn't respond, so Star tapped her on her leg. That must have hurt a little. Janet moaned in pain a bit and moved her head.

"Jimmie, please. I can't lift you. You have to get in..."

Another sizable aftershock rolled through the area, this one waking Janet. She looked around a moment and then down to where she was sitting.

"What the hell?" She rolled her head around like it was trying to come loose and then caught Star's eye.

"Please, Jimmie, please get in the car right away," Star pleaded.

Janet tried pushing herself up from the chair, but the pain dropped her right back in with a heavy groan.

Sirens were going off everywhere, including now the civil defense wailing of an impending emergency. Star turned to look in the direction of those and saw smoke plumes all over the city. She worried it might be lava, but quickly dismissed that as silly. Just fires from the quake probably, knocking over things, gas lines and all that, she thought.

Janet pushed herself up again, this time anticipating the pain and powered through it. She pushed the front seat forward and dragged herself into the backseat.

Star had the engine started and as soon as Janet cleared the door she put it into reverse and quickly backed up. Another tremor was shaking the trees all around them, this time dropping small branches heavy with the avocados that were still too green to fall the first few times.

As she reversed her car the passenger door slammed shut and the wheelchair bumped into her side mirror, wedging itself there. Star was in a bit of a panic at this point. She wasn't about to get out and pull the wheelchair away, so she reversed up the parking lot. It was still attached. For some reason it struck her as demonic, a Stephen King prop.

"Be gone! I don't believe in you!" Star screamed, terrified now. She saw a telephone pole slowing falling across the street, dragging wires down with it.

Slamming the car brakes didn't dislodge the chair either. Finally she was backed all the way back up into the doctors private parking spot. The wheelchair followed until her rear wheels went up on the curb and the angle freed the chair from under the mirror.

Star slammed the gear shift into drive and floored it, until she realized she was going downhill, and again hit the brakes hard. Janet was moaning with pain in the back seat with every violent move of the car. As she stopped again, the wheelchair ran into the back of the trunk.

"I don't believe in you! I don't! Be gone!" Star screamed again, pushing ahead on the accelerator again. As she moved down the steep driveway, she looked back in her mirror. The wheelchair was rolling toward them, weaving slightly left and then right, but following her nonetheless.

At the bottom of the driveway she had to stop, going left looked bad. A block down there were poles crisscrossing the road. As she looked uphill, to the right, the wheelchair slammed into the trunk again.

"Shit!" she quickly spun the steering wheel to the right and floored it. The front wheel drive spun the tires in a scream themselves before grabbing and pulling Star and Janet rapidly ahead.

Star looked in the backseat quickly. Janet was curled up in a fetal position, moaning softly. She looked back up into her rear view mirror to see the wheelchair racing down the street in the opposite direction, toward the intersection below and the downed power lines.

~~~

Alice and Jack at the Hawaiian Volcanoes Observatories were actively trying to determine one thing and one thing only. Where would all this magma exit the earth? Jack was fielding the phone calls from the high level government types while Alice was gathering as much information as she could.

Her seismographs had now recorded seven aftershocks of 5.5 or greater. Literally hundreds of swarm quakes, measuring around 1.5 to 2.5 were coloring the graph paper with short little arcs.

The problem with this, was that all of her seismographs were doing this, all locations were showing the swarms. She felt like there must be magma moving under the entire southern flank of Mauna Loa.

"No sir, we don't expect Hilo to have any problems. The summit is not inflating. Stable up there, so we don't foresee any lava exiting to the east and the airport or the town," Jack was telling the Governor on a conference call that included all the other island mayors as well.

He walked over to where Alice was busy scribbling a synopsis for him. She handed him the hand written paper with hands that were incapable of not shaking.

Jack looked at her, concerned. He leaned over and kissed her on the top of her head. "It's going to be fine, Alice." They both appreciated the attempt to calm his and her nerves with the soothing lie.

"Sir, our problems are on the southern side of Mauna Loa. We are experiencing massive magma movement underground in the entire Volcano village area, through Pahoa, Kapoho and beyond the coastlines."

Larry was approaching Halema'uma'u crater at 1000 feet above the ground level. The clouds around the massive pit were gone, vaporized by the heat of the venting gases. He figured it looked like at least twice the volume coming out, but the crater itself was obscured.

"Jack, this is Larry over Halema'uma'u. Over."

Jack heard his friend calling and put the conference call on standby. "I have a report from the field now, we managed to launch a motorized paraglider before the earthquake. He is still airborne and over Halema'uma'u now...standby."

Alice leaped up out of her chair to stand next to Jack, hoping to hear some news. Jack noticed she had put her hand on his back as she stood close.

"Go ahead, Larry, over." Jack said, a smile hidden in his voice.

Larry was staying upwind of the massive plume, careful to avoid any contact with the sulfuric dioxide super heated gases. Small explosions could be heard from the half mile wide pit as well.

"Halema'uma'u looks to be double the normal volume plume, but the crater is hidden at the moment. Let me see if I can..."

Jack and Alice, and even those on the conference call heard the distant voice on the walkie talkie pause. In such a dangerous situation as this people got nervous immediately. It was quiet for half a minute.

"How is your man there Jack?" Governor Abercrombie asked.

"Larry, you got cut off. Say again. Over."

Larry couldn't believe his eyes and had to look over his shoulder as he turned his paraglider again, keeping well upwind. A burst of trade winds was threatening to push him downwind with the plume but it was also clearing the mouth of the crater.

"Jack! Jack, we've got a problem. The crater is full. I say again, the crater is full. It even seems to be spilling out the south side!"

Everyone heard that.

Alice sat down quickly and grabbed her calculator. They regularly measured the volume of space occupying Halema'uma'u with lasers, its depth on a normal day, measured against its current width. As she punched in the numbers she felt sweat trickling down her back.

"Roger that, Larry. Understand the crater is full and spilling over." Jack repeated for both Larry and the conference call. "How is your fuel now? Over."

Larry looked down at his gauges and with the current winds, if he wanted to use any of his preferred landing areas in this wind he had about twenty five minutes left.

"Jack, I've got fifteen minutes left, over." Larry always kept ten minutes of fuel to himself. Life insurance.

"Roger that Larry. Safe landings! Call me when you are parked. Over."

Larry signed off and headed toward his house, another mile or two upwind. The clouds were nearly gone with the day's heat, probably helped a little with all the stress the poor humans were feeling down there as well.

~~~

"Jack, come here a moment would you?" Alice asked.

"Another moment guys, I may have one more data point for you." Jack put the phone down and walked quickly to Alice's desk. He leaned over, putting his hand on her shoulder.

"Look, I figure that we now have a fresh 22 million cubic meters of magma, well lava now, in the crater. Ring any bells?" Alice turned slightly, enjoying Jack's touch as she peered into his eyes.

"Hmmm, not really. Should I know that number Alice?"

"1960 Kapoho, Jack. That was the volume held in Halema'uma'u that time. When the lava tubes below finally couldn't handle the pressure it all flushed out like a giant toilet bowl. Right into the downhill tubes leading to Kapoho."

Jack looked into Alice's eyes, loving her look. That look of knowledge, that look of danger. He never thought vulcanology would be this exciting, in all different kinds of ways.

"Evacuation?" Jack asked walking back to the Governor's conference call.

"Yes!" Alice confirmed. "I've been right once today," turning back to her computer screens. "I'm afraid I'm going to be right again."

~~~

Star saw blinking blue lights ahead on the road toward Pahoa, where she would have to turn to get to her seaside cabin in Kapoho. Janet was still asleep in the back seat, snoring lightly now. As she slowed to a stop behind the other cars she rolled down her window.

The civil defense sirens were wailing like lost children. She quickly turned on her radio to A.M. 1060 KHBC. Her car no longer seemed to ingest FM radio.

"...catch Uncle Kimo and his band tonight at Tiwaka's Tiki Bar and Grill, home of the famous Coco Loco Moco. Remember Tuesdays are Ladies *and* Dudes night. $3 Hinano and $2 Primo. Come on down. All empty bottles are being donated to the Build a Lava Dyke Around Hilo project."

"Not funny," Star sneered and switched the radio off. Cars up ahead of her were turning around, being directed by a very tall police officer. She used the opportunity to move forward, intent of getting through the road block.

Finally she was stopped at the barrier. Another police officer, somewhat of a familiar face she thought, approached her window.

"Sorry, ma'am. Road is closed, you need to turn around."

Star looked at the guy for a moment and then recognized him as the son of one of the fishermen who lived down at her cove.

"Henry? It's me, Star." She leaned out the window.

"Auntie?" He came closer and leaned down to talk with her. "Sorry, Auntie, the road is closed. No can go. You felt the earthquakes, yeah?"

"Yes, I sure did. Look, Henry, I need to get to my place, get some clothes and all. Plus, my friend, here in the back," she pointed to Janet. "She has all her stuff at my cabin too."

Henry stood up and looked over at the really tall officer he was working with, shook his head and then leaned back down.

"Look, we were letting only residents through until about half an hour ago. Now, they're telling us nobody."

Star was fearful she wouldn't be let through, even knowing the cops. Her mind was racing with options and alternatives.

"Henry, where's your dad? He's down there right?"

Henry shook his head no. "No, Auntie. I talked to him already. All the guys took their boats out to sea right after the first quake. Tsunami you know. Better to be in deep water."

Star leaned back into her seat. "Tsunami?" she whispered. Her heart was sinking. Opening the car door, she had to try one more thing.

"Henry, dear. Look, I'll be OK. I just need my stuff, you know?" she looked him directly in the eye. "You know, I don't have much. I need my stuff, my cats, Henry."

Henry wasn't saying anything, trying to look away at the increasing line of cars behind Star.

"Henry, did your dad say there had been any tsunami yet?" Star implored.

Henry looked at her, eager to solve this and get on with his traffic duties. "Auntie, yes. He said they thought there was a small one, but there were only looking through binoculars from their boats, yeah?"

He came closer to her, whispering. "You might not have anything left down there anyhow, you know?"

That thought was the one thing Star would not accept ever again. She remembered vividly being told the same thing when in 1960 the lava had claimed her parents house and eventually their happiness. She was too old to start somewhere new.

Then she had a great idea, Henry would have to go with this.

"How about this? I have my cell phone, your dad has his. I will stay in touch with the guys on the boats, and if I get in trouble, they can come pick me up." She looked at him with her best 'pretty please with mango sugar on top' look.

Henry looked over for his tall co-worker again and noticed he was walking up the long line of cars, telling everyone the news.

"OK Auntie, you sure stay stubborn lydat. Here," he said moving the barrier to the side. "Hurry up!"

Star jumped in her car and quickly pulled through, blowing Henry a kiss as she found second, third and finally fourth gear. In a couple of miles she took the left turn, down toward the ocean and Kapoho.

Janet was still sleeping in the back, but Star remembered well the first time they'd both driven down this road. Funny, she thought, Jimmie is all messed up again, but at least it's not raining this time.

Quickly moving through Pahoa town, she saw dozens of people quickly packing their cars and heading uphill, evacuating to Hilo and places north of there. As she drove deeper down into the jungle, closer and closer to her home, she looked over to the still standing cinder cone from 1960, on her left.

She had to stop her car to confirm. There was no other cars on the road now. She got out and stood perfectly still, afraid to wake the monster.

Janet moaned a little as she woke and propped herself up. Looking at Star through the rear window she wondered what she could be staring at, until she saw it too.

White plumes of steam were rising out of the cinder cone, twisting lazily up into the blue sky.

~~~

Larry finally got Shirley on the walkie talkie and confirmed she was still at home. She still had the little dogs and supplies in the SUV, with the windows down, in case she had to make a run for it. The aftershocks, however, had stopped during the last hour.

"Shirley, I'm two minutes out, over." Larry announced, lining up his landing zone.

"I've got a bottle of red open dear, clear to land!" She could already hear his engine above the trees to the north. Walking out across the street where he would soon be landing, she carried the wine and two glasses.

Larry swooped over the house and then the landing zone to Shirley's cheers. Seeing the wine and glasses he reached down and punched the button on his electric Peterbilt semi-truck horn. Twice.

Swinging around to the southwest so that he could land with the northeast trade winds at his face, giving him a bit of air braking, Larry dropped below the Ohia trees and quickly planted his tires onto the hard packed soil with the kiss of experience.

He cut his engine quickly and pulled the lift dumper spilling the remaining air out of his parafoil. It collapsed nicely onto the ground, happy to have a rest finally.

"Congrats Larry..." Shirley smiled walking over and pouring a glass as she did. "...as soon as you get airborne all hell breaks loose."

She handed him the full glass and added, "Just what did you do to piss off the mountain?" Laughing, she poured her own glass.

"I dunno. All I did was throw tennis balls at her. I'm a little surprised she found that reason to complain so much." Larry had his helmet off and had unstrapped, standing now next to Shirley.

"Kiss me now, or I'm going back to throw basketballs!"

Shirley leaned in and tasted the sweet red on her husband's lips.

"Sweet as wine, baby!" Larry confirmed. "Thanks for the arrival drink."

They both spent fifteen minutes securing the paraglider, folding the wing and pushing it back into the garage.

"The dogs are still in the car?" Larry asked, a bit surprised.

"Yeah, they seem to like it, for now. The aftershocks were less dramatic inside. You should have seen them freaking out, They were jumping like kangaroos."

"Well, look, let me call Jack and get the latest. If he thinks things are calming down we can probably bring them back in the house." He looked around the garage. "I guess we didn't get any damage in the house?"

Shirley looked at him a moment, wondering if he had forgotten. "No damage in here, no." She waited.

Then it hit him. "Oh no! My wine cellar!" Quickly he ran around the side of the house and out into the middle of the half acre yard. There, in the opening to his lava tube, extending down into the ground some twenty feet was a lingering odor of spilled wine. He wasn't about to crawl down the ladder, for fear of another aftershock, but he could see the broken bottles all over the floor.

Sadly, he stepped back, turned on the walkie talkie and checked in.

"Jack, Larry on the ground. Over."

Jack took a few moments to answer. Alice still had her hands running through his hair, hidden as they both were in the locked ladies restroom.

"Go ahead Larry, you're safe and sound?" He kissed Alice again before remembering, "Over, big guy!"

Larry looked at the walkie talkie like he had heard something strange going on. If only it was a video talkie. "Look, Jack, I don't know what you put in those tennis balls, but whatever it was, it caused my wine cellar to implode. Over."

"Heard about that. So sorry. Look, Larry, I've got something going on over here. Can I call you back?" He laughed out loud. "Over. Over."

Larry suspected a serious distraction in Jack's world. He could call back, but remembered he wanted to ask about the latest news.

"What's the latest on the magma Jack?"

Jack took a full minute to answer, having shed his shirt and shoes now. Alice was sitting up on the bathroom counter beckoning him with her finger.

"Uh, Larry. Let me see," Jack tried to make this quick. "Belt Highway is closed between Hilo and Pahoa and again south of Kona. We think the magma is flowing downhill, soon if not already." He smiled broadly at Alice. "Things are heating up buddy. Be careful out there. Over. And out."

Larry looked at the radio and turned it off. He figured it might be a good idea to fuel the paraglider up right now in case the roads remained closed and the volcano really started acting up. He attended to his flying machine, checking the oil.

Jack moved in close to Alice, feeling her warm skin against his. They kissed deeply even as they got even closer. A small rumble moved through the ground.

Alice laughed right into Jack's kiss. "You make the earth move baby!"

~~~

Star could still see the steaming cinder cone in her rear view mirror as she approached the ocean. All of the vacation rentals appeared empty, strangely vacant of Mustang convertible rental cars, and Jeeps.

As she turned right onto Aloha Lane the first thing she noticed was the layer of sand, everywhere. The road was covered with it, hiding the asphalt so well that she had to use memory to stay on the road. Making her way slowly toward her cabin she noticed their little three thousand gallon community water tank over on its side, completely off the concrete foundation they had installed it on.

Pulling further into their little compound was a shock, a fist in the face blow to her fragile emotions. The fishing shacks were flattened, piled up in haphazard collections of tree branches, plywood and PVC pipes. Her own little cabin was sitting on the ground, completely swept off its post and pier foundation. The roof looked like it didn't quite fit on the walls correctly. She pulled up, turned off her car and took a moment before she got out.

"Tsunami," she whispered, trying to explain the chaotic scene to herself. She looked quickly out to sea, and there the Champagne pool was full of debris, several large pieces of some kind of building material wedged into the coral, others simply floating.

"What happened?" Janet finally spoke, now awake.

Star turned to look at her. "Stay here a moment, until I can see if it's safe to go inside." When Janet didn't respond, she spoke a little louder. "OK?"

"Sure, Star. Sure."

Star had seen large swells from distant hurricanes pour over the lava pools before and pile up a little sand here and there, but nothing like this. As she stepped inside her cabin the first thing she noticed was the light. It was different.

Twenty some odd years in the same small space and she could tell in an instant that the shadows were in the wrong place. Most of her furniture was still in the right place, give or take a foot or so. A few pictures were missing off the wall.

"Oh, Nemo," she moaned softly. Picking up the broken pieces of her fish bowl, once the home of a small yellow Tang from the pools, she became afraid she would soon find a dead fish. Piece after piece of rounded glass was gathered into her hands, but thankfully no fish.

As she stood again she placed the pieces in her small sink below a driftwood framed window. Looking out she saw Janet peering out the rear windows of the Tercel, patiently waiting on her. That was strange though, she thought, she had always looked out this window at the mountains, not her parking area.

Spinning around quickly she looked out her front door. There, instead of the lava pools, she saw the ocean, and on the horizon, several fishing boats at anchor. The cabin had been spun around quite a bit.

Star felt like crying. But as she walked back to her front door, and sat down with her legs now touching the fresh layer of sand below, she took a slow, deep breath. Remembering a dream of her mother she recently had, she smiled. The incoming ocean had come into her home and knocked her fishbowl onto the floor, shattering it.

Nemo, her little fish, was free.

~~~

The Hawaii Air National Guard 204th Airlift Squadron C-17 taxied out toward the Reef Runway, also known as 8R on trade wind days, or 26L on a Kona wind.

"Tower, we're ready when you are," the first officer announced as they approached 8R. Surfers paddled after head high rollers in the restricted area just off to the right. They would certainly get a whiff of Jet-A fumes when they turned the massive aircraft toward Diamond Head and hit the throttles.

"Roger Pele two niner. Cleared for takeoff runway eight right." The Honolulu tower air traffic controller triple checked his radar data with that of the Center, confirming the airspace for the large jet was clear of traffic. It was clear for miles.

Adam and Agatha were both grateful to be included with the two dozen news reporters and government officials being flown over the volcano for an aerial inspection before a relief mission landing in Hilo.

Agatha looked around, a little claustrophobic with the lack of windows and the three large bulldozers crowding the center of the cargo bay.

She leaned over to whisper to Adam. "How are we going to see anything, I can't see any windows?"

Adam smiled. They weren't going to get any viewing done. "We're just bumming a ride to a closed airport dear." He nodded toward the

Governor and some of his party as well as the official photographers accompanying his entourage. "Those guys will get a peek from the cockpit."

Agatha sat back in her seat, a little disappointed. She was glad Adam had somehow secured them a ride, and wouldn't dare complain about anything, but she had assumed all aircraft had windows in the back.

She could only feel what was going on, and that was unnerving. The plane, still taxiing, made a slow sweeping turn of about ninety degrees and paused for a moment, waiting on instructions, she figured. They had been taxiing for almost ten minutes at this point. They had to be on the runway by now she hoped.

"Ready?" Adam leaned over and kissed her lightly on the cheek.

"Sure, but when..."

The consistent noise of the engines at idle began to increase slowly as the co-pilot pushed the four throttles slowly forward, watching his gauges for any indication of failure. The captain was glancing out the window as well, scanning the runway, the nearby ocean and the sky for anything unusual.

Adam reached over and grasped Agatha's hand firmly as the engines rapidly spun up to maximum power. He could visualize exactly what was going on in the flight deck, having flown many a mission in this same aircraft.

Agatha was shocked how noisy it was. Having been used to commercial planes that took some effort to insulate for noise, this C-17 wasted little precious weight on such issues. The engines were roaring with some kind of anger, in a battle with the great dragon Gravity. The aircraft shook and rattled as it accelerated down the two mile long battleground.

She soon could feel the rear tail dipping as she quickly looked toward the flight deck. Seeing it rise slightly and then her own seat lifting up off the ground was a sensation she knew, she prayed, she never would get used to. It was unnatural, this and all massive flying machines.

As the great engines continued breathing fire, lifting the beast higher up into the safety of the sky, she marveled at its persistence, its ability to fight with so much energy for so long.

trade winds being what they are, inconsistent at times, a sudden drop in the aircraft as it lost a little support from headwinds stiffened her grasp on Adam. Was the dragon going to pull them down again?

"No worries, just a bump on the road." He put his arm around her and squeezed. "Be there in about an hour."

"Thank you," she whispered unsure if he had even heard her. Agatha suddenly realized this was a type of military aircraft that her son James might have ridden on. She looked around in wonder at the complexity of the textures, at the wonder of engineering capable of moving this kind of mass through the air.

All around her were little traces of soldiers that had traveled in this great beast. A misplaced hat, a stray candy wrapper, a boarding pass. Closing her eyes she tried again to find her James Madison, focusing on the same signals she had always found before.

Ignoring the roar just outside the metal walls her hope, her very heart sought out that thing she would never be able to describe to anyone else. A mother's intuition was what her friends might call it, and that was a fine description for dinner parties and afternoon teas.

Agatha knew it was more than that. It was a bond that was now broken, a bond that she was trying to reconnect. It was a bond that had often faded in and out of her life, but one that she always sought to preserve. James had often joked that she could find him faster than any Ranger battalion, but might have trouble extracting him from a firefight.

She was still hearing nothing, feeling nothing, sensing no feedback from wherever it was she sent her mind in search. That had never happened before.

Adam figured it was just too noisy to attempt a conversation with Agatha now about her son James. As she was boarding the C-17 at the Hickam Air Force ramp an intel officer had approached him with a thin manila envelope.

"Sir," the young warrant officer announced, not quite at attention for a civilian. "I have the documents you requested from General Wong's office." He extended his hand and studied this guy who had somehow got himself and his girlfriend a ride on a high level flight. He studied the eyes of this civilian who had solicited some personal information, for his girlfriend no less, which had sent a flurry of activity through the General's office unlike anything he had seen in over a month.

"Thank you," Adam graciously replied. Looking at the young officer he nodded, subtly acknowledging the effort it had taken to get this delivered so quickly. "Please tell the General, and his staff, I am very grateful."

"Yes sir."

Adam looked over at Agatha now, her eyes closed.

"Maybe she is sleeping," he thought. "Maybe dreaming of happier times."

He leaned his head back against the netting, attempting a moment to relax as well. The documents though were racing through his mind.

He could see the logo at the top of the pages announcing its source as Naval Intelligence Service, Pearl Harbor, Hawaii. He could also see it was personally signed by a Captain John G. Gimber, N.I.S. The first sheet of paper had tracking information on it, and he knew most likely was embedded with a RFID chip. The last sheet simply said "Destroy After Reading"

But, it was the second, the middle sheet that had stuck in his mind. Stuck worse than his old Jeep at the beach, no way to get it out and no good way to explain it.

Private First Class James Madison Turner U.S. Army is AWOL as of 23December.

An initial investigation, performed at his last known whereabouts, the Kilauea Military Recreation Area in Volcano, Hawaii has been completed as of 0900hrs 30December.

An official finding has yet to be determined, but per instructions from General Wong, the lead investigator, myself, has been instructed to offer an early assessment.

As to that point, it is my opinion on this date, that Private First Class James Madison Turner, U.S. Army is dead.

His fiancé is being sought for questioning in what we now have upgraded to a murder investigation.

Sincerely,

Captain John G. Gimber, N.I.S.
Pearl Harbor, Hawaii

Agatha had long ago acknowledged her optimistic tendencies.
She had learned to work with them and take the extra effort to question
her first inclinations. That had tempered her early reputation as a
idealistic dreamer. It had also saved her considerable embarrassment
when playing bingo. She had to finally admit that the universe couldn't
possibly give her winning numbers every evening.

It was with that healthy attitude toward failure that she came to
realize that she was no longer going to be able to sense James,
regardless of how much she tried, or how much she wanted to. It was
heartbreaking nonetheless. Leaning her head gently against her new
love's shoulder and taking a deep breath she sadly acknowledged what
had to be. It was inevitable, eventually she would have lost him, given
his occupation.

She felt a little embarrassed that the Governor himself and
reporters from every radio and newspaper in Hawaii might see her
tears. Glancing up shyly, eyes full of water, she saw the Governor
himself, looking at her. He nodded gently and with a gentleman's
respect turned back to his work.

Somehow this gave her the permission she needed to cry. Putting
her head down into her hands she let it go, let it all go. The hope that
her young James would somehow come to her and say it was all a
mistake, a bad idea, was gone. He was not ever going to hug her
again, or bring her a box of chocolates from Germany.

Visions of birthday parties with balloons and other little kids running through the house, visions of cake smeared grins and bare feet were dancing there behind her tightly closed eyes. She felt the heavy tug of history and time. Death sorted itself out from life, leaving the past behind for elderly daydreamers. She felt as if she were an old lady now, with no husband, no family, no son, never to play with grandchildren.

Adam was gently rubbing her back as she let her heart melt. She sighed heavily after a while and sat back, letting Adam wipe the tears from her cheeks. She had surrendered. She knew that her only son, James Madison was gone.

It was just at that point, somewhere over the island of Maui, directly over the mystical summit of Haleakala, in a C-17 some four miles above the ocean my message arrived.

Agatha caught her breath in surprise. "No," she thought, "it's my grief playing tricks." She applied her time honored tradition of cautiousness and skepticism. "I mustn't torture myself," she said to herself. She looked up at Adam and smiled a little, thanking him silently for being there.

She turned back to her thoughts. "That was different," she reasoned, thinking it must be a trick of her mind. "Never was it this clear," she felt she might actually be losing her mind. She had heard about that happening to people in her situation.

How could such a burst of joy be an appropriate response to what she now knew to be true about James? She continued to analyze, tearing herself down, tearing her own dignity away in strips of self doubt.

As the military aircraft flew over the weathered northern point of the Big Island, over the village of Hawi and across to the eternal Hamakua coast our message, Poho and I, came through unmistakably.

"We are happy and we love you."

~~~

Alice unlocked the door to the women's restroom and peered cautiously outside into the hallway. Seeing no one close by, she waved at Jack to follow her out. They were practically giggling, still high from the danger and the adventure.

"You animal," she whispered loudly to Jack, who was right behind her.

"Lion tamer!" Jack answered back.

They almost rounded the corner into the operations room together, but at the last moment, Alice stopped, put her hand on Jack's chest and said, "Wait here, count to ten or something." She smiled her best 'That was fun' but Jack saw only 'I'm done with you for now'.

"That's cool," he replied, looking down at his feet for some reason.

Alice disappeared into the bright lights and action, someone immediately calling out her name.

Jack figured he could use a drink and turned to find the soda machine in the break room. He felt a little lonely for the briefest of moments. Sure, he thought, I'm a big stud. Yes, I just had sex in the woman's restroom, but here he was, again, by himself.

Being a middle aged single guy wasn't all it was purported to be, despite what the movies might suggest. Freedom? Of course, freedom to enjoy massive amounts of loneliness.

He pulled two one dollar bills from his wallet, remembering when a Sprite used to cost thirty-five cents. That was when he was a young buck, when it wasn't just desperate scientists in remote locations that found him attractive.

The can fell solidly into the slot and he waited for the change. A long silence followed. Looking up at the price, it had just changed from a few days ago of $1.50 to $2.00.

"Unbelievable," he murmured, popping the top.

Tipping up the can to take a full mouthful, he gargled with the bubbling drink, like he used to in college. For some reason, he couldn't quite remember, it was supposed to freshen your breath better than Scope. Something about the scrubbing action of the bubbles...

"Wait a minute," he stopped and thought. "Scrubbing action of the bubbles?" He thought about the viscosity of the magma, and if it had more dissolved gas then it might travel farther, scrubbing the old lava tubes. Less gas might keep it from traveling as far.

Excited to tell Alice about the idea and to see if they might get a sample from the field he walked briskly into the operations room. Several people were crowded around Alice's monitors. As he got closer some peeled away and went back to their workstations, shaking their heads, or pulling out their cell phones.

"Alice!" Jack said a little too loud. "Alice," he said a bit softer, having gotten her attention now. "I've got an idea about the travel time of the magma..."

"Jack, wait," Alice said putting up her hand. "Halema'uma'u has drained half of its volume in the last hour."

"No way!" Jack exclaimed. "No way. That's what? Eleven million cubic meters?"

Alice nodded. She patiently waited for his obvious follow up question.

"Where the heck did it all go?"

"Kapoho. A large amount of magma has moved into the Kapoho tube system."

~ ~ ~

Star and Janet were finished with what little cleanup they could do for the afternoon. It was getting dark quickly with the large vog cloud hanging to the west, blocking the sun.

Janet wanted to ask Star about the steaming cinder cone they had stopped at on the way in, but she could see from Star's face that now was not a particularly good time. She simply sat with her, at the edge of the Champagne pool, letting her feet gently stir the water.

Star looked over at her and nodded a silent thanks. Thanks for being with her now, at the scene of what Star thought might be her own eventual destruction.

"How are you feeling, Jimmie?"

Janet hadn't thought about it for a couple of hours now, but pretty good for the most part. She had a strong build and was young. Plus the pain pill she had taken at the cinder cone stop was perfectly matched. No pain, no side effects.

"Not bad," Janet answered, trying to smile a little. "I want to say thank you, you know. Thank you for driving me there." She put her arm around Star. "I know it wasn't something you wanted to do."

Star bowed her head a little, trying to shut out the images of what she knew had happened there. She couldn't hold back the few insistent tears forcing their way out.

"Damn wheelchair nearly freaked me out," she laughed slightly.

Janet looked at her, trying to remember. "All I remember was a lot of stopping and starting. Did you run over a curb too?"

Star laughed at that as well. "Two or three I think."

They sat in silence for a while, watching the ocean tousle with the wind and the horizon. The guys could still be seen anchored out in the deeper water.

"Do you think there might be another tsunami?" Janet asked.

Star hung her head. Of course there might, she thought. They were foolish to be next to the ocean while earthquakes were happening. But, she had to be here, she had to stand firm on the last piece of land on this earth she could ever call home.

"Yes, perhaps." Star took Janet's hand and pointed out several coconut palms close to the damaged fishing shacks. "See those trees there?"

"By the shacks?" Janet asked.

"Yes, see the wooden steps nailed into them, I think there are four or five trees that have them. If there is another earthquake, big, like you have to catch your balance. That big. If so, run over to one of those trees and climb it as high as you can."

Janet didn't understand that. "Why wouldn't we just drive up the road, up to the main highway?"

Star tilted her head to one side and nodded a little. "You could of course. But, you probably wouldn't have time."

"No way," Janet whispered. "Really? That fast?"

"Sure, you can always look out to see if the water has receded. That is probably your last warning. If it's dark, you can try and listen for where the waves are breaking, or just climb the tree."

That evening, in the warmness of her familiar surroundings Star slept soundly, despite the dozens of small barely perceptible tremors emanating from up the road, at the cinder cone.

Janet was up at every one of them, looking at the ocean with her flashlight to see if it the water was pulling back. It never did. By dawn, she had been up half the night.

One of the fishing boats was on its way in, coming ashore, having seen their lights during the night. Star ran out happy to greet them and share some information about the tsunami and to get some fish from the guys.

Janet stayed back in the palms and watched Star explain she would remain here, despite the danger, and keep an eye on things. The guys gave her a big hug and a jug of water and made their way back out to sea and safety, trailing a baited hook with them.

Finally, around 10 in the morning she felt her eyes too heavy to keep open and blissfully drifted off to sleep in the hammock.

Star managed to get into Pahoa town, itself well within the evacuation zone, and found the grocery store owner still there, with a shotgun. "NO LOOTERS" was painted on the window covering what used to say "Pahoa Shop -n- Save".

She picked up a week's worth of can goods, water and as many bananas as they had. He gave her the bananas for free.

On her drive back she stopped again at the cinder cone, steaming quite fiercely now, venting with a noise she could easily hear from the half mile distance. The ground wasn't shaking with earthquakes as much as it was continually vibrating. It reminded her of a trip to Chicago and how her friend had told her the vibration in the sidewalks was the underground subway trains.

As she climbed back into her Tercel, she caught a brief glimpse of a glow on the far side of the cone. She drove forward a little to get a possibly better angle. There, she could see a distinctive orange glow slowly spilling out of the top of the cone.

~~~

Adam and Agatha thanked their hosts for the ride over and walked across the deserted airport to the rental car booths. The airport was closed to commercial traffic, no one was around. Adam got on his phone to call a taxi.

"No, bruddha, I cannot take you to Volcano. You heard right? They stay evacuating the whole area!"

"Yeah, OK." Adam looked around the rental car booths. "Too bad I can't rent a car myself."

The taxi driver jumped out of his Buick Estate Wagon and pulled some keys out of his pocket.

"I can rent you one car right now," and walked over to Billy's Certified Rentals, at the very end of the long line of rental booths.

"Great!" Agatha said. "How much?" she asked out of habit, even if Adam was paying for it.

"Well," Billy, the apparent owner said. "Good deal this week, we call it the lava special, you know."

Adam was expecting to get fleeced when the affable old guy said something quite unexpected.

"$100 for the week, but you gotta buy full insurance." He looked back over his shoulder toward the ever darkening plume toward Volcano. "Bad mojo now, and I know you're headed that direction."

"Deal!" Adam laughed, slapping down his AMEX Centurion Black.

Ten minutes later they were driving a late '90s Ford Fusion up to the roadblocks just outside of Hilo, on the road to Volcano.

As they approached it, there appeared a chaotic mess of cars trying to turn around all at once. A police officer with a flashlight in his hand was waving the world back, as another officer drug the barrier behind him, widening the evacuation area a little more. In the near distance a cinder cone was crowning itself with a glow of orange and yellow. Plumes of white smoke were pouring out of it as well.

"Looks like trouble," Adam said automatically, half wishing he had not said it out loud. Turning to Agatha it was apparent she was now convinced this chase for her son, into the Volcano area, was a bad idea.

"They look scared," Agatha whispered to herself.

"What?" Adam was busy turning the car around. "What did you say?"

She turned to look at Adam as he looked out the rear view window reversing in his lane.

"They look scared, Adam," Agatha repeated loud enough to get Adam to turn around and look. He stared for a moment straight ahead.

"Yeah. They do."

"They're too young..." she paused a moment before finishing, afraid she might offend Adam. She watched him twist around again, backing the car up. He could handle. "They're too young to be that scared."

He laughed shallowly. "What? Are old folks the only ones that should be scared Agatha?" He scoffed a little at that as he got the car turned around, headed back toward Hilo.

She didn't answer right away, watching instead the jungle slide past her window. Adam had the radio on, but Agatha reached over and turned the volume all the way down.

"I have a friend with a nice house up in Pa'auilo. Great ocean view, horses, quiet. Let's go wait this out over there," Adam suggested. "No lava out that way."

They drove on in silence for several minutes, eventually crossing the Hilo river bridge and into the pastoral beauty of the Hamakua coastline. Here on the slopes of Mauna Kea, the land would never host lava again.

Agatha had her window down, her elbow out. Adam knew she was disappointed. He figured she would eventually say something, when she was ready.

Laupahoehoe was so spectacularly different from the area they had just left. Cobalt seas used their immeasurable skills to carve coves, rock beaches and cliffs into textures impossible to ignore. Agatha had never imagined anything like it. She could feel the natural beauty slowly peeling some of the stress from her skin. Warm hints of plumeria and ginger forced her uneasiness to surrender. Finally she reached over to find Adam's hand on his seat.

He squeezed back. That made him feel better.

"Agatha, don't be scared anymore." He wanted to follow that up with some kind of reason or explanation, but dropped it. There really wasn't a reason or explanation to not be.

She was gazing at her hand, atop his. Both of them had weathered their own unique decades of life. Both of them, she knew, were well past their middle years.

"Those boys," she began softly. "Back at the barricades..."

"The police?" Adam guessed.

"Yes," squeezing his hand a little more. "They reminded me, somehow."

Adam looked at her a moment and then back to the road. The scenery demanded almost as much attention as the driving. The road was diving into another valley of lush green worshiping its own waterfall god high up in the mountain reaches above.

"I *am* scared Adam," Agatha admitted. "I'm scared of old age, of dying."

"Oh, we have a long time to go before any of that," Adam reflexively replied. He personally never gave it a thought.

"I'm not afraid that there won't be a place, an afterlife," Agatha explained. "It's not that, not at all."

Adam was slowing down to turn up Pohakea road, upcountry from the ocean view highway they had been on. Soon, he turned again onto Pa'aulilo Mauka road and began a slow beautiful climb through rolling pastures and the dark eucalyptus forests that watched over them.

"Adam, I'm just afraid that it will be so different."

They pulled into an unmarked driveway that wound them through avocado and mango trees, and finally up to a broad veranda wrapping around a one story home. The ocean softly caressed the view far below as the gentle greens of pasture fell to it.

They both got out of the car slowly, soaking up the scene with the thirst of new explorers, of artists in a new museum of wonder.

Adam pulled Agatha to him, both of them sitting on the warm hood of the car. He held her tightly, his chin on her shoulder as they both breathed in the view.

"Agatha my dear, heaven can't be much different from this right here."

18

From a distance lava always looks enchanting, almost hypnotic. Watching it on a television can even make it appear beautiful. Perhaps it could indeed be all of that, but not when it was in your own backyard.

Like most of nature's creative tools, it completely disregards human opinions and certainly ignores whatever dreams or wishes people have. It is a force that cannot be redirected or delayed, negotiated with or compelled. Planetary forces rarely cut humans a break but at least Hawaiian lava gave them enough time to get out of the way.

This event was no exception. There were no surprises here. A continuous thirty year eruption at Kilauea had convinced the world that time had a whole other meaning here than it did to humans in general. Past lava flows demonstrated quite convincingly that what had been pristine pools and beaches could within weeks be covered in over twenty feet of molten rock. Earthquakes alerted everyone to a process that had started here on the Big Island of Hawaii some four hundred thousand years ago.

Yes, Hawaii could destroy and create but it never snuck up on you, it never surprised the observant.

Star knew all this. The history was clear. Yet her history was just as clear in her mind; the history she would maintain, the history she intended to live, here at her home by the sea.

It wasn't that she was fearless, no, not that at all. Hurricanes, tsunami, floods, earthquakes, lava. They all owned a little piece of her nightmares. It wasn't that she was crazy, she knew the risks and had balanced them with her pride.

Star was going to make her stand here, among the palms and the clear pools, the black rocks and the blue ocean. She was going to use all of her heart to do as her hippie mom had always told her, to create her own reality. And, if that didn't work, she would evacuate by sea.

Janet had slept the entire afternoon before, through the night and was only now just stirring two hours after sunrise. Star watched her like a mother might her hung-over teenage daughter, with a touch of contempt floating atop a large pool of compassion.

Despite her faults, Star found Janet a companion who was willing to share both her dreams and her fears, and most importantly, her papayas.

~~~

Alice felt like a college girl again. She was all infatuated with a new guy and immersed in a big science challenge, all at once! What could be more perfect?

"Nothing, that's what," she thought to herself, happily typing queries into her magma projection software.

Twenty-two million cubic meters was a lot of anything. It could, she quickly deduced, cover the entire island of Manhattan ten inches thick. Five inches of coverage had just disappeared into the underground lava tube system and was heading for Kapoho, again.

She turned to look for Jack, she needed an observation of Halema'uma'u. And she wouldn't mind just looking at him a moment. It had been a while since she had felt like this. His hair, she daydreamed, was long enough for her to fill both of her hands. Shaking that thought off, she returned to the task at hand, without the hair.

"Jack?" she called, walking into the break room.

Jack looked up from his prepackaged ham sandwich, then quickly to his left to see if anyone else was in the room with him. Besides Alice there were two others, reading a paper. He dropped his initial thought.

"Yes, Ms. Alice?"

She stood askance, one hand on her hip, the other up to her chin.

"I need something from you, right away."

Jack stood up, watching her like a cat.

"Yes, I need it right now," Alice said, getting the attention of the two others in the room.

Jack was a little surprised she was talking like this in front of others, but still managed to smile.

"Am I the man to give it to you?"

She nodded slowly.

"Oh yes, yes, you are. I need a volume reading on Halema'uma'u big boy."

Jack grinned broadly. He looked to the two newspaper readers, one of them smiling and then returning to his paper.

"Well then. I shall give it to you right away." He picked up his sandwich and walked around the table.

Alice immediately turned and went out the door. She looked back over her shoulder as he followed her into the hallway. That man, she said to herself, was going to make her job worth every penny they should be paying her above what they actually were.

Jack practically ran to the laser room to retrieve what he needed and then in a moment was in the observation room where he and Larry had watched the hikers that night.

The crater was obscured again with massive amounts of plume, and thus he would indeed need his laser observer. With this, he could fire toward the pit and get a reading about the level of lava.

Lining up his view finder Jack pressed the trigger and immediately got a return.

"That can't be right," he shook his head, putting his eye back to the viewfinder and firing another laser shot.

"What the heck?" The answer was the same. He thought he might actually be shooting at the rim by accident and not to the middle of the pit. He calibrated it on a known distance marker rangers had setup for just such a purpose.

For the third time he picked his point as the center of Halema'uma'u and squeezed the trigger.

"Holy shit," he whispered to himself after seeing the same answer for a third time.

Quickly, he got on the phone to Alice.

"Yes, big guy?" she answered.

"Alice."

She hesitated a moment, catching something in the tone of his voice. "What, Jack? What is it?"

"Alice, Halema'uma'u is full! Again!"

~~~

The tide and winds had done a great job of clearing the debris out of Champagne pools. Janet and Star luxuriated in its cool clearness as the noon tropical sun did its best to melt them. Impossible as that was, with them dunking their heads under water every few minutes, the sun was relentless. And, so was the cinder cone two miles away.

Star could hear it now. Hissing and spitting and other obscene sounds the jungle or the beach was never supposed to bear. Fortunately the trade winds were keeping the fumes and plume behind them, pushing the great clouds away from the coast.

They both seemed adept at ignoring the problem. Wally called them twice a day from the boats offshore, begging Star to come with him, to the safety of the sea. Neither Star nor Janet could leave, despite the ominous volcano. Star told Wally she would wait it out here, giving her strength to the land, and taking strength from it. But, she did find it extremely comforting that he could swoop in and rescue her if the lava got too close.

Both women luxuriated in a splendorous denial. Taking long walks along the beach, looking for shells and smooth stones kept their minds off the unimaginable. It was however getting more difficult to ignore it all.

The ground was constantly rumbling softly under their feet, the fishermen were still anchored in the deep water a half mile out and the pools were completely empty of tourists, locals and for some strange reason even the turtles. Paradise seemed under siege and its only defenders, two women of undetermined fortitude were unprepared for such a battle.

It was a peaceful scene on the surface. Both Star and Janet were singing old hippie love songs, eating papaya and coconuts. Star had found some old chocolate chip cookies she had stashed for special occasions. Swinging in their own hammocks under the deepening blue of a late afternoon they finally discussed the volcano, like they might an old boyfriend.

"You know," Star said, chewing softly on the sweet chocolate dough. "I've dated worse."

Janet laughed out loud. "Really? Worse than hot tempered, blowing his top, pissing everyone off around him?"

"Well, maybe similar," Star pushed her foot along the cool sand under the tall coconut palms so she could swing a little higher. "Certainly some with about as much hot air and definitely several with just as toxic of breath!"

Janet giggled like a little girl. "And that complexion! Seriously!"

Star enjoyed her cookie for another moment thinking of more insults.

"And, I've dated a few, handsome types, even beautiful, that thought that once you fell for them, you know, totally in love, when you became dependent on them, then they could do as they please..."

"Yeah, bastards," Janet agreed.

Star continued. "They could just up and destroy it all, lay waste to everything good around you, and then act like I've should have known better."

Janet could see that Star was getting upset, that her eyes were closed as she swung lightly in the hammock. She was squeezing them tightly shut.

Janet swung around to let her feet hang out the side of her hammock and stopped swinging. "Star," she tried to say but saw her friend now crying harder. She stood and went over to her, putting her hand on the still swinging hammock. "I feel lucky, for you. I feel you will be lucky here."

Janet looked around for a moment. It was indeed the most beautiful place she had ever been, and it wasn't just the postcard qualities that abounded everywhere. It was the mana, the feeling in the shadows of the palms, the soft whispers of the gentle breezes and the constant singing of the ocean. It was manifested most obviously in this older woman who had come to her rescue on the side of a rainy road.

"Star, you always say the volcano must destroy in order to create." She lightly stroked the hair of her still crying friend. "But, why would it destroy what it has worked so hard to create?" Janet looked across the bay, sparkling in the late afternoon sun. "This place, this wonderful, wonderful place has created you. This island has spun you from the sand, from the sky and sea into its loving expression. You are, my friend, the very thing paradise must breathe through." Janet looked out at the first star of the evening, shimmering in the clear tropical air. "Without you, here in your cove of palms and hammocks, and chocolate chip cookies the world would be just another rock in the darkness of space."

Star opened her watery eyes in a great big smile. "That's beautiful Jimmie. Thank you." She wiped her tears as best she could with her paisley shirt. "I've never heard you speak so ... I don't know, so, well sweetly."

Janet dropped her head to watch her own toes flex in the sand, embarrassed a bit by her eloquence.

"It just felt," she wondered how to explain it. Looking up she blinked and added "It just felt like my heart had it to say." She stood up and walked slowly back to her own hammock. Sitting back down, she got quiet a moment, all the while staring at the ocean beyond.

"I feel like I have destroyed too, Star. But for me, I have created nothing."

"Oh Jimmie, don't do that," Star said gently, sitting up herself now. "Don't go there now, it's too soon."

Janet pushed herself against the sand and lifted her feet so she could swing. "I know, I know. But, it's true, and it won't be any less true in a month. Or a year."

Star kept silent, letting Janet continue.

"The volcano, here," Janet continued. "It destroys but it rebuilds what it took away. It eventually makes it all right." Leaning back into the hammock she placed her fingers into her hair. "Star, I've destroyed things I can never bring back. Ever."

Star felt a wave of grief emanate from Janet, but one that quickly receded into a puddle of sadness. She watched Janet sink into that puddle, slowly. If she could offer any hope it must be something that could speak to her recent trauma at the clinic in Hilo. Maybe that, she thought, could offer some consolation.

"Jimmie, look, that baby wasn't right for you, wasn't good. But you can always have another, find a good guy, you know."

"No. No Star. You see, my curse is that I don't want to create anything." Her voice gave away some emotion, but Janet kept it well masked. "I don't know what I want actually. Nothing I guess. I want nothing."

Star watched the young woman say words that made no sense to her. She tried to let the words fashion some kind of meaning as she silently listened, but that idea was quickly overwhelmed by a large explosion behind them.

Both of them jumped a little, especially when they heard the artillery type sound whirling over head. Quickly they both got out of their hammocks and walked out toward the beach for a clearer view of the sky.

"What is that?" Janet asked, looking up into the dusk.

Crackling and popping in the purple sky above them was what they first thought to be a meteor. As they watched the arch it followed they saw it splash only a few hundred yards out into the ocean. Quickly, two others followed, smaller and splashing closer.

"Shit!" Star hissed. "Lava bombs!"

Another larger, heavier explosion some distance away rumbled the ground with a shock wave. It was followed immediately by what sounded to Janet like a waterfall. A very large waterfall.

Janet looked to Star with some hope of an explanation. 'Lava bomb' didn't make any sense to her. She grabbed Star's arm.

"Lava what?"

Star was shaking but didn't realize it until Janet held her. "The volcano honey. It's shooting out big rocks, popping them out like corks."

Janet let go of her arm, horrified. She ran around to the driveway, looking for the cinder cone. She couldn't quite see it so she ran a few yards up the road just in time to see a steaming, glowing rock about the size of a basketball rolling toward her along the asphalt road. The cinder cone, in the far distance looked like a giant firework, the kind other kids were always allowed to set up in the street. The kind that shot fire and sparkles and tons of smoke out of its top to the cheers of all around.

Those had always been so beautiful to her. *This one* was of course quite different she thought, turning to run back to Star. *This one* would not stop in thirty seconds. *This one* looked alive, and somehow hungry.

Janet took a few steps before it hit. A burst of static swept through her head, surprising her enough to stumble and pause. Quickly putting both hands up to her head she tried to push her increasingly long red hair into her head. Anything to quell the noise, the chaos. The static, her personal monster, her resident demon simply shouted louder.

"Jimmie!" Star was yelling above the increasing volume of the cinder cone. "Jimmie! Are you hurt?" Star ran over to Janet, saw she wasn't injured and quickly moved out to the road to see what Janet had seen.

She noticed several still smoking lava bombs on the road where the asphalt ended but her eye was immediately drawn up toward the cinder cone. Star had seen it all before, on TV of course. But, now, right in front of her she could hear it. Her ears told her she was too close. Too close - to the massive amount of liquid rock fountaining over a hundred feet into the early evening sky. Too close – to the splattering sounds of the falling lava, louder than her own racing heart. Too close - to escape.

She turned and ran back to where Janet was still immobilized, now on the ground, on her hands and knees.

"Jimmie!" Star had to shout about the roar. "What's wrong honey? Come on, I'm going to call the fishing boats and see if we can get out of here."

Star tried to pull Janet to her feet. She could hear her friend moaning pitifully, but managed to get her almost up when they both were thrown to the ground. Another earthquake, somewhat larger, had moved through. A large rumble continued to move under them.

Janet had rolled over, curling up now, holding her head. Star was dazed but managed, as she sat back up, to catch a strange sight. All the coconuts in her grove fell at the same time, thumping the ground so solidly she could feel it.

Suddenly, by certain instinct of having lived so close to the ocean for decades, she stood up and looked over at the beach. There she watched horrified as in the remaining dim light she saw the water receding.

"Oh my god!" The words never made it to her ears with all the other noise around them, but she felt them in her heart. They spoke as a dagger of fear thrust deeply into her chest and twisted back and forth.

She turned back to Janet quickly. "Get up, Jimmie! Now!" She pulled on Janet's shirt, trying to find her armpits to forcefully pull her up. "Now!" she screamed.

Janet was completely overwhelmed. She could barely hear her friend yelling at her. It was just too much to move. She could feel her friend pulling on her shoulders and relented a bit, but felt she could not cooperate, could not move right now. The stress, the fear, the bubbling insanity just below her consciousness was rapidly rising.

Star was hitting her now, hitting her on the back. "Get up! Now!" Looking with trepidation she turned again to the ocean. It was obscenely misplaced, the entire bay was a hollow bowl of coral and sand. The dark ocean had left it there, alone. Movement caught her eye off to the right, around the point. It didn't make sense to her mind, this large frothing movement where there should be none. A strange movement where there was only a point of land extending out to sea.

In a momentary flash of clarity that spoke directly to her primal survival instincts she stood, dropping her hands away from Janet. Frozen with terror, she managed to find a fragment of control for a split second, enough to scream an alert. An alert to all who might hear the last warning, the last chance to save themselves, indeed the last human voice they might ever hear.

"Tsunami!"

~~~

Up in the high jungles of Volcano village people were still shaking from that last earthquake, a frightening reminder that it wasn't just lava that could destroy.

Larry and Shirley, with their two little dogs right under their feet, were looking at the incredible plume rising above the jungle. It was indeed impressive, beautiful, amazing and historic. Unfortunately, it was only two miles away as well.

They had lived close to the volcano for well over a decade and knew the risks and the protective terrain between them and Halema'uma'u. Lava from the massive crater would certainly never flow into their yard. Statistically it was safer than living on the beach, considering hurricanes, storm surf and the occasional tsunami.

However, volcanoes had other bad habits besides simply pouring lava all over the landscape. Fumes from such massive plumes could be quite toxic, lava bombs could pepper the land for up to two miles away – putting them within range, and earthquakes could tear the ground and your home's foundations apart.

"You know, Shirley, I better give Jack a call and see what the latest is."

"OK Larry," Shirley said, leaning down to pet her nervous dogs. "I'm going to go see if I can squeeze any more stuff into the car."

Larry nodded to her as he listened as well to the ringing of Jack's cell phone. He stood and watched the plume roll like a thunderstorm pouring into some hole in the sky.

Jack's phone answered but sounded like it was still in his pocket.

"Hello? Jack?" Larry looked at his phone to confirm it had indeed connected.

"Larry...we're..." Wind noise or rustling was distorting his voice.

"Jack, what's going on over there?" He looked at his phone again. It was still a live connection.

"Larry...we're evacuating for God's sake..." Suddenly his voice became clearer. "I'm running to my goddamn car."

Larry felt a tinge of fear creep into his heart. "Jack, you said you're what? Evacuating?"

Jack was only steps behind Alice and all the other Hawaiian Volcanoes Observatory employees running to their vehicles. He jumped into the passenger seat of Alice's Ford 150, closed the door and pulled the phone from his shirt pocket.

"Larry, we're getting the hell outta here! Halema'uma'u is overflowing and that last quake took out most of the windows and some walls."

Jack leaned over and gave Alice a big kiss on the cheek as she accelerated out of the parking lot.

"Larry, you still there?"

"Yeah, Jack." Larry had that sinking feeling that things were growing dangerous. "Where are you headed?"

Alice was the lead car and rocketing toward the exit to the National Park when she slammed on her brakes, getting a lot of attention from her co-workers just behind her.

There were large cracks in the asphalt ahead. Several trees were down as well, partially blocking the road.

"Larry, gotta go, roads are fracturing as well. You and Shirley better head for Hilo, that's where we're going." Jack hung up, stepped out of the truck and began walking ahead, giving Alice directions around the worst parts.

"Shirley!" Larry yelled from the porch. He was still watching the plume when he saw something glowing inside of it, rising rapidly through the gray and black.

"Yeah baby?" Shirley stuck her head out from the open kitchen window.

Larry was watching more and more of the glowing balls rising inside the plume and saw one arching outside of the smoke.

"Lava bombs," he whispered to himself, incredulous at the very mention of the words.

"Larry? What?" Shirley sensed something wrong watching her husband stare at the plume for so long.

"Get in the car...lava bombs," Larry was still whispering to himself. He watched as another glowing ball of lava rock arched out of the plume toward him, toward his home, toward his exit. He couldn't quite believe it, surreal as it appeared. It reminded him of an old medieval movie where they catapulted burning balls of fire at the castle walls.

Shirley came up behind him, put her arms around him and looked up at the plume as well. She saw it too and screamed just as it hit the trees across the yard, tearing through them and bounced once, twice and then rolling up against their outdoor grill. The large lava rock was still molten, crackling and smoking as it rested against the stainless steel.

"Holy…" Shirley was about to say, noting it was as big as the grill.

"Propane! Run!" Larry found his voice and pulled Shirley with him through the house and to the garage.

"Are the dogs in the car?"

"Yeah! Holy…"

The explosion of the propane canister, some seven pounds of liquid fuel, broke windows behind them as they opened the door leading into the garage. Larry hit the garage door opener button and jumped in the driver's side, Shirley waiting for him to pull out so she could get in.

They always left their keys in the ignition, if the car was in the garage, a safety habit they had practiced since moving in. It was a good idea, as the keys were always in the same place, and if you had to leave in a hurry, they were in the best place.

Larry got the car clear of the garage wall as Shirley opened the door, her dogs barking in encouragement to hurry up.

"Come on, baby!" Larry yelled. He was looking up in the sky for more incoming lava bombs just as Shirley heard more trees being torn apart. Another mass of lava, glowing and hissing red hot, hit the pavement twenty feet behind them and off to the side rolling out of view.

He didn't bother trying to find the garage door opener in the car so the door remained opened. Larry looked inside to his paraglider with a bit of sadness as he rapidly backed out. He honestly wondered if that was the last time he would see it, or, for that matter, his home.

Speeding down the road, Shirley got her breath back enough to ask Larry about his phone call.

"What did Jack say?"

Larry was consciously aware that he could still kill them all in a simple car crash if he didn't focus on keeping his speed down. As he rounded a turn and had a bit of a straight section he shook his head, amazed at his answer, that he would ever say such a thing.

"They've evacuated, to Hilo."

Shirley looked at him, amazed as well. It was the first time that it must have ever happened. "Holy..."

Larry slammed the brakes just in time to keep the falling monkey pod tree from smashing them. Even with the great job he did, several branches covered their windshield. Immediately putting it into reverse he stopped several feet back and jumped out to see if there was a way around.

He could smell something acrid in the air as he looked for a path around the tree. More and more lava bombs were falling sporadically in the distance, each heralded by braking tree branches and thuds in the ground. The ground was muddy all around the asphalt until it met a ditch that made it stupid to even try an attempt around the fallen tree.

Being the only road out of their neighborhood made it even worse. Larry turned to look back at Shirley through the windshield. She was waving him back to the car.

As he got back in she was pointing. She couldn't quite speak, with either fear or overwhelming excitement but she sure could point.

"What, what is that?" Larry asked trying to follow her finger.

"There...they...bulldozed. Last week!"

Larry reversed back, turned around and made his way over to where she had directed. It was a clearing through the jungle being carved out for several new houses. Maybe, just maybe they both thought, it would connect to another road.

They followed the path off road, bumping around at speeds too fast for freshly cleared ground. Both of them were scanning ahead for any sign of a road, but it looked so far to be more trees in the near distance.

"I don't see anything!" Larry said loudly. The dogs were still barking. He looked back at them irritated and then to Shirley. "What *are* they saying?"

Just then the car lurched to a stop, impaling the front bumper on a stump he had not seen. Both airbags deployed.

"Watch out, I think." Shirley said, stunned beyond sarcasm but still within her sense of humor.

Larry stumbled out of the car, ran around to the front just in time to see both front tires deflating. Fluids were pouring out of the engine.

Shirley ran out as well, a backpack on her arm, the dogs in close pursuit.

"Holy..."

"Shirley!" Larry yelled, looking back toward their home, about a quarter mile away. "Follow me!" He began to run back up to the road and toward their home.

Shirley and Larry, both weekend runners, were soon shoulder to shoulder, the dogs right behind them.

"You've always wanted to go flying with me, right?" Larry asked.

She just looked at him, a little smile creasing his nervousness.

"Well, today's your lucky day baby!" Larry laughed as he watched the sky for more lava bombs.

"Holy...Guacamole!" Shirley finally said.

~~~

"Tsunami! Get the hell off the ground!" Star screamed one last time, already looking to the coconut trees.

Somewhere deep inside the static of Janet's head, somewhere in the midst of the familiar battle between her core and the noise, a voice distant and urgent rose above the fray. It wasn't Star's voice.

It was a voice she had never heard before. Insistent and kind, ripe with clarity and command, it spoke to her directly. Unlike the static that was always a conversation *about* her, this voice was polite. 'You have other work to do.'

Star gave Janet one last tug, this time with a handful of her red hair. She figured she might drag her as far as she could and only abandon her when she was forced to save herself. The coconut trees, with the steps built onto them, were only a few yards away.

The frothing, rolling mass of angry ocean was spilling over itself in some race to consume anything unfortunate enough to be within its reach. The massive glow of the cinder fountaining behind them was lighting up the sky, and throwing shadows around like leaves in the wind. Between those shadows it lit the onrushing flood.

Janet's eyes popped open. Star was pulling her hair and the noise suddenly all around her seemed deafening. She stood up finally and stared blankly at Star for a moment.

A braver soul would have left Janet long ago. Perhaps some people were just not survivors, could not fashion a response to certain death. Star wasn't such a person. Her friend, the young troubled woman she had found wandering a rainy road, deserved a helping hand, one last time. She slapped her hard on the face, turned and ran toward the coconut trees.

"Follow me!" She yelled, looking back. "Climb the coconut tree!"

Some human instincts are obviously built into our genetic code, inherited from the successful lives of those that survived by following them. One such instinct is: when there's a crisis, follow the others that are running. Janet wasn't quite clear in her head yet, but her friend was terrified and running toward the trees. She would, too.

Strange sounds filled the air. The bay, a few moments ago empty and flushed with only hapless fish and sand left behind was now filling with a raging waterfall of chaos. The land itself, the 'aina, had been under assault now from earthquakes that tore it asunder, lava that burned its flesh and now the sea herself threatened to rupture its face and drown it. It groaned deeply under the onslaught, casting a cry to the heavens themselves.

The coconut palm, an amazing creation, one that had no doubt been given to islands in some divine gratitude, were well suited to disaster. Hurricanes would bend but not break them. Tropical heat only promoted their growth. Growing together in groves, their massively connected roots, spreading out five times their own stature, anchored them all as a family. They provided sterile water to those who opened their fruit and lifesaving height to those that climbed them.

Star reached the first tree with the built in steps and passed it to make for the next one. Hopefully, she thought, Jimmie would be able to reach the closest tree in time. Already the trade winds were blowing the salt spray from the arriving mass of water onto her, stinging her eyes. She could hear it so very close, a rushing wave already sweeping up the small beach to this tiny mound of sand and trees just above.

Star grasped the third step on the tree trunk, pulling and leaping at the same time to get at least one foot up to the first. Quickly she used every bit of energy her body and adrenaline could provide. Scrambling up to the fourth step she screamed in anger and fear feeling the cold sea sweep beneath her, splashing her legs.

Janet saw Star reach her tree and quickly saw another was right in front of her. Suddenly, seeming too fast to be real, the water was upon them both. This first wave was small, only a few feet high, but it swept Janet right off her feet tearing away her grasp of the first step.

Star had turned to look, only to see Janet rapidly move backwards in the rushing water toward her little cabin, itself now being pushed up against the trees behind it.

"Jimmie! Hang on!" Star yelled before moving farther up the tree.

The small first surge quickly moved through trees and back downhill of the coconut grove, taking a moment to pause before beginning its retreat back to the sea.

Janet had been forced underwater twice, but fought hard to find a bit of air every time she bounced off some object hard enough to surface again. After only a minute the rolling mass of water changed. Incredible! she thought, the water stopped moving and she found her footing. Standing now on rocks and debris she was up to her waist in water. She could see Star climbing higher on her coconut tree when she turned and yelled something at her. Maybe it was over, she wondered.

"Climb! Jimmie! Climb, Jimmie!" Star was yelling, competing to be heard with the onrushing second wave, the volcano and the wind. It was the wind that carried her voice back to Janet. It was the wind that tried but failed to stop the water that now wanted to rush back to sea, to fall back to its natural level.

Janet felt her feet swept out from under her again, this time falling backwards, this time sweeping her toward the dark sea ahead, the churning bay and coral and certain destruction. The water picked up speed as it fell back to the beach, dragging Janet with it, holding her up a little better. She was headed right back to the coconut grove, spinning through the first few trees. Briefly she saw Star ahead and above it all, yelling mutely, waving one of her arms.

Janet was bumping into things unknown, rough and sharp but they didn't hurt, nothing hurt in the fascination of surprise and confusion. The silence was somehow comforting as the water pulled her through the trees and toward the gaping maw ahead that wanted to consume her. She tried to get her feet back down, so she might stand up against the rushing water. Having bounced off what she thought was the bottom a few times, the flood couldn't be that deep.

She was pushed into a coconut tree, tried to grab it but was spun up and around it quickly, sweeping her backwards now. Another tree smashed into her back, banging her head hard. It seemed the water was picking up speed somehow, it seemed so hungry, so desperate to take her.

Janet flailed wildly with her arms, trying to grab onto anything. She was being pushed up against another tree now, enough to stop her progress to the sea, the water now rushing over her instead of with her. Flipping herself around to face the tree her arms found something, a piece of wood, a board. She sunk her fingers, the very bones of her fingers deep into it. The water was furious now, angrily tearing at her fragile grasp of life, intent on returning home with its trophy human flesh.

If she could just climb, her mind told her, if she could just get a step up onto this tree she might win. She might live.

Rubbish was flowing back into the sea with the returning tsunami, chairs, books, couches, most of Star's cabin, in pieces. Janet, her head well above the water, still hanging on with one hand to the first step, noticed Star's car bumping among the trees like a pinball.

Something moved underneath her, something buoyant, something hard, bruising her legs with a crushing force. Instantly, she was a few feet higher; she found the second and third steps and pulled herself up just as the large propane tank spun around off her tree and fled toward the chaos in the bay.

"Climb, Jimmie! Climb higher!" Star's frantic voice was coming in loud and clear now from the tree next to hers, urging her to live, to find the will.

~~~

Larry felt like the little dogs were barking just behind him in some kind of encouragement. "Go faster, big guy!"

He did. Soon he was rounding the corner to his house and the open garage. Shirley was two seconds behind him.

"Put the dogs in your backpack!" Larry said, running into the garage and rapidly pulling the motorized paraglider out to the driveway.

"They won't fit, baby..."

Larry ran back into the garage and got his tandem rig, used to carry a passenger. Quickly he spun the bolts, latched them and looked over to Shirley.

"Honey, both of us on here will take a lot of takeoff power. The dogs..."

"They only weigh twelve pounds, together!" Shirley pleaded.

Larry nodded, this was no time to argue. He knew the engine could lift three hundred and forty pounds, in perfect conditions. He laughed out loud at that last caveat.

"What's so funny, Larry? They do, only twelve pounds, I swear!"

"Help me push this out to the side road."

The lava bombs were still peppering the area every few minutes. As they rounded the corner of their yard to line up the paraglider with the side street Larry saw two large rocks steaming about a hundred yards down the road, smack in the middle of his rural runway. Just beyond, about another fifty feet, were the first Ohia trees, which they had to clear. He calculated they would need absolutely every inch of take off roll with the added weight. The dogs were going to be a problem. That and the darkness.

The parafoil laid out nicely for once on the first try, ready for a breath of wind. He ran over to the paraglider, checked the bolts to the parafoil and to the seat and relied on his last engine prep to be a good one.

"Shirley, the dogs will most likely be OK here. They will hide until this is all over, and then we can come back for them." He sat down in his pilot seat and strapped in, pulling Shirley into the tandem harness.

"If we get close to the tree tops, you'll have to let them go and that won't..."

"Larry, they're twelve pounds!"

He pushed the electric start while holding the brake, and flipped on his 10,000 watt halogen lights. Shirley held the dogs under each arm once she was strapped on. Her backpack sat in her lap.

The gauges looked strong and Larry let the brake go, the parafoil behind them already inflated. They began a painfully slow roll down the street. Larry was leaning to the side to see around Shirley and she was looking down at her little dogs. They seemed to be enjoying the wind in their face.

His first obstacle was going to be the large rocks in the road. They were approaching them straight on. If he couldn't get enough speed in the next three seconds, he thought, he would have to abort or risk crushing Shirley, the dogs and eventually himself into the still steaming mass.

The parafoil above them shimmered loudly with some external wind. It might be twirling thermals or a bit of tradewind making its way into the open area of the street. Larry looked back at the rock ahead and up to the parafoil quickly. It was full, already flying for the most part and just waiting on him to give it a chance to rise.

Out of the corner of his eye he saw another lava bomb ripping through the trees to their side, screeching and tearing and leaving fire and smoke behind it.

Risk. It is certainly a part of flying. Too much risk was foolhardy, as the saying reiterated: Old, bold pilots simply don't exist. Conservative pilots understand risk as something to manage to the nth degree. Never underestimating it, never ignoring it, but always understanding it. Often in the complex environment of flight, it was a matter of balancing multiple risk factors. In such cases a choice had to be made, if for no other reason than to rid oneself of at least one risk factor.

Larry saw the massive rock ahead approaching and he saw new ones falling all around them. Should he abort and try taking off the other direction, or should he bet on his lift being sufficient to clear it?

His engine sounded strong and deep inside his consciousness he knew he had one more advantage. He had always been a lucky guy.

"Lift your feet up! Now!"

He released the hold on the parafoil, allowing it to fill completely, letting it lift them up. Immediately they left the ground, a few inches. The dogs were barking excitedly, urging them all higher.

The largest rock was only ten feet away and they still had at least another foot to rise to avoid it. Larry attempted a slight turn to at least avoid hitting it head on. A side hit would spare Shirley and the dogs and maybe just hit his stainless side tubing.

The parafoil above them fluttered again, in the presence of a burst of wind, from where Larry could never guess. But, it was enough to clear the rock by some small immeasurable amount and they sailed a bit sideways, still climbing slowly and now clear of the rocks.

"Go, Larry, Go!" Shirley started chanting. "Go, Go, Go!"

They were some twelve or fifteen feet off the ground now, Larry figured, and needed another ten to clear the now approaching Ohia forest that began the jungle canopy for the next several miles. As they got within fifty feet, Larry knew they did not yet have enough altitude and he turned sharply to the right. They swung around back toward their house staying in the small opening of theirs and a neighbor or two worth of clearing.

"We need more altitude, Shirley!"

She just hugged the dogs closer to her body.

Larry circled another time, still needing more room to climb. But, the engine was not giving them anymore for now. They were just too heavy.

They were high enough, though, to see the plume a little better. Both of them could see the glowing rockets rising within the smoke and falling out to the side.

Shirley turned as best as she could to see Larry.

"Can we climb anymore if we keep turning?"

"I don't think so! I think we are too heavy!"

Shirley looked down into her lap and sighed. The two little dogs were squirming, excited to be flying, but quite a bit apprehensive about the fact that their little feet were dangling in space.

As their next turn pointed them directly at the plume, both of them watched as another huge lava bomb rocketed up and out of the smoke, this one headed their way.

Larry tried to pick a line that would steer them clear of the missile, but he had to keep turning to stay out of the tree tops. Hating to have the plume at his back for more than a few seconds, he turned early this time, to spy the approaching rock.

As it did he saw it was going over their head, by a few feet. They could hear it crackling, pushing the tropical air out of its way, rushing to crash into the edge of the clearing and bombing into the edge of the Ohia trees there, knocking one over.

"OK, OK, Larry!" Shirley yelled over her shoulder. "I know we're too heavy." Larry leaned forward to kiss her on the back of her head, then looked over at both little dogs with a heavy heart. Turning again, he kept an eye on the plume as he knew Shirley was making one of the most difficult decisions anyone could. The dogs, after all, were part of their family.

At that moment, he felt the paraglider lurch up at least ten feet, released of some significant weight.

"Whoo hoo!" he yelled, knowing they could now clear the downhill side of the tree line. Above his own shouts he could hear the dogs barking. It was enough to bring tears to his eyes.

"Larry!" Shirley was shouting. "We're climbing!"

And, the dogs were still barking! Larry looked down and there they were, still nestled tightly in Shirley's arms.

Larry was incredulous. How could that happen?

"What did you drop?"

Shirley twisted around, a little sadness embedded into the happiness that they were now clearing the tree tops.

"My backpack!"

Larry nodded. Whatever that was, he thought, it must have weighed at least twenty or thirty pounds.

"What was in it?"

Shirley was quiet a moment, but when he asked again, she had to say it.

"All the Bordeaux. And the 1945 Haut Bailly."

It was enough to bring tears to his eyes.

~~~

Even as Star was urging Janet to climb higher, she herself was about as high in her own tree as she could go. The last nailed in board stopped just shy of the first fronds. From that height she looked back to the cinder cone for a moment. It was vomiting lava straight up into the air uncaring as to where it splattered, uncaring of the vast mess it was making of her little slice of heaven. Her smaller and smaller slice of heaven.

Janet was obviously injured. Her shoulders looked to be bleeding but the lighting was sporadic, depending on outbursts from the cinder cone. The little moon there was could only tell Star that Janet was now half way up the tree. Her moans as she pulled herself higher told everything the light could not.

Another wave, a bit larger, was sweeping under them now, splashing on Janet but safely below her. Despite what comfort that might have given anyone, Janet was terrified. Terrified of heights.

"Star!"

"Jimmie! Are you OK?" Star had to repeat herself over the noise of the water rushing furiously below them. She watched as large parts of what must be her cabin roof swirled around the area just below them. The second wave was now retreating back to the sea.

"Star! How much higher?" Janet begged, hoping not another inch. Even as the sight below her was horrific, it was far below and her dizziness was overtaking her.

"All the way! Up to the branches Jimmie!" Star was finding her voice getting hoarser. "All the way up!"

"Oh, my god," Janet murmured, trying desperately not to look below her. Her ears were painting a scary enough picture. Rushing water below her, strange booming sounds out in the bay followed by cascading crashes of water and the deep rumble of the cinder cone behind it all.

The fact that it was dark helped Janet make her way up into the fronds themselves where she wiggled her way into a spot she could sit. Her legs were bruised and her feet were aching, bleeding from a thousand little cuts. Her hips were sore, to the very bones it seemed, from whatever she had bumped into while being swept around in the first wave.

As a third, even larger wave moved beneath them, some eight feet deep, they both felt the trees shaking in the turbulence.

"Are they falling, Star?" Janet screamed from her perch at the top. With the wind and the shaking from below she clutched the crown with a baby's grip on a parent's hair.

"No way!" Star guessed. She was thinking what she would do if they did indeed fall. The roots needed something to hold on to. More waves would surely sweep all the sand away, from all the trees of the connected grove.

"If it does Jimmie, stay with the tree, don't let it go!"

She looked out to sea for the first time, trying to see the fishermen in their boats, safely in the deep water. Once or twice it seemed she saw a dim red light, or two.

She could hear Janet crying now, sobbing in the tree next to her, hidden in the top. For some reason, she realized, she had not herself collapsed. With the loss of her cabin, and her car it seemed all the things that had supported her in this sanctuary had abandoned her.

Except the trees.

"Please, hold on," she whispered to her tree, hugging it tightly. "Please stay with me. Please stay here."

As the most recent wave seemed to continue rushing in for over three minutes now Star thought she heard a new sound, in the direction of the cinder cone. Was it a bubbling sound, or after listening to it a bit longer, was it more like a sizzling sound?

The waft of steam that reached her confirmed it was a boiling sound. The last tsunami wave had cleared all of the remaining brush and low bushes from behind where her cabin used to be. Star could now see an advancing line of glowing rock replacing that which the ocean had attempted to stop.

"What's that smell?" Janet managed to ask, a shivering in her voice.

Star shook her head in amazement. The ocean, as destructive as it might be, was trying to hold back the volcano, the lava, by assaulting it head on. Memories of her favorite Japanese creature films came to mind, something like Godzilla versus the Sea Monster. The movie trailer played out in her mind: In the dark tropical night, two desperate women hide from a marauding sea on one side watching lava approach from the other, the tops of coconut trees their only hope.

"Star!" Janet yelled weakly. "What is it? What is that smell?"

As shock finally settled into Star's mind, she retreated into the comfortable fantasy of her memories. She wasn't sure which monster would save them, Godzilla or the Sea Monster. The first light of dawn, some hours away, would tell. Hopefully, she wished, it would be the winner.

"Jimmie, it's the smell of battle."

~ ~ ~

The Pacific Ocean a half mile away from the fountaining cinder cone was just as should be, pacific. Light winds and small swells gently rocked the flotilla of five boats anchored in the deep water as the darkness slowly moved west.

Wally was scanning the coastline with his binoculars, a few minutes evidently before there was enough light to do so. He turned to the east to see if clouds were obscuring the sunrise. None were, just the earth.

"Come on!" he said to himself, knowing the sun would never listen.

His son, in the next boat anchored near his, was pulling in another aku on a hand line. Wally watched his strong young body flex and bend and win the battle. The teenager reminded him of himself, on a good day.

It was a proud moment in a pool of doubt, doubt about not insisting his girlfriend Starshine come with him. It was something he had been used to for many years, the conflict between his local practicality and her hippie wishfulness. Those contradictions are probably what complimented their one similarity.

"Ready Dad?" The young man was looking to the coast as well.

Wally was shaking his head, then looked back into the binoculars.

"Why she gotta be so damned stubborn?"

Both of them, on their respective boats watched the cinder cone near their cove, their home, continue belching fumes high into the air. Wally scanned the coastline looking for something familiar, Star's cabin, or her car. He couldn't even find the vacation rentals on the opposite side of the cove.

His son had his binoculars out now and quickly saw a debris field uphill from where the two story rentals had been.

"Dad, the vacation houses!" He lowered his binoculars a moment to confirm with his own eyes, then brought them back up again. "They're gone!"

Wally looked at him, then back again.

"What the hell?" He stared for a moment, whistling.

"I don't see any lava there, so, they never burned down or anything?" His son was pulling out his cell phone to call his Auntie Star.

"Another tsunami?" Wally whispered. Turning to his son he said it quite a bit louder, worried. "Another tsunami? Must have been one during the night!"

Both of them searched for signs of Star on the beach or near the cove. They searched in a silence that spoke loudly of their common fear, that Star had been swept away during the night.

"Her cabin is gone too, but I don't see her car." Wally noted. "Maybe she left before it came?"

"Dad, check Champagne pool, the car is there, upside down."

Wally swung right to look at the pools, where he and Star had spent many a magical evening. There, impaled on some underwater ledge, tires up in the air like a dead cockroach, was Star's Tercel. Wally tossed his binoculars onto the seat cushion.

"Come on, son! She might be holding onto some flotsam." He fired up his twin 250hp Yamahas to idle and pulled up his anchor.

His son was drawing up his anchor as well, retrieved his fishing lines and started his engines.

"Headsets, Dad?"

"Yeah!"

"Guys," Wally said to the other three boats on the CB radio. "Tsunami looks to have swept our area clean. Go south a mile or so, with the current. Star might be hanging onto something. Might be more people, too."

All five boats got moving immediately. Both father and son were soon full throttle toward the beach, drawing beautiful white arches behind them in the blue water.

"Check, check." Wally asked, testing his headset.

"Got you five by five," his son answered.

"Good, look, you stay offshore about two hundred yards. Keep an eye out for any wave activity, any more damn tsunami signs. OK?"

The young fisherman wanted to be on the front line helping, but if he had to be lookout he would, for his dad.

"Sure, got it."

"Thanks, I'm going up to the beach. If you see anything, I mean anything that could be a person, hit your air horn."

"Got it."

Wally was closing in fast when he had to quickly slow down for rubbish in the water. Floating logs, plywood, plastic and a big propane tank bobbed in the otherwise pristine water.

"I'm going to blast my horn son. Three times. Anything after that means I need your help." Wally moved cautiously through the debris field, avoiding anything that might damage his boat, looking at every piece that floated. He also knew that if the worst had occurred, he would also find Star this way.

~~~

Exhaustion is a very effective agent of compromise. How else might the top of a thirty foot coconut palm seem actually comfortable?

Star was stirring with the increasing light of dawn. She had followed Janet's lead by climbing all the way up into her own tree where she might rest without having to hold onto anything. She could hear her injured friend switch between snoring and moaning in pain.

Somehow she had managed to move into a position between the rising fronds that kept her safely inside a little nest. From here she could still see the cinder cone inexhaustibly continuing to pour lava in a steady march toward the bay. She could also see that the lava had surrounded her little enclave now with slow moving fingers approaching the beach to the south. To the north she looked for the vacation rentals but couldn't find them. The tree tops were obscuring the view in that direction.

Below, the sand was swept clean, shimmering in the pink light flowing in from the east. No coconuts on the ground, no leaves, no sticks, no home and no car. Nothing, nothing but sand.

Wondering if it was wise to climb down she tried to remember if there had been any earthquakes during the night, after they had climbed up into the trees. Nothing she could remember, she thought. Yet, it might be safest to remain in the trees for a little while.

The tsunamis from the night had swept through around 10 P.M. and it was now somewhere around 6 A.M. Surely it was over by now. Still she remained in her tree, wondering what to do next.

The three loud blasts of an air horn, coming from the sea, answered that question. Turning to look she saw one of the fishermen's boats motoring in slowly. Rescue!

"Jimmie! Wake up! We've got us a ride!" Star was yelling as she gingerly tried to make it down to the top step. The tree top had not seemed so high up in the air, with its protective shield of fronds, but the top of the trunk, where her feet were now, seemed precarious.

Her legs were sore and her arms had a few cuts she had not noticed until she hugged the tree on her way down the next several steps. Looking up to Janet's tree she saw nothing of her.

"Jimmie! Come on! You wanna stay up there all day?"

No response.

"There's a boat coming for us! Let's go, girl!"

Some rustling in the tree told her Janet was at least alive.

"I can't move, Star," she said too softly to be heard. "My legs are not moving..."

Star looked up at Janet's tree, just as high as hers was and then down to the approaching boat. It was Wally!

"Wally! Wally!" she yelled, waving at her boyfriend, looking all the white knight on a horse.

She saw his head tilt up to find her in the trees, having been scanning far lower for something. He hit the air horn again, as he waved wildly now.

In a moment he had beached his Boston Whaler on the clean sand, jumped out with his bow line and an anchor, and then run to Star's tree.

"Babe! What? Are you OK?"

"Am I glad to see you!" Star exclaimed, still gingerly moving her stiff legs down the last few steps of the coconut tree.

"Hey!" Wally said into his headset to his son. "I've got Star! She was up in the trees!"

Reaching up to guide her down, he marveled at how smooth her skin felt, how strong her legs must be and how lucky she was.

"Tsunami. I guess you saw it all, Star."

"Not good, Wally. Not good. Jimmie nearly got swept away."

Wally looked around. "Jimmie?"

He forgot the question for a moment as Star hugged the breath right out of him.

"Thank you so much! Thank you for coming to look for me!"

Wally laughed a little shaking his head.

"You're one crazy wahine, Starshine Aloha! Surrounded by lava on one side and tsunami on the other. But, I love you no matter." He kissed her hard and squeezed a little too hard.

"Ouch," she moaned, still kissing him back. "I'm kinda sore. The beds here at Hotel Coconut are a little hard."

Wally pulled back a few inches and looked at her smiling. "Yeah, but they sure are convenient when you need them." He and his fishermen crew had installed the steps years ago, never thinking they would ever get used.

"Help, please." A weak voice from the trees pleaded.

Wally looked up confused. "Hey, who is that?"

"My friend, Jimmie, she got swept away in the first wave, but made it to the tree when it started sweeping back to sea."

Wally looked at Star for a moment, incredulous that anyone could manage such a feat.

"I think she's injured Wally."

"No doubt!" Wally got on his headset and called his son into shore to help while moving up to the tree to climb it.

"Hold on there..." he turned to Star from the second step. "What's the name again?"

"Jimmie."

Wally looked up in the tree and then back to Star. "Our Jimmie? The girl you picked up hitchhiking?"

Star nodded as she watched Wally move higher into up the tree. She could see Jimmie's face, bruised and dirty staring down like a scared monkey.

"Hold on, Jimmie, I'm on my way up."

Star noticed Wally's son rapidly approaching the beach in his boat. The ocean was a deep azure in the low morning light, smoothly textured in the light trade winds. She watched as he beached his Whaler close to Wally's on the beautifully swept sand, as beautiful as she had ever remembered seeing it. If you didn't look behind, toward the cinder cone and it's lava progeny, if you looked only to the brilliant tropical sun filtering through the pristine skies into the equally magnificent waters you might think you were in the lap of heaven. You could wander into the compelling shade of the coconut palm grove, climb into a hammock and easily be persuaded that this was indeed one of the planet's little known gems.

Perhaps it was an appreciation common to those who have had near death experiences, an appreciation enhanced by surviving. Star looked around for the few moments it took for Wally's son to run up to her and saw a special place worth saving. She just wasn't quite sure how she might do that.

He gave her a big hug and a kiss on the cheek.

"Auntie, I'm so glad you're OK."

"Thank you. Me, too!"

"Dad!" his son announced. "What do you need me to do?"

Wally was just reaching Janet up in the top of the coconut palm. His brief three years in the Army had exposed him to injuries of all types, and methods for dealing with them in the field, away from professional medical help. Here he saw a classic blunt force trauma with complimentary lacerations where the skin had given way to pressure.

"She can't climb down, get me all the rope you have, and something we can sit her in." Wally looked out to sea for a moment. "And get one of the guys on tsunami watch OK?"

"I'm on it!" the young man got on his CB radio while rounding up nylon rope and some seat cushions.

"How you feeling Jimmie?" Wally asked, knowing she must be in some considerable pain. Bruises covered her entire torso, from her shoulders, down her back, and onto her legs. It looked like her stomach was purple as well.

Janet was shaking again, in fear. She could not get the events of the previous night out of her mind, thinking that the sea might come back for her any moment.

"I'm scared," she whispered. "Why are you up here?"

"I'm here to help you…"

"Is there another wave coming?" She yelled, then quickly began moaning in terror, the static flooding her overwhelmed mind.

Star and Wally's son both looked up into the tree at that. Star quickly turned to look at the beach and the young man scanned the southern points of land.

"Dad?"

"Go to my boat and get my medical kit. Hurry!" Wally knew Janet was too injured to move without first giving her some pain relief.

"Do you see another wave Wally?" Star asked. The concern in her voice struck Wally deep. His love, his companion of many years, was now afraid, afraid of the sea. Great, he thought, and I'm a fisherman.

"No, baby, nada!" He took another look just to be sure. The horizon was clear, the points of land on either side of them were old black lava rock against blue sea. No white water. He looked over toward the vacation rentals to his left. They were gone.

"How is Jimmie?"

"She's all buss up Star. We gotta get her to a hospital."

His son soon had climbed the tree with sixty feet of rope and the seat cushions. He also had the small medical kit that Wally kept in his boat. Injuries at sea, while fishing, could be debilitating. If the weather turned bad you couldn't afford the luxury of pain, you had to get to port.

"Thanks son," Wally whispered. "Here, help me."

Both of them used their one free hand, the other holding onto to the tree, to prepare the syringe. Wally had prepared 15mg of morphine capsules, which he now stuck the needle into, drawing out the liquid.

"Let me see your foot, Jimmie," Wally said with the certainty of a man determined to fix a problem.

Janet moved her leg as best she could, giving Wally a look. Several of her toes seemed broken, but the veins on the top of her feet were what he needed.

"A little poke and you will be a lot better. OK Jimmie?" He looked into her eyes, beyond the clouds of confusion and deep into what he knew were cascading spasms of pain. "Here you go, girl."

It took them half an hour to get her down and into Wally's boat. Star seemed quite a bit better, walking normally now. The other fishermen had returned from their search and rescue mission and had anchored offshore again.

Wally, with Janet comfortably secured in his boat, prepared to leave. His son had his anchor in his boat as well, ready to push away.

"I'll take her over to Hilo bay, where we can get an ambulance."

"Good," Star said, leaning into the boat, touching Janet's hair softly.

"Hop in, Star," Wally said.

She hesitated and turned to look back at her home, now virgin beach and coconut grove. Wally noticed her reluctance.

"Starshine! There is nothing left. The waves took it all. Nothing!"

"I know, I know."

"Look, even those two story vacation rentals are gone, Star."

Star looked quickly over to the other side of the bay, where three beautiful homes had been built, where many a party had celebrated what she herself could every day. There was nothing but rubble, and sand.

Wally watched her closely, hoping to find an angle to convince her into getting into the safety of his boat. He knew Star's story well. She had grown up in this area, decades of living at the very boundary between earth and heaven.

"Come on Starshine, we can come back in a few weeks if this thing blows over and see what we have left." He looked at her, imminently afraid of her unpredictable behavior when it came to her heart. "OK?"

Star was unable to look into his eyes, afraid of his persistence, his undeniable logic. She was watching the little yellow tangs play around her feet as she stood in the shallow water.

"Star! For God's sake, we gotta get your friend to a doctor. Get in!"

Wally's son was already moving away from the beach into the deeper waters, looking back as he did. He knew his Dad's girlfriend, his Auntie, was a free spirit. She had a big heart that seemed rooted in the land deeper than anyone he had ever known himself. He was proud of her for that, if not worried sometimes about the decisions she seemed to make.

Star reluctantly climbed into Wally's boat. He immediately pushed off the sand and dropped his twins into the water, threw them in reverse and quickly retreated.

The waters were still of floating debris, forcing Wally to pick his way carefully. His son had already stopped, clearing rope from his propellers.

Wally pulled up next to him to see if he could help. He was still worried that they were close enough to shore to get caught in another tsunami.

"Small kine," the young man said. "There!" he tossed the old nylon into his boat, so no one else would have the pleasure.

"Good job," Wally proudly said. "Let's pick our way out carefully." He looked at Star, still staring back at the beach. "Star, can you stand watch on the bow please? Look out for logs and such?"

She looked back at Wally and then down to Janet, asleep on the seat cushion couch in the shade of the boat's bikini top.

"Sure." Walking slowly she made her way to the front of the boat, immediately yelling out. "Log!"

Wally threw his engines into reverse for a moment, enough to stop their forward progress. Nervously he looked back at the beach. At fifty yards they were still too close in case another earthquake decided to stir things up.

"Move left about two feet or so," Star directed. "Slowly."

Wally's son moved slowly in behind them, following their cleared path. Both boats were running at just above idle. Star was constantly looking back at the beach, until Wally would point ahead.

"Stop! Stop!" she suddenly announced.

Both boats came to, with the son's boat sliding easily up to the right side of Wally's.

"What, Star?" Wally demanded, frustrated with their slow progress.

Just ahead in the clear waters were dozens of green sea turtles, all headed to the shore. The Hawaiian sea turtles, or Honu, were large, certainly a hundred pounds or more.

"Honu!" Star said, almost laughing. "Wally, the honu are returning," she looked at him with conviction and a sparkle in her eye. "They're going home, Wally."

Both fishermen had a lot of respect for the turtles, as both competitors for bait fish and as a sign that the ocean waters were healthy. But, few had made the mystical connection between them and humans like Star had. Wally knew this and was rapidly getting worried as he watched them swim by his boat.

"Star. That's a good thing, maybe they are exploring the flotsam for food."

"Yes, it *is* good." Star was watching them fly beneath the boat, surfacing at times for air and a quick glance at her. A light wind moved her pareo, tied above her breasts and hanging to her knees, as a colorful flag.

Wally had seen this before with his long time girlfriend. She was tuned into nature to the point of being blind to the inherent dangers there. He would have bet she would have been hurt or died a dozen times since he met her and he would have lost each time. Something in nature, something in the universe, loved her right back. Something there kept her out of harm's way, despite whatever she did.

"Star," Wally attempted. "We can come back tomorrow, check on things you know. The turtles," he silently cursed their timing. "They'll be around for you to play with then."

Janet woke a little, surfacing from her morphine nap to find acute pain in her back, in her feet and in her head. Still she tried to sit up when she heard Star talking about turtles.

"Where?" Janet said hoarsely. "What turtles, Star?"

"Hey there!" Star smiled. "Are you any better?"

Janet shook her head, and tried to stand, falling back into the seat. Wally moved over to help her stand, putting her hands on the windshield.

"There, Jimmie," he pointed. "The turtles are swimming right past us."

"Wow!" Janet laughed. "Look at them all!"

Star was walking back to the stern of the boat, now leaning on the engines as she watched them.

"Beautiful, aren't they, Jimmie?"

Wally kept an arm around Janet as he continued to prop her up so she could see.

"Oh, yes!"

"And brave, too!" Star added. "Heroic, actually."

Wally had never heard that said of green sea turtles, but he knew he would hear an explanation soon, one that would color Star's personality even brighter. Crazy as she might be, he loved that she embraced all creatures as special. Fishermen had a degree of that as well, except that they ate what they appreciated.

Star had taken off her slippers and had climbed up on top of the railing of Wally's boat.

"Star..." Wally moaned. "What are you doing?"

She turned to look at her boyfriend, and then over to his son, and back to Janet.

"They are going to the beach, to protect it. To guard it against the lava."

"Auntie!" Wally's son was getting the same thought that his dad had.

"Jimmie," Star said, now turning to her injured friend. "Honu have a connection with the sea and the beach. They know when it is safe." She turned back to watch the last of the turtles move past the boat on their way to the white sandy stretch Star still called home. "They are defending the magic, and I must go with them!"

With that she dove into the clearness, took several long strokes underwater, as if she might mimic the turtles themselves, and finally surfaced twenty yards away.

"Dammit, Star!" Wally exclaimed. "That's insane! Come back to the boat right now!" He knew his voice would simply skip off the surface like a flat rock thrown just as hard as those words.

Her brightly lit smile was hard to argue with.

"I love you Wally!" She splashed the water with her arms like a little kid would playing. "I must defend the magic, my home!" With that, she turned and started swimming into the beach, just behind the large group of turtles leading the way.

"Go, Star! Go!" Janet managed to yell before collapsing in a burst of pain.

"Dad? Should I go pick her up? At least give her a ride to the beach?"

Wally looked at Star, swimming strongly and confidently behind dozens of sea turtles toward a white sandy beach line with stunning coconut palms, a brilliant blue sky behind them all. The plume from the cinder cone just beyond spoke to her mission like a soldier's charge at the enemy. She was the bravest woman he had ever met, and maybe the craziest.

"No, son," Wally answered. "Joey's got a tent on his boat. Can you go get that, some water and food and drop them off for her?"

His son nodded and throttled up slowly to meet with the other boats in the deeper waters.

"I am going to take Jimmie here to Hilo," Wally told him. He looked to Janet, now back on the seat cushion couch, fighting her own battles.

He pushed his boat slightly beyond idle into a slow forward slide. Looking back one last time, he could still see Star swimming, closer now to the beach. It was her home, he knew, it was her only home. It was a home almost completely surrounded now by a six to ten foot wall of slowly creeping a'a lava. Another week and it would all be gone, he figured. Turning back to sea, he moved his boat out farther and farther.

"Your friend," he said to a sleeping Janet, "is brave, crazy and..." he paused. He fought a supreme sadness at leaving his love behind with an ever increasing hope he was learning from her.

"...and I'll never bet against her."

19

Two days had passed since the reports of tsunami waves sweeping the Kapoho area had been broadcast on television and the internet. People all over the world were fascinated with the Hawaiian volcano, the destructive lava and now the impressive power of tsunami.

The Hilo airport air traffic control folks had to set up a temporary tower of sorts just outside the evacuation zone to work all the helicopter and over flight traffic. Everyone who had ever heard of Hawaii, with all it's natural blessings of sun, sand and surf now wanted to see the destruction. The rest of the world was having a quiet news week, so this was the top story everywhere.

When word got out that a woman was hold up on a tiny sliver of her land, trapped between the sea and the lava, it put a human face on the nature story. Every airborne flying machine that could adjusted their flight path to include a low pass near Star's beach.

At first she waved to them all, but on the second day it was easier to ignore most of them. She was busy building her little ahu structures everywhere she could, especially near the edge of the slowly approaching wall of semi-cooled lava. Ahu, or cairns, had taken on many meanings in Hawaii, from trail markers to sacred beacons.

Using small rocks, pieces of coral, abandoned coconuts and driftwood, Star created her own version of the ahu, stacking them in short piles. When they were done, she sat back at the beach, cross-legged in the sand, facing the sea, hands upturned on her knees and her head slightly back. It made a fantastic shot for the news, but in her heart she only focused on the lava, focused on asking the great mother to spare her home by the sea.

Civil defense boats were keeping out dozens of boats that wanted to land fans there and join Star. The authorities reasoned that Star owned the land she was on and could stay, but due to the obvious danger, no one else could approach. Wally was supplying her once a day, pleading with her to leave each time, but slowly understanding her resolve. He brought her food, water, hugs and kisses and then returned to the deep waters offshore.

~ ~ ~

Janet had been met by an ambulance at Wally's request as soon as they made the small dock at Suisan's Fish market in Hilo harbor. Her injuries were for the most part severe bruising and lacerations that would all heal. In the two days she had been at the Hilo Medical Center she had begun to walk again.

The police had been there briefly to interview her and file a report. The doctors were all fascinated with her survival story and a few news reporters had been trying to reach her, unsuccessfully. But, it was a small island, a smaller town and a much smaller community. Everyone in the hospital knew her story, of how she survived a tsunami by climbing a coconut tree. Quickly the connection between her and the now famous Star were made, cementing Janet's fame as well.

As Janet sat in the cafeteria, trying to force down the strawberry Jello a young man approached her, took her picture quickly and left.

Little did Janet know, but within minutes he had posted her picture and the story, as he had heard it on his Facebook profile.

Within hours several fan pages had been created featuring both Star and Janet as the Heroes of Kapoho. Youtube videos of Star's brave stand against the lava were interspersed with the story of how she and Janet had been swept by the sea to within inches of the hot lava approaching from the other direction, then swept back through a grove of coconut trees in the retreating wave.

Every television in the hospital had the news on with the continuing coverage of the volcano. Janet was on her third jello when another segment about Star came on, this time via CNN. They showed an aerial view of the cinder cone and how it had now covered some 500 acres of land and, including to the south of Star, over 10 new acres out into the sea.

It was shocking to see how little land was left for Star. The slowly moving a'a was piling up in the last remaining low area behind the beach there. It had already consumed Champagne pool on one side and the entire southern coastline was suffering its final gasp before succumbing to the lava.

Video of Star praying toward the sea was overlaid with the fountaining cinder cone. Her stacks of rocks and sticks, ahu, were shown while the commentator talked of this brave woman who was holding her own against the powerful volcano.

A close up of the coconut grove led into the story of how Star and a companion, now in the Hilo Hospital had climbed them to escape several tsunami waves.

That was the moment Janet saw her picture flash onto the television, along with Star's.

"Both women," the commentator reported, "have various fan pages on social networks and blogs where you can keep updated as to their progress."

The story then focused on her. The entire screen filled with her image, the one taken by the young man.

"This young woman was taken to Hilo Hospital where she remains recuperating from her horror with the destructive tsunami wave. Reports tell us that she was swept to within inches of the approaching lava and then back against trees, rocks and almost into the ocean. We haven't any news on her, but we are wishing Jimmie a speedy recovery."

Janet immediately stood up to leave, as several in the cafeteria were clapping for her. Horrified she almost ran back to her room, except that it hurt to move too fast.

Here she was eating jello in the comfort of a warm place, one of healing and her friend was camped on a beach in a tent, being attacked by a volcano. She had to get back to Star, to stand as one with her, against the lava. There was something about Star, something quite incredible, even miraculous, that made Janet feel Star would win.

As she entered her room it was dark, her roommate there snoring behind her curtain. Janet turned on their shared television, but kept the volume off, as she tried to follow what else might be said about Star, and what, God forbid, might be said about herself.

She sat in the dark silence following the glow of the broadcast, now showing archival footage of the 2004 tsunami in Thailand.

Comparisons were being made to the ones that had struck her and Star, and the entire coastline southeast of Hilo.

"It could have been much worse," Janet said softly in her mind. "It could be worse...next time." The thought of going anywhere near the ocean seemed...impossible.

Yet, there she was, on the television yet again, in her yoga pose, with the expression on the silent reporter's face telling the world what they were all really thinking: that this old lady on the beach was insane.

"She's trying so hard," Janet said to herself, unaware she was talking out loud. It seemed easier to think that way now that the static had returned.

"Who's that, honey?" The curtain talked right before a boney hand pulled it back around and out of the way.

"Oh," Janet said. "Sorry. To wake you, I mean, I was trying..."

"No problem, honey. No problem. I'm need to pee, anyhow." She swung her half covered legs down perfectly into some furry slippers and stood up slowly, letting her bones find their balance.

Janet watched the old lady walk in front of her, coughing hoarsely a couple of times and cursing under her breath at something unseen. She thought she had the look of a career alcoholic, perhaps one of who had risen to president of her local drinking club.

For a moment, Janet saw herself, decades into the future, just like this dying woman. Liver shot to hell, struggling to walk and in a dark hospital room peeing in someone else's toilet.

Just the thought of such a fate made her strangely thirsty. If a single drink was offered, she would feel safe taking it, right now. If only one.

"Poor old broad," Janet heard from the darkened bathroom doorway.

"What?" Janet said into the corner. "Who?"

The old lady moved awkwardly from the blue shadows of the television and back in front of Janet's bed. She waited to answer until she had completed the almost overwhelming task of getting herself planted again in her own bed.

"That poor lady on T.V." she pointed at the screen. "That's who." She turned up the volume with her own remote.

Janet watched a shot of Wally resupplying Star.
This time it was Fox News and the commentator brought up a question as to what kind of boyfriend would leave his girlfriend on the beach in such a situation.

Their Facebook fan page, the Heros of Kapoho, was displayed next with just such a question. Janet noticed 347 comments noted below.

"She's a good person." Janet looked over at her roommate, ready to argue for her friend.

"Oh, I can tell that, too." Propping another pillow behind her frail back she looked up at the screen and continued. "But, she can't stop that lava."

Janet believed if anyone could it would be Star and she said so emphatically to this pessimistic old lady next to her.

"Ha!" She shook her head at the young woman's comments.

Janet was getting furious, the static rising up from the vast reservoir she must have. Holding her hands up to her head, trying to quiet the storm, she nearly spat.

"Star is a powerful force in this universe! She's a survivor! If the world has a scrap of compassion, it will let that poor woman alone on her little strip of sand."

"I know, honey, I know. I went to school with that lady, know her well, I do. Starshine Aloha, I think that is her name." She turned to look over at Janet. "Am I right?"

Janet nodded, her hands coming off her head slowly. "Yes."

"Yes," the old lady confirmed, looking back up to the television. The lava pool at Halema'uma'u was the center of attention for the moment.

"An eye for an eye, that's the only thing that will stop the damned thing."

Janet felt a sudden sinking deep inside as the static began to get louder again.

"Yep, someone did something bad. Did it to the volcano they did. Ain't gonna stop until that is made right." She looked directly at Janet now. "Eye for an eye honey."

Janet found that idea distributing. She looked into the old lady's eyes. She looked so damned old, so sick, that maybe, Janet thought, she had been to hell, heard her murdered fiancé Jimmy's story and returned. Returned to torment her. She shook her head a little, trying to free that crazy thought so it would leave her head.

"Why?" Janet tried to ask, holding her head again. "Why would a volcano give a damn about..." Her head was pounding now with the static. "...anything?"

The old lady pulled her legs up to her chest, bringing her sheets and covers up and out from where they had been tucked nicely. She scooted herself up higher against the pillows.

"My old man, drunk bastard that he was, took my car one night. Didn't ask me or nothing. Just stole my keys and took my car. Sure as shit he ran into a tree and messed it up real bad. Messed himself up real bad, too.

"I was pissed at him, stupid drunk! My car was trashed! My only way to get around, gone. I didn't even care that much about him being in critical condition at the hospital, I was so pissed off at him."

She was rocking slightly back and forth now, telling Janet something she had probably told no one else.

"My car was dead and in another two days, so was he."

Janet mimicked the lady's rocking motion unconsciously. "Oh, my god! He died?"

The old lady stared at Janet. "Yeah," she looked back up at the television. "And, you know what?" she asked without looking back. "I felt a lot better. Eye for an eye."

~~~

The next morning shoved aside the darkness in its rush to flood the sky with some of the best light it had ever come up with. The air was pristine over the entire state with the passage of a frontal band. Freshly washed with rain and cool air the island literally shimmered in the early rays of orange and yellow.

The only blemishes on the battle for contrasting brilliance were the plumes of the Kapoho cinder cone and Halema'uma'u and a sea entry in the park boundary. Three boiling columns of dark gray pouring upward into purples and blue.

Star felt the eyes of a thousand cameras on her as she watched the sun crest the edge of the eastern sea. Her focus was now quite capable of ignoring the gawkers. The conviction that fed her now was stronger than ever. The little yellow tangs that swam between her feet, in and out of the gentle surf, looked brighter somehow.

However, the sound of the waves on the beach could no longer entirely drown out the sound of the crackling and popping a'a' lava mound as it slowly piled up higher behind her. Some fifteen feet high it was an approaching cliff eager to embrace the sea, eager to reclaim what the sea had been wearing down and then some.

Wally had moved his boat in close, to within fifty yards. He knew a breakout could happen at any time, pouring liquid lava from beneath the wall of a'a'. Such a thing would give him only ten or fifteen minutes to get to Star and get her safely away.

Watching his woman, his love, attempt to do what he was sure no power on this Earth could was painful. It was obvious though that keeping her from trying or belittling her was infinitely more so. Besides something inside his fisherman soul, the one that saw wondrous things constantly, tugged his heart with a pull of confidence. She was a most powerful force of nature herself. She was, after all, a woman.

~~~

Janet was woken by her entire bed shaking and rattling. Sitting up quickly, eyes wide with the fear of yet another earthquake she saw the old lady.

"Wake up kid!" She shook the bed again, standing next to Janet and literally falling against it each time. "Got some uniforms downstairs asking about you." Coughing and clearing her throat from so much effort she managed to add "You in some kind of trouble with military types?"

Janet shook her head twice, trying to shake off the static. Coffee might have helped, or maybe a beer. She looked at the old lady and grabbed her firmly by the shoulders.

"Get me outa here! Now!" She swung off her bed, pulled on her jeans and Hilo Hattie t-shirt and looked for her shoes. "Damn! Do you know...did you see my shoes?"

"Yeah, yeah, in the closet." The old lady moved back into the hall and looked in both directions. "I figure you got about five minutes, maybe less." She turned to look at Janet with a knowing eye. She too had had a few run ins with the law. "There's only two of them. I suggest we start with the stairwell across the hall. They'll be on the elevator."

Janet pulled her second shoe on and demanded, "How do you know which way to go?"

"Yeah, right!" The old lady ignored the silly question. "Look, I've been here long enough to know where the nurses hide and where the doctors go to screw. Trust me."

Janet ran out into the hall, pushing the old lady forward as nicely as she could. "Let's go then! They can't find me!"

~~~

Larry and Shirley had finally returned to their home. Amazingly, the only damage was to the windows facing the exploded propane grill. The yard had a couple of new rock features, but Shirley honestly thought they fit in nicely with her landscaping.

Halema'uma'u had calmed down quite a bit since they had fled by paraglider. Jack and Alice had returned to the Observatory, even as temporary repairs were being done. The big driver in everyone's optimism was the lowered level of the lava lake. What had only three days earlier been an overflowing pool of magma was now a pool a hundred feet below the rim.

Several Volcano residents had seen fit to sneak back in past the less than strict barricades and see if there were any cold beers at the Lava Lounge. There were.

Agatha Turner and Adam had managed to get a helicopter tour of the area. When they flew past Star's beach Agatha felt a strange connection to the woman, but the feeling passed. Adam agreed to stay on the island with her, at least one more week. He was enjoying Agatha's company, and the mangoes.

~~~

Janet and the old lady found their way down three floors and out into a rear parking area big enough to hold two dumpsters and some discarded furniture. The area was littered with big olomea tree leaves.

There was a quick moment of relief, having escaped, but immediately it was followed with the panic of "what now?"

The old lady stood stoically looking toward two mopeds parked up against the olomea tree. She raised her thin arm to point with her boney finger. Janet had a flash of an old movie where death was showing you your future. The moped was a good idea though.

"How do you start one of those?" Janet wondered out loud.

"That kind? Just roll 'em down the hill, pop the clutch. Off you go."

Janet ran over to the first moped and found it chained to both the tree and the second moped.

"Shit, they're locked up."

"Nah!" the old lady laughed. "Only fake. Try look, the chain doesn't connect."

Janet pulled the chain away from the one moped and sure enough it was only looped on to appear locked. She pushed it forward enough to throw a leg over and to retract the kickstand.

"Good luck there," the old lady waved. "You going to tell Star I said hi?"

276

"Sure," Janet nodded, anxious to get going. "But, I never got your name."

The old lady smiled at that. She knew she had never mentioned it to this brash girl. "Memitim. Tell her Memitim said good luck and all."

"Memitim," Janet murmured. She pushed forward enough to let gravity pull the moped along and then popped the clutch. In two puffs it was running on its own. Upon exiting the parking lot, she made her way through the back streets of Hilo out toward the barricades between her and Star.

~ ~ ~

Star was patrolling her increasingly smaller and smaller perimeter. None of her ahu rock and driftwood piles had been overrun yet, but they were uncomfortably close to the approaching a'a hill.

Her little island of sand and coconut trees had always been on a slightly higher piece of ground than several acres of jungle that had been behind her. That had protected them against the winter flooding that might have left her on many occasions with inches of mud and debris.

She looked over to where the vacation rentals had once been. They had avoided the flooding issue by building directly onto the lava. She knew that was tempting fate, and sure enough, they were gone now, burned and buried under several feet of fresh cooling lava.

Walking back to the water's edge she stood hands on hips and looked out at the dozens of boats offshore, the occasional helicopter tour and Wally. They all seemed to be watching her, and the approaching inevitability behind her. With the possible exception of Wally, she knew they were all, news people, gawkers, tourists, expecting her to eventually bail. How could an old lady stop lava? With her thoughts? With her prayers to some long forgotten hippie god of love?

Would she be another Harry R. Truman of Mount Saint Helens fame, dying a silly death in the face of certain destruction? She wiggled her toes deeper into the soft sand, flexing them in frustration and not a small amount of embarrassment.

She turned away from the sea and her fan club, a celebrity in doubt. The creeping hill of black was imposing and the occasional bursts of orange from still molten rock blinked on and off like a living monster winking at her.

"Soon," she imagined it to say. "Soon I will eat all of everything, and you too if you test me."

If only she had someone here, to talk her through her doubts. All anyone wanted to do was talk her onto a boat. Her only true supporter, Wally, from a long line Big Island people, understood that the volcano did this kind of thing. It was nothing to stop, but something to deal with, to live with and move on. Hawaiians had been doing that for centuries.

Her story, though, was quite different. Her mom and dad had arrived bright eyed and full of adventure from a place where snow and ice trapped you for six months every year. Where gloomy weather took a massive toll in suicides and mental health and where every teenager that could, got up and left.

Hawaii was a true paradise in that respect, warm, inviting and beautiful. A paradise not just for your skin and toes but for your mind and soul. People like her mom and dad, and herself, thrived here. They bonded to the new land like their own ancestors had done in North American when they had left Europe. This was home, this was quite beyond special. Leaving, and therefore failing, was inconceivable. Short of certain death she had to stay, even if it terrified her.

Star looked to the sky above her, to the swaying majesty of her protective coconut palms against the blue and wished. She wished for a miracle of the universe to save her one last time. The volcano could have this land, later, when she was long gone herself.

A sound of rolling and tumbling rocks from the southern edge of her perimeter caught her attention. The a'a pile had moved up to her ahu stack there, and as she watched in awe, it knocked it over, overran it and several steaming stones rolled over the sand and into the ocean.

~~~

The old lady found her way back to the elevator to ride back up to her hospital bed. In the lobby where she waited she watched the military policemen talk on their phones before looking over to her and the opening elevator.

They got whatever information they needed, and walked quickly over to ride with her to the third floor.

Four of them came into the small elevator, one of them nodding his head in acknowledgment of her, but none of the them talking.

"Where you boys headed to?" All of them had to be well over six feet tall, making them tower over her.

"Good morning, ma'am."

The old lady waited for an answer but that was all she got. As the elevator arrived at 3 they rushed out the door, forgetting all about her. They rushed into her room, opened the bathroom door and as she finally made her way into her room, they were looking under both beds.

"Where is Janet Turner?" The leader demanded.

"Good morning sir," the old lady responded with some indignity. She remained in her doorway while they continued to look in smaller and smaller places until there was no further place any human could have hidden in.

"Your roommate, ma'am, where is she?"

The old lady watched their eyes and saw deep wells of hate and anger. These men were hunters. She had a place for them too, just as she had for Janet.

Raising her thin arm, pointing out the window with her boney hand, one long weathered finger shaking slightly with the effort she simply stood still.

The four military policemen turned toward the window, one of them running over to look through the open glass and to the ground.

"Did she jump?" The leader was barking. "Is she climbing down?" He turned abruptly back to the old lady, demanding an answer from her. She only offered her pointed finger.

"Let's go!" The four of them ran past the old lady and down the stairwell.

The old lady smiled and lowered her arm. She looked beyond the open window and to the rising plume of the Kapoho cinder cone plume, climbing high into the brilliant blue sky.

~~~

Janet made her way up the climb toward Kapoho and past the unmanned barricades across the road. The moped was perfect, since she could manhandle it around the concrete blocks. She was close to the turn where the road to Kapoho met the main belt highway, but decided to check her fuel anyhow.

She had been riding for almost an hour and surprisingly the fuel seemed near the top. Hopping back on she motored up the few remaining miles, looking back often for her pursuers. At this speed though, she figured, if she ever saw them it would be too late.

Thinking of Star, the wave of static pulled back a little, clearing her mind for a moment. Despite her desperate desire to stay away from the ocean she felt compelled to help Star somehow. Perhaps she could run supplies to her and then retreat uphill away from any more tsunami waves? Maybe just a hug from a friend would help? It sure would help her, Janet thought.

The turn off was only another mile ahead. The plume from the cinder cone was dramatic, rising sharply into the clear sky as a column, then spreading out in a fan a few miles above. Janet wondered how Star could possibly survive anything that thing could throw at her. Her heart was breaking slowly, melting under the stress of overwhelming odds. No person, no sorcerer, no earth-mama or hippie love child, no one could stop a volcano!

Star was a soul though, unlike any Janet had ever encountered. She was a light that penetrated her own dark static, one that showed a promise where she had never seen one. Star had a grasp on happiness that Janet had never known could exist. She was bravely standing her ground.

Janet pulled over for a moment, to alleviate her legs aching still from the battering of the tsunami. Star had saved her there too. If not for her coaching she would have died that very night.

The ocean stretched beyond the green jungles as it always had. Star only wanted a little more time on a little stretch of land. The universe, the world, this island had enough to give, all three had enough to share.

"Whatever you need Star," Janet said out loud to that same trinity. "Whatever it takes."

She looked back toward the barricades, some seven or eight miles below and behind her. Two sets of flashing blue lights were paused at the concrete barriers while a yellow construction machine of some sort moved them aside.

Immediately she climbed back on the moped, her thighs aching in pain and headed for the Kapoho turnoff. The static was thickening.

~~~

Despite Janet's adventures Poho and I remained distant, and I felt that situation would only increase with time. A bigger picture was showing itself to me, of which Janet was becoming a smaller and smaller portion.

Poho and I moved as one in our new space. Everywhere we went, everything we did was together. Whatever one might call this grand place; heaven, nirvana, paradise or the cosmos, it was a dynamic place with many comings and goings.

Ms. Debbie, the one who had first greeted me had already left, on to her next adventure and Poho and I were to replace her, as official greeter. It was an amazing request but one which we were not afraid to take on.

It's funny, looking back, how fear keeps people from enjoying what they have been given. If anything, you learn this first after crossing over. It's probably impossible to eliminate it completely as a human, but the contrast is shocking when you no longer have humanity as an anchor.

Our hearts went out to those whom we knew before, those living with fear and dread. We tried, Poho and I, to send them signals in dreams, music, and sometimes embedded in the happiness of people they might meet. Signals that they might do better, without fear.

It was, of course, challenging. It seemed a lot like talking with hand signals, in a different language, difficult to get through. Impossible, if not for one thing – humans were just like us, they just didn't know it yet.

~~~

The stop sign at the corner of the belt highway and the road down to Kapoho was bent over halfway to the ground, apparently run over by someone in a hurry. Janet paused a moment as she made the turn to look back down the road, toward the barricades and the police she presumed were chasing her.

There was nothing to see beyond the last curve, Ohia trees were hiding her view of the distant road. They must be getting close, she thought, especially if they were speeding. Flashing blue lights had that habit.

She dropped down the descending road toward Kapoho and saw the cinder cone, still active and in the distance the cobalt sea, dancing as it was in the bright light of noon. A smile moved up from whatever depths she had been storing them in, pushing some static aside and giving her a welcome pause. Star would be only a few minutes further.

The moped seemed to welcome the break from a constant uphill struggle and almost purred as it idled in the gentle pull of gravity down toward Kapoho and Star's beach.

Something seemed wrong, though. Something didn't match the last time she had come down this wonderful road to the sea. This time, this last time, Janet saw that the road abruptly ended ahead. Covered in lava close to the cinder cone, it became clear that there was no passage from there on. There was no path to Star, or the beach or sanctuary. Her heart sank as the static rose up.

There was also no escape. Looking back uphill she saw the two police cars, light still flashing, just making the turn down hill. Quickly, she pulled her moped off the road and buried herself and the moped several yards into the jungle. If they hadn't already seen her, they never would find her in there.

The first car slowed quickly as it approached the cooled black lava covering the road. Some three feet high the a'a had easily assumed control of the entire landscape.

The second car screeched to a stop, both officers jumped out, including the leader from the hospital raid.

"Shit, I would have bet she would have been down here."

"No way she can cross this sir," a younger officer said with some unknown expertise. "No way."

"Get on the radio and have the watch boat tell me who is on the beach with that crazy old witch." The leader was angry for two good reasons obvious to the other three officers. First, they were being outsmarted by an obviously mentally ill woman, and second, they had yet to even spot her.

"No one there but the one lady sir."

"Shit! OK, lets get up to the Volcanoes Observatory. We might see her on the road."

A minute later both cars were rocketing up toward the belt highway, leaving the jungle and the lava to its devices.

Janet was hyperventilating, her knees deep in the mud and ferns, her hands up against her head trying desperately to push the static noise out. With the exit of the police she finally broke, sobbing uncontrollably.

"Goddammit Star! I tried!" Janet screamed into the empty jungle. "I can't help you now..." She rolled onto her side, sinking a few inches into the jungle muck. With the police hot on her trail her options were narrowing. "Star! Starshine!"

Janet opened her eyes in a few moments, gazing blankly through the jungle and out to the cinder cone. It was turning paradise into a mass of gray and black rock, destroying everything that might have saved her, destroying the heart of her most amazing friend. Star, Janet knew, was all alone in her fight to save her home beach, her last remaining slice of all that was fabulous and happy and hers.

The cinder cone was belching large balls of smoke up into the sky, angry at *something*. It spat in disgust at *something*. It would continue to destroy this wonderful place because of *something*. If nothing changed, this island would indeed be just another rock in the darkness of space. The volcano was angry at *something*, and Janet was beginning to understand what.

~~~

Wally approached the beach quickly, beaching his boat and running over to Star, who was staring at the breakout of lava at the southern end of her little cove.

"Starshine! Come on, we gotta go! Look, your ahu is gone and it's gonna wrap around from the south."

Star moved away from Wally and walked briskly over to the now covered ahu and the new a'a rocks starting to stack themselves up. She grabbed a handful of wet sand and threw it at the new land, in anger, in fear. It steamed its nonchalance.

"Stay away from my beach!"

Helicopters hovered overhead getting it all on camera. Star looked up and flipped them off, with both hands. "You, too!"

Wally wasn't sure when it would be appropriate to just pick her up John Wayne style and throw her in the boat. If not right now, really soon.

Star walked back over to him, and his boat. He reached out to take her hand.

"No, Wally." She implored him with her great big green eyes. "Wait here with me." She took his hand then. "Please?"

Wally looked at her closely. She wasn't out of her mind, she wasn't being anything other than herself. She was brave and resolute and if she was wrong, he would just have to be there for her. "No worries babe, I'm gonna wait right here, with you."

Star gently let his hand go. Walking slowly over to a higher part of the beach, she knelt down to both knees, put her forehead down into the sand and kissed the earth.

"Pretty please..." she whispered.

~~~

The static in Janet's head had finally overwhelmed any defenses she might have had left to mount. The battle she had attempted to wage had only made it chaotic inside her mind. Now, with no choices, no options to weigh, one thing became clear. The static moved into the background, replaced with a very soothing voice. It sounded so much like the old lady she had met in the hospital, Memitim.

Pushing the mud covered moped out of the jungle and back onto the road almost exhausted her. Not bothering to shed any of the mud from her own clothes she mounted the machine. However, she couldn't start the machine pointing uphill. Rolling it back around to face the lava wall toward the ocean she let the machine roll downhill picking up speed before popping the clutch and kick starting it.

Moving toward the lava, drawn to its glow, its texture of consumption seemed the right thing to do. She hit the leading edge of the already cooled layer with her front tire and immediately stalled, the machine falling off to the side.

"Damn it!"

This didn't seem quite right. Her new master, her new voice in a head finally relieved of the static said try again, try again elsewhere. Janet got up, turned the moped back uphill and pushed it to where she had started.

As she looked back downhill again, toward the lava, she grinned, squinting her eyes, unaware of the drool moving down her chin. She let the moped roll toward the lava again, popped the clutch and immediately got on her brakes. Slowly turning the machine back uphill she spun the accelerator back toward her and went as fast as she could uphill to the belt highway.

~~~

Larry and Shirley were still cleaning up broken window glass when he got a call from Jack at the Observatory.

"Howzit going Larry?"

Larry put down his broom and walked outside for a better signal. "Good Jack, how about you guys?"

The Hawaii Volcanoes Observatory was operational again, as long as it didn't rain too hard. Many windows were still missing but plywood was going up where it could and plastic sheeting where the plywood couldn't.

"We'll manage. Hey, look, Larry, you feel like a short observation flight? You know, something to get you out of housework?"

Larry grinned. Of course. "Sure Jack, what's the mission this time?"

Shirley stood up straight from her sweeping and looked at her husband with a bit of a scowl. If he was going to go flying she was going to sit down with her current book, In the Middle of the Third Planet's Most Wonderful of Oceans. Its feel good theme about life on Maui would take her mind off the mess here.

"Great Larry. We just need a survey of the roads surrounding Halema'uma'u. The trails as well. We want to send some rangers out but need to know what they might expect in country."

"No problem," Larry held a thumbs up to Shirley. She gave him one back. "I can get airborne in ten."

~~~

289

The military police hunting Janet had run through the few roads they could navigate in the National Park. Nothing, no one. They had even looked inside the Lava Lounge. Only the bartender was there, sweeping up broken bottles.

The leader was beginning to question the anonymous tip they had received. They had not seen anyone on a moped, much less the redheaded woman they were seeking.

They made their way back out to the belt highway. At the intersection, as they were turning left, Janet came screaming around the corner on her muddy moped, heading into the National Park.

She looked at the officers for the briefest of moments, her face a maddened, wide eyed mess.

"Shit, is that her?" The younger officer said over the radio.

Everyone turned in their seats to see the rapidly disappearing moped rider.

"Has to be right? Only moped for miles. Let's go!"

The wet jungle mud on either side of the asphalt forced them all into four point turns. By the time they were headed after Janet, she was out of sight. Both cars put their sirens on as well as their lights.

Janet heard the banshee behind her, the screams of the monster with the flashing blue eyes. The new voice in her mind told her to look for a side trail, to get off of the road. She did, finding one that ran the edge of the vast crater wall of Kilauea caldera. She hugged the railing as she rocketed down the little paved tourist pathway.

The police cars kept heading down the road.

"I'm going to slow down and look around these side trails. You guys head to the lookout and the trail head," the leader told the other car of officers.

"Roger that, sir." The young officer was excited to be in an honest to god suspect chase.

"Finally, eh?" he said, turning to his partner. "We get to actually apprehend a live one!"

"Yeah, well, sonny," the seasoned partner deadpanned. "It's the crazy ones that will hurt you the worse. Biting, spitting, who knows what they'll do." He looked out the window trying to find a clue to Janet's position. "Personally, I prefer the ones that are already passed out."

Janet's trail was going to intersect the trailhead down into the crater in a few yards, right where the second police car would be in moments. As she saw the parking area appear from behind the rapidly thinning Ohia trees she caught a glimpse of Halema'uma'u's plume in the distance - the lava pit within the massive Kilauea caldera, the same lava pit where she had taken Jimmy Turner.

She knew the trail head was there, could see it just on the other side of the park garbage cans. The jungle path that wound down from here to the floor of the massive crater would be a perfect place to escape the screaming banshee chasing her.

Except now there was one pulling into the parking area, ahead of her. Her mind froze into a single determination. She would not stop for them, convinced they would certainly eat her very skin, which the voice was insisting they would do.

As the young officer and his partner pulled up into the lot, sitting comfortably in their car, Janet sped right past their front windshield, headed down the trail head.

"Oh shit, there she goes!" The young officer leaped out of his seat and half ran after her.

"Suspect in sight, headed down the trail into the crater. On her moped!" The older officer reported on the radio.

"Goddammit! Go after her!" The leader barked, not really knowing what he was asking.

The young man, full of adrenaline now and excitement called back. "I'm on it!" He began running toward the trail head and quickly found himself picking his way down rocks and a dirt trail riddled with roots. He saw Janet not too far ahead and yelled at her.

"Stop! Your under arrest!" stumbling on a root and falling to his hands. "Bitch!" Quickly he got up and continued his chase. This collar would make his reputation on an island where boredom was all anyone could claim.

Janet saw one officer running after her as she made the first hairpin turn. Her moped was small enough to maneuver well down the trail, but it was beating against her sore hips and legs terribly. Somehow in her compromised mind she thought the banshee, sirens still screaming in the parking lot above, devil still chasing her along the trail, was actually eating her flesh now. The pain was excruciating, but the horror of being consumed was overpowering.

It propelled her faster and faster. She could see the exit of the trail head not much farther ahead. From there it was a relatively smooth path across old pahoehoe lava to the plume. Her moped would easily outdistance the blue devil gaining on her.

Janet took one turn too quickly and fell, the moped falling on her skin and the hot exhaust searing her bare leg.

"Ahhh!" she screamed. She saw the officer only one switchback above her, his eyes wide with anticipation. He would surely devour her where she lay! Quickly, she was up, the moped still running. Hopping back on she felt another severe shot of pain rocket up into her brain from her now broken ankle.

"Stop! Police!" The young officer knew that with his natural speed he could probably catch the moped in the first twenty or thirty yards of flat lava. He picked his way down the trail carefully, even if it was leaps of six and seven feet at a time, downhill.

Janet made the flats of the old lava crater and immediately found the smooth trail she and Jimmy had walked that dark night so very long ago. She slowed a moment as the memory hit her hard.

The plume ahead was probably a mile away. It looked safe, inviting, far from the monsters that wanted to capture her. Her attention focused a moment too long on that thought.

The young officer, fast and sure, made a flying tackle on Janet and the moped, crushing all three of them into a rolling ball along the ground.

"Got you!" he yelled as they rolled to a stop. He reached for his handcuffs.

Janet didn't feel any more pain at this point. Her hips, legs, left ankle and now her back would have been screaming in agony if it had not been for the incredible fear driving her to escape. She flailed her hands at the blue monster and found something to grab onto. Grasping it firmly, she pulled it.

The young officer was still laying prostate on Janet with his handcuffs in one hand. He was about to sit up when he felt the cold steel barrel in his stomach.

He didn't know what to do. His own gun was sticking harshly into his flesh, the mad woman wild eyed and mumbling nonsense as she pushed it even harder into him.

"OK, OK, you win," he thought to say. What could he say, he was about to be shot with his own gun. Classic screw up, he thought. That will be my last thought. He expected the shot to happen instantly, any moment.

"Go away," Janet spat. "Go away." She looked into the handsome young face of a man, not a monster. Somehow, as she thought lucidly for a brief moment, she had confused the two.

The officer slowly lifted himself up and off Janet, dropping his handcuffs as he did so. He got to his knees and put his hands up.

"Don't shoot, please."

Janet rolled over, still holding the gun toward the young man. The pain was attempting to take her attention away again. The gun was heavy, and her hand was falling under its weight until she stood quickly.

A shot exploded from the muzzle just missing the officer, scaring both of them.

"Don't shoot!" he yelled, getting up and running away from her.

Janet looked at him briefly. Something seemed harmless about the young man, dressed in the blue outfit.

"Leave me alone!" Janet screamed as more of the pain manifested. Her voice, her new master summoned her to keep going. Throwing the gun in the opposite direction of the young officer she mounted the still running moped and sped away toward the plume.

He wondered how he might have been so lucky. His own gun stuck into his gut. Training films had said this was how most cops died in hand to hand confrontations. He had survived. Watching the moped speed away, bouncing along the rough trail in places, he felt his courage return.

Looking over at his gun laying next to the trail and then back to the moped and the crazy redheaded woman, he reached for his radio as he began to run.

"In pursuit!"

~~~

"Jack, this is Larry, over."

Jack walked away from Alice's desk to the open deck facing the crater of Halema'uma'u.

"Go ahead Larry, what do you see? Over."

Larry was turning north in a gentle arch, toward the end of the jungle leading up to the great crater opening.

"Trails on the north side look fine. Heading to the lava pit now."

Jack nodded. He might be able to send a team out this afternoon after all.

"Great Larry, can you see the lava level in the pit yet? Over."

Larry was just clearing the two hundred foot cliff walls of the crater, jungle dropping away to a gray hardened lava. In the near distance was the pit of lava. The great floor of the crater was always impressive, some fifty times larger than the smaller internal pit where the lava and plume were.

Movement caught his eye in an area where you would never see any, especially lately. He turned his paraglider in the direction of the trail leading up to the old abandoned lookout.

"Jack, you got people in the crater? Over."

"No," Jack said. Looking for his binoculars, Alice handed them to him. "No one is in the crater, Larry."

"Well, you got someone! There looks to be a guy running toward the pit. And, it looks like a moped or motorcycle is ahead of him. Over."

"What the hell?" Alice complained. More crazy tourists came to her mind. It was like bugs to a flame.

"I see them," Jack said looking into his binoculars with some fascination. "What are they doing? Over."

Larry shook his head. That was a great question. They probably didn't know the answer either.

"I'm going to fly low and warn them off. Over." Larry dropped his speed until he began a descent, and then headed on a path that would intersect the moped.

The young police officer, huffing and puffing by now, caught sight of the paraglider descending toward Janet ahead of him. Was this some kind of elaborate rescue? Just like in the movies?

"Damn!" he muttered, impressed with the drama of it all. He sped up as fast as he could.

Janet was rocketing toward the plume, her voice telling her it was the right place to be. This would help Star, this would save Starshine Aloha and her little beach. It would make things right with the world. The static Janet had fought for years was a comfortable hum in the background of her new voice. It was such a relief, like the few good days she had at Star's beach, when the world seemed friendly to her.

Visions of Star pushing back the lava with her bare hands, burning her fingers and her hair filled Janet's mind as the plume filled her vision. She would save Star! She, Janet, would get the volcano to stop its attack.

Larry could see the moped rider clearly now. It was not a tourist, not with the dirty clothes and battered look. He was aiming for a point about ten feet in front of the rider as he quickly descended. The guy chasing her looked like a police officer!

Swooping down to about ten feet, between the boiling plume and the moped rider only another couple of dozen feet away Larry looked over to see the redheaded woman.

"Turn around!" Larry yelled at the top of his voice, as he swooped past her, pulling up and turning behind her now. He climbed up higher to get back to a safe altitude and tried to circle around again. The police officer below him was watching him, as he stopped running.

"Larry! What's going on down there? Over." Jack couldn't believe the flight maneuver his friend had just pulled off.

"Damn crazy moped rider!" Larry was climbing still and headed toward the plume. In a moment it came to him. Red hair! Could it be the same Cabin #94 wild thing he had met before? Could that be why the police was chasing her?

"Jack, police office giving chase down here as well. Red headed girl on the moped. Might be that murder suspect. Over." He continued to slow his forward progress. There was no way he could make another pass this close to the plume. Wondering what the moped rider intended to do when they got close to the edge he watched.

The young officer was completely winded. The paraglider had not rescued his suspect after all. He couldn't continue though, didn't want to get any closer to the active volcano either. The plume was magnificent, he thought to himself, in a terrifying way. He watched the moped moved faster toward the plume, now framed completely by the boiling column racing up into the sky.

A burst of tradewind from behind Larry pushed him a little closer to the plume, causing him to turn slightly. From his height now, some hundred feet, he watched as the plume fell to the side, showing the yellow and orange lake of lava below.

Janet felt content, she was a savior. She had redemption at her hands. Starshine Aloha needed saving and the island needed saving from the lava. She herself needed saving from her own sins. Jimmy's death had been a mistake, even if he deserved it. She felt the voice kiss her goodbye as she flew past the broken down barrier at the edge of the lava pit.

Larry couldn't believe it. The moped and its rider were sailing over the edge of the pit, into the brief space between life and certain destruction.

The young officer watched in some confusion as the moped seemed to drop from view. He began running a little closer, maybe she had fallen down and he could still capture her.

Janet felt her heart racing as the moped slowly fell away from beneath her. Spreading her arms out wide, she finally felt free. The static was gone, the banshee left behind, the pain in her legs forgotten. Upside down and slowly spinning backwards she wondered for a moment if the boiling lava would hurt when she landed.

It didn't.

~~~

Larry circled around another two times, half expecting what he had seen to have been an illusion. The wind shifted back to calm and went back to hiding the lava lake. He watched the police officer turn and began hiking back to the trail head. The radio was trying to get his attention.

"Larry! Larry! The moped!" A pause. "Over."

Circling higher and higher, moving slowly upwind and away from the plume Larry called in.

"Jack, moped went into the lava lake. Over." His voice fought to control the emotion. Crazy or not, suicide was depressing.

The radio was silent for almost a full minute before Jack got back.

"Roger that Larry. We ..." His radio stopped abruptly.

Larry figured Jack must be talking with someone else, until he felt the rumble in the air. Long low sound waves were moving up toward him, pressing into his skin. He looked down to see several of the cliffs of Kilauea crater collapsing.

"Earthquake," he whispered to himself. "Shirley!" Larry yelled out. Quickly, he called her on the cell phone. He got two rings and then heard the connection click dead.

Circling around Larry watched as more of the crater walls slid down, carrying trees and large parts of the jungle with them. He could hear them now, and a ripping sound like aluminum foil being torn.

"Geez, this a big one."

Larry flew closer to the Volcanoes Observatory, watching more windows break out and a part of the roof slump down. It looked like everyone was outside in the parking lot, waving at him.

"Jack, come in! Jack!"

All he heard was static, a massive release of static that made him look at the tuner, thinking he had gone off frequency. In a few seconds it cleared and he heard Jack calling back.

"Jack," Larry said. "You guys OK down there?"

"Yeah, I think so. That had to be a 7.5!" Jack's voice was wavering. It could have been the electricity in the air from the quake, but Larry thought it was probably that he was scared to death.

300

Circling once more Larry noticed something dramatic in the lava lake. Halema'uma'u walls had collapsed as well, sending vast amounts of cold rock into the lava lake, and the plume had vanished!

~~~

Wally felt the quake easily through the sand of the beach, turned to Star, grabbed her arm and literally pulled her into his boat. He dropped the engine into the water, slammed it into reverse and backed away. Three minutes later they were both in the deep water, approaching the flotilla of boats parked there.

"Oh, my god!" Star exclaimed, looking back to the beach.

Wally figured the tsunami was already sweeping the beach and turned to look. Nothing.

"What Star?"

She was crying though, and jumping up and down on the deck, throwing her arms out in a victory dance.

"What? Star?"

All she could do was point, not to the beach, but toward the cinder cone.

"Shit!" Wally whistled. The cinder cone eruption had stopped. Stopped pumping lava and smoke. The last of its plume could be seen several hundred feet above it, slowly rising, disconnected from his creator and dissipating.

He looked to the southwest for Halema'uma'u's plume and saw the same thing, a small cloud moving up and away from where a semi permanent column had been for years.

With the trade winds working their magic it only took about twenty minutes for the southern Big Island coastline and rising land behind the sea to once again shine. Shine clear in the sparkling tropical air. In the distance the snow capped Mauna Loa summit shimmered against the dark blue of a distant sky.

20

The Lava Lounge had been open a week now after the massive 8.2 quake had silenced the 30 year eruption of Kilauea, Halema'uma'u and of course the Kapoho Cinder Cone. Scientists from all over the world were packed inside enjoying their first Lava Lager along with Larry Larson, Shirley and the local crew.

Jack and Alice felt it was time to let it all hang out in public and were smooching it up in the corner booth. All the Volcanoes Observatory crew were there. It had been an intense couple of weeks since the Kapoho event had begun and everyone was enjoying some relaxation on the tab of the Lead Scientist.

Word was out around the world that the longest recorded eruption of modern times was over. The people that lived on the Big Island were especially thrilled. The vog had finally cleared, swept away for the last time by some nice trade winds and their showers. It was the pristine Hawaii that everyone remembered from their small kid days.

Larry watched the door to the bar open again, this time to whistles and hoots.

"Oh my god, those guys! Again?"

The bartender looked over at the door where Larry was staring.

The five head lamp characters were back, sans the headlamps but wearing blue and white striped ball caps this time. They all sauntered up to the bar, saw Larry and immediately surrounded him.

"Hey, Larry! How you doing buddy?" Everett asked.

Larry turned around, smiling. It was going to be a party after all.

"Let me see now, Pat, John, Dave, Tim and of course, Everett."

"Wow, great memory Larry," Pat remarked.

"Of course," Larry laughed. "Bartender, two Lava Lagers for each of these fine gentlemen. Except Everett. He gets only one!"

They all laughed at that. Everett never could handle his lava.

"So, what are you guys doing back?" Larry asked. Tourism in the Volcanoes National Park usually attracted those in search of a picture of lava. Those days were gone now.

"Oh, we're here to buy some real estate!" John exclaimed. "We're headed to Kona tomorrow morning, got our eyes on some great places near the water."

"Really?" Larry wondered. "What if the eruption starts up again?"

"We don't think it will," Tim said, looking over to Dave.

"Yeah," Dave said. "We left dozens of gin bottles all around the crater the last time we were here."

Larry turned to look at Shirley, at her knowing smile as she nodded to him.

"Remember that crazy red head you guys were flirting with last time?" Larry raised his eyebrow.

"No, no." Pat laughed. "That was Dave."

"Thanks Pat." Dave deadpanned. "She isn't here is she?" He looked around quickly.

Larry shook his head in disbelief, just thinking of the story he was going to tell them later.

"Come on over for dinner to my place tonight. I've got a story for you."

~~~

Poho and I had completed our first meet and greet. It was something everyone here seemed to take turns doing. We were thrilled not only because we were able to help a new arrival through a few of the mysteries, but that we found ourselves capable of infinite compassion.

Our first arrival had had a rough one, having had a shortened life full of darkness and confusion. It had been a case where the good soul within had been attacked constantly by an insidious poison. A poison in the mind that some poor humans get stuck with, or fall prey to.

The real joy was seeing the release from those shackles as they moved into the light and took each of our hands, Poho and I. We could immediately tell from the nature of her smile that this was the first time she had ever really been clean, been happy.

Poho didn't really recognize her but I sure did. I'd explain it to him later, but for now I was just happy that Janet was finally free.

~~~

Wally was putting the finishing touches on Star's new cabin, and as primitive as it was, it was far more special than any mansion. It was set up high on large telephone pole stilts and had a commanding view of the ocean through the coconut palms.

"I think this will keep you for a while," he said over a glass of wine that evening.

Starshine Aloha, true to her name, pointed out the first light in the evening sky and leaned over to kiss her hero. They both sat on the small outside deck in the warm light of candles and each others attention.

"I love you, Wally," Star whispered just above the quiet.

"I love you more," Wally grinned. He had finally understood just how much. Star was a beacon of hope, proving to him that optimism was quite capable of carrying the day.

The gentle ocean moved tenderly at the edge of the sand mirroring the movements of the palm trees high above. Star watched it all and her mind drifted off to wonder how her friend Jimmie was doing, if she had heard the good news about the cove yet. Watching the stars twinkle just beyond her reach she soon curled up with her love and fell softly asleep.

I listened in on Star's dreams one last time. Sometime just before dawn when the sky still sparkled against the tropical black she drew a deep breath. Star appeared just then, swinging lightly in her hammock, framed by the beach she had fought so hard to protect. An angel appeared and told her how this island had spun her, Star, from the sand, from the sky and sea into its loving expression.

I turned and looked back toward the rising light. Poho was calling me with his gentle laughter and I left here forever.

~~~ the end ~~~

the playlist

(mahalo to Michael Peacock for many of these)

A Letter From Home	Ulrich Schnauss
The End	Track Star
R.I.P.	3Oh!3
Secrets	One Republic
Yellow	Alex Parks
Mad World	Alex Parks
Twin Peaks Theme	soundtrack
November Rain	Guns n Roses
Kathy's Song	Eva Cassidy
Bring Me to Life	Evanescense
Kandi	One eskimO
The Light	Human
If I Die Young	The Band Perry
Cough Syrup	The Jakes
Invocation	Ty Burhoe
Lightning Crashes	Live
Shine	Collective Soul
Frozen Charlotte	Natalie Merchant
Fade Into You	Mazzy Star
One	U2

If you enjoyed the "magical realism" in this story, you might also enjoy the three books below. All available on Amazon.com as paperback or Kindle book. Search for "Everett Peacock"

Aloha!

Made in the USA
Lexington, KY
29 January 2012